Kidd's Country Grocery

enjoy !! :)
Patricia Woodard Synan
God's Blessings

Patricia Woodard Synan

authorHOUSE®

AuthorHouse™
1663 Liberty Drive
Bloomington, IN 47403
www.authorhouse.com
Phone: 1-800-839-8640

First published by AuthorHouse 9/22/2011

ISBN: 978-1-4634-0300-3 (e)
ISBN: 978-1-4634-0301-0 (dj)
ISBN: 978-1-4634-0302-7 (sc)

Library of Congress Control Number: 2011908041

Printed in the United States of America

DEDICATED

To my "sister-cuz", Barbara Krivacs,
who inspired me, and had faith
that I could write this book
I love you.

and

IN LOVING MEMORY

of my husband, David Ray Woodard,
who encouraged me and stuck by me;
and was delighted with each chapter I wrote.
"I'll always love you."

Acknowledgments

I am so very grateful for my friends and family that helped me carry my story to fruition. To my sister, Karen Alexander, who read, edited and made suggestions up to the last minute. I love you dearly and appreciate you so much. To my new friend, Thomas Rain Crowe, who let me mail him the manuscript and then took his valuable time to read, encourage and make suggestions – I valued each and every one of them. Thank you. To my very good friend, Betty Wolf, who read and edited – always ready to lend a hand, thank you so much. To my friend and fellow lover of bluegrass music, CharLy Markwart, who read and wrote such an encouraging endorsement for me – thank you. You're a great writer and the words meant the world to me.

Also to the ones who read and encouraged me: Adrienne, Tara, Barbara K. & Barbara W., Aunt Thelma, Aunt Helen, Mom, Dr. Rob Merritt – and last but not least, my sons, Davy and Chris and their great families, and my wonderful husband, Russell. Thank you all from the bottom of my heart.

The gratitude in my heart is only surpassed by the love I hold for you guys.

Table of Contents

Chapter I

The Dollar

November 1, 1981

The quiet Sunday morning air was filled with the smell of wood smoke and the deep blue sky promised to chase away the chill that lingered from the cold night. Barbara took a deep breath. *I love the smell of autumn...the crisp air, the smoke, the sourwood trees.* She let out her breath with a loud sigh. Ray looked over at her and smiled. He knew how she loved to smell the air when it was fresh...or smoky...or rain-filled... Barbara absent-mindedly held five-year-old Jaime's hand as he skipped across the parking lot that stretched from their little rental house to the store. They were nestled in the mountains on the border with West Virginia just outside of Pocahontas, Virginia. Barbara looked up at Peeled Chestnut Mountain that towered behind the store. She noticed some more of the yellow, red and orange colors had dropped to the ground during yesterday's rainstorm. *Pretty soon the mountain will be brown.* She knew everything about this day would be imprinted on her mind. She shook the image from her head and raised her free hand to her pounding heart as she watched Ray slide the key into the worn lock and jiggle the glass door. Today she and Ray would open their own business – a small country store that they were buying from his parents.

Jamie looked up into his Mom's face. She brushed a piece of lint from his dark blue shirt as he asked if he could have a bottle of pop. She sighed. "No, Jaime, it is too early for pop. Wish I had taken time to press your shirt."

Jaime pulled the shirt away from his body and looked it over. He shrugged his shoulders and walked through the door that his dad held open.

Barbara walked behind the counter and opened the brown paper bag she was carrying. She withdrew a bank deposit bag and took out their starter bills of ones, fives, and tens and put them into the cash register.

Ray turned on the lights and gas pumps. "We're ready for business," he announced. Barb's hand flew to her thumping heart again.

Ray walked over to the glass door. "Here comes our first customer. It's fast Eddie…and, here comes Junebug from the other direction. Don't forget about the first dollar."

"Don't worry. I won't," she said.

She nodded to Eddie and Junebug as they walked in the door. Eddie headed for the wine cooler. Junebug walked up to the counter. "I need a bottle of that cough syrup." He pointed as Barbara turned to get him the bottle from the display of medicines and beauty aids that were on the shelves behind her. She sighed. *Thank goodness our first sale won't be the bottle of cheap wine that I know Eddie is going to buy.* Barbara rang up the sale. "One dollar and eighty-four cents," she smiled at the young man. Junebug handed her a five-dollar bill. Her smile faded as she looked at Ray with raised eyebrows. Ray grinned at her and shrugged his shoulders. She bit her lower lip, furrowed her brow and then opened the register and traded the five dollar bill for five ones. She laid the five bills in Junebug's outstretched hand. He stared at her as she took two of them back. She laid one beside the register, put one in the register and took out sixteen cents. She then counted out the sixteen cents change to her first customer. "Thank you," she nodded and smiled as Junebug stood staring at her. Finally he nodded, turned his head and coughed.

"May I help you?" Barbara had turned toward Eddie as he handed her two one-dollar bills. She realized he already knew the price of the wine was $1.66. She handed him change and put his wine in a paper bag. "Thank you," she said.

Eddie picked up his bag. "You're welcome." He walked out the door behind Junebug. They stood in the driveway and talked awhile. In this small neighborhood everyone knew everybody and many of them were kin to each other. Junebug and Eddie were first cousins.

Jaime looked up at his Dad with the same warm, dark brown eyes that he had inherited from him. "You gonna put a pit-cher in that, Dad?" he drawled as Ray took the frame that held their licenses down from the wall.

"No, son. I'm gonna put a dollar bill in it."

"Why?" Jaime cocked his head and looked up at his dad.

"Well now, since this is the first dollar we just made in our new business, we're supposed to keep it. It's supposed to bring us good luck. We want our store to grow and make us a good living, don't we?"

"How's puttin' money in that frame gonna do that?"

"I don't know, Jaime, but superstition or no, we're not taking any chances."

"Oh." Jaime looked up into his mom's green eyes. "What's super--- super-ti-tion?"

"Well, it's when you do silly things to bring you good luck!" She laughed and tickled his belly as he squealed and scooted away.

Ray hung the frame back on the wall, stepped back to measure its straightness with his eyes, and cleared his throat. "Well...what do you think, *Mrs.* Kidd?"

Barbara grinned. "I think it's just fine...*Mr.* Kidd."

He walked outside with Jaime, as she lingered behind the counter staring at the frame and chewing her bottom lip. *Well, I guess this is for real. We've done gone and bought ourselves a store...or at least we signed the loan to buy it. It's too late to turn back now. We'll have to make the best of this.* She looked around the store and her shoulders sagged. The shelves were mostly full and it was clean, but the roof leaked badly. The floor had dirty looking tan linoleum patched up with darker brown tiles covering the broken and worn places. A line of coolers sat in front of the windows hiding most of the daylight. The fluorescent lighting didn't do much to chase away the dreary look inside. The building was one hundred twenty-five feet long but only twenty feet wide. Attached to one end of the store was a two-bay garage. On the other side of the garage sat a modest green house that they were renting from her father-in-law. Running behind and slightly below the store was a little dirt road with small makeshift houses sitting between it and Laurel Creek. Known as "The Bottom," it was where the poor people lived. Peeled Chestnut Mountain rose behind the creek. In front of the store ran a two-lane country highway and across from it a subdivision where the houses were made of picturesque bricks and frames owned by middle-income residents. Ray's plan was to open the garage and earn money as Barbara worked the store.

Thinking that this whole venture was going to be a challenge, Barbara's thoughts were interrupted when the wind chimes that hung over the door rang out as it was opened. "Hello, how are you?" Barbara asked.

3

The customer smiled back at Barbara. "I'm fine, thank you. Just need a pack of Winstons."

"That'll be $1.25 including the tax." Barbara said as she handed him the cigarettes.

"What! I'm gonna quit if they go up one more time! I remember when I used to buy them for ten cents a pack."

"I know," Barbara said. *Back when it took you a whole day to make a dollar.* Barbara smiled as she handed him his change and kept her thoughts to herself. She continued waiting on customers with Ray talking to them all as Jaime played while asking childish questions.

Lunch time arrived along with Ray's brother, John, and his wife, Shirley, and their three kids, Sarah, Seth and Billy. Barbara ran back and forth between the counter and the kitchen, which was at the far end of the store, trying to make lunch while waiting on customers. She sliced ham and tomatoes; unwrapped cheese slices and slapped them onto large slices of white bread.

After eating her sandwich, Shirley headed toward the door. "John, watch the kids. I'm going to run up to Mom's."

John and Ray walked straight outside as Shirley left. "Let's go check out the garage, John. I want to open it as soon as possible," said Ray.

Barbara ran back and forth the sixty feet between the kitchen and the counter to clean up. She froze as Jaime screamed. "Mommm! Billy hit me in the head with the ball."

"Put the ball *uu-pp*. You *know* you're not supposed to be throwing a ball in the store," Barbara said – slowly and deliberately.

"I told ya, Billy," ten-year old Sarah smirked.

"Yeah, she told ya," nine-year old Seth mocked.

Jaime rubbed his head while six-year old Billy grinned. Barbara turned away trying to contain her urge to strangle him as another customer walked in.

"Hello," she sighed with a false smile.

"Ouch!" yelled Billy.

"Got what you deserved," Jaime spat back.

"That's enough of that!" Barbara said, aiming her impatience at the two children while apologetically raising an eyebrow to her customer. "Sorry," she said.

"That's okay, but how *do* you do it?"

Barbara grinned and shrugged her shoulders. *I'm just trying to cope until their Mom gets back.* She rang up the chips and soda and thanked the lady. "Come back," she said.

"I will."

Barbara turned to the children. "Kids, if you have enough energy to fight, you might as well use it to fill up the pop cooler. And *quit* running in the store."

They looked at her as if she had asked them to stand on one leg and repeat the Gettysburg address. They opened their mouths to protest, but hesitated as she clamped her mouth shut and squinted her eyes.

"Okay," they moaned. They each got a few bottles and laid them in the old horizontal, bright red Coca-Cola cooler. Before too long they escaped out the door and up to the churchyard that sat just beyond their little rented house. She sighed as she heard them screaming and laughing. *I guess I should have kept them inside where it's warm.* She finished the pop cooler and swept the floor in between waiting on customers.

The day passed as the customers came and went and the children played and argued, running in and out of the store. By now, it was time for supper and Shirley had not returned. Barbara sighed as she peeled potatoes at the counter. *I can mash these but what meat can I fix while I divide my attention between customers, stove and children.* She took the potatoes to the back, washed them and threw them in a pot of water on the stove. She spied the hamburger in the meat cooler and patted out some burgers and opened a can of corn. The wind chimes rang out as she put the last burger into the skillet. She turned the burner down a little. "I'll be right there," she called to the customer.

She met Jaime half way up the aisle. "Hey, Mom, can we have a pop?"

"No. Supper will soon be ready. Go tell your dad and the others to come and eat."

Jaime ran out the door yelling for his dad as Barbara waited on her customer. Another customer came in just as she said thank you to the first one. "What can I do for you?" she asked as she nervously thought about the food on the stove.

"Well, let me see. Where do you keep the pop?"

"Over in that corner." Barbara pointed to the Coke cooler. As the mother and daughter walked to the cooler, Barbara sprinted back to the kitchen to flip the hamburgers and turn off the potatoes and corn. The woman waited patiently as Barbara hurried back up the aisle and slipped back behind the counter. "Sorry you had to wait."

5

"No problem," she said.

Barbara rang up the sodas and was about to tell her the amount when she noticed the little girl reaching in and out of the candy display. "Do you want me to add the candy she got?"

The woman turned around. "Oh, no, you don't," she said as she started pulling candy bars and packs of bubble gum from the little girl's hands and tossing them back into the candy case. The little girl started to wail, but the mother ignored her.

She paid for the sodas and turned to leave when the girl stomped her feet and sobbed, "I want some candy...I want some candy."

"Oh, all right," the mother said as she reached down and got her a Cow's Tail and laid it on the counter. "Kids. You can't bring them into a store," she said as she reached back into her billfold. As they were leaving the little girl grinned and reached in the display again for a Milky Way. The mother slapped her hand as she took the Milky Way and threw it back into the candy shelf. "One is enough," she said as she pulled the little girl out the door.

Barbara rolled her eyes as she started straightening the candy and putting them into the right boxes. Ray walked in with John. "Jaime said supper was ready."

"Almost." Barbara straightened up as she smelled the hamburgers beginning to burn. She raced back to the kitchen and turned off the stove. Grabbing the potatoes, she started draining the water and got them mashed in record time. Ray stayed at the front waiting on the customers.

"Mom, I thought you said supper was ready," Jaime said. Barbara turned as the kids walked into the kitchen.

"It is," Barbara said.

"Don't look like it to me," Billy said.

"Here," Barbara said as she sat the pot of mashed potatoes she had finished back onto the stove. She nodded to Sarah and Seth. "Get a plate and get you some food. What do you want, Billy?"

"Just some potatoes and a hamburger," he said. "I don't like corn."

She filled his plate and turned to Jaime. "What do you want on your plate?"

"Some potatoes and corn. Those hamburgers look burned."

"They're not burned, just a little well-done," Barbara said as she flipped them over.

"I want a bun to make me a real hamburger," Seth said.

Barbara sighed. "Go get a pack from the shelf."

John and Ray appeared in the kitchen. "Burned the hamburgers, huh?" Ray said.

Barbara glared at him. He didn't seem to notice as he filled his plate. She filled her plate and poured glasses of milk for the kids. "I wanted pop," Billy said.

"Me too," Seth, Sarah and Jaime said in unison.

"Drink your milk," Barbara said as she headed toward the counter with her plate in hand – eating from it as she walked.

Dinner done, dirty dishes to wash and customers to be waited on, Barbara thought as she sat her plate in the sink and started scraping the dishes. *I'm so tired. Wish I could go home and crawl into bed...I'm going to run an X tape when I get back to the register to see how much we've done.* Barbara grabbed her stomach as the excitement of their first day in business made it flutter.

She finished the dishes and walked back up the long aisle with the mop in her hand just as Mrs. Fox walked in. Barbara had spent most of the previous two months working in the store with her mother-in-law as they waited for their licenses, loan approval, etc. She had learned much about running the store and at the same time became familiar with many of the customers. She knew how Mrs. Fox loved to talk, complain and exaggerate. She nodded her head and sat the mop down as she went and stood her place behind the counter and waited for Mrs. Fox to do her shopping.

"You know," said Mrs. Fox, "I'm sure glad Ray's Daddy give him this here store. I'm just sure you young folks will have more energy to run it. Why it was just awful the people they hired to work for them!"

"Pa didn't give…"

Mrs. Fox ignored Barbara as she continued on. "There's nothing worse than gettin' a box of cereal home and findin' the date more than two months old. I just tell ye, Barbara, I wouldn't have it. Why I'd just march right back up to this here store and say to your mama-in-law, 'Now listen here Betty, this here cereal's done got old. I want my money back'…Course sometimes I'd trade it for another kinda cereal with a better date. Some people don't pay attention to dates. But, no sir, not me. I pay attention to those kinda facts."

"I've noticed," Barbara said.

"Some people's just lazy, ye know. They couldn't care less iffin they're workin' for somebody and lazin' around when they should be moppin', dustin' and checkin' dates. Know what I mean?"

"Yes, I do; and I'll try to watch those dates." *It's a wonder my face doesn't get sore from all this smiling.*

Mrs. Fox laid a loaf of bread, a gallon of milk and a box of Fruit Loops onto the counter one by one as she held them up to the light to read the expiration dates. "Can't see no date on this bread," she said.

Barbara started ringing them up. "Oh, the bread man picks up the ones we have left everyday and puts in new loaves," Barb assured her.

"I guess," Mrs. Fox said with a sigh.

"That'll be five dollars and eighty-nine cents," Barb said as Mrs. Fox was rummaging in her purse. Barbara patiently waited as she extended the palm of her left hand and rubbed her neck with her right hand. She rolled her head as she idly looked around. Suddenly she froze – stifling a scream. On the wall directly behind Mrs. Fox a bat was hanging – upside down.

Barbara stared at the bat. Mrs. Fox laid a five and one-dollar bill in Barbara's outstretched hand. She felt the motion and looked down at her hand. Mrs. Fox turned toward where Barbara had been staring past her. She shrugged her shoulders and turned back around.

"Here's your change," Barbara slightly groaned as she shoved her hand toward Mrs. Fox.

"You know, Barbara, maybe you need to rest a little. You look a mite poor. This store work can get to you."

"No, I'm okay. Here's your change." Barbara glanced back to the bat. Mrs. Fox glanced around again.

"Eleven cents. Here's your eleven cents, Mrs. Fox." Barbara pleaded as she tugged at Mrs. Fox's sleeve.

Mrs. Fox looked back at Barbara with the corners of her mouth turned up. "I'm serious, Barbara, you don't look so good. Maybe you need some rest."

"Yeah, I guess so." Barbara laid the change in Mrs. Fox's hand. "You have a real good day now," she said.

"Oh, I will. You do the same. Oh, yeah, that reminds me, did I tell you I need some ten penny nails?"

"No, I don't think we have any of that size nails."

"Don't ye think ye oughta give it a look-see?" Mrs. Fox cocked her head sideways and rubbed her chin.

"No, I'm sure we're out. Now you have a good day, Mrs. Fox, and come back real soon." Barbara moved from behind the counter and took Mrs. Fox by the elbow. "Let me help you carry your stuff," she said.

"Good Lord, I don't need nobody to help me carry this little bit. A body would think you're tryin' to git shed of me, Barbara."

"Oh, no...no. I've just gotta get this floor mopped. Don't want to be wasting your time."

"Well, now, iffen I thought ye was wastin' my time, I'd done been gone. I'll see ye tomorrow."

"Yeah, tomorrow," Barbara said as she glanced up at the wall.

"You git you some rest and things will be better by and by. Ye look a might pale," Mrs. Fox chuckled as she walked out the door. She turned back and saw Barbara watching her. She nodded her head and grinned.

Barbara stood at the door just long enough to see her out of sight as she walked to her house in the Bottom. In the meantime, she kept one eye on the bat. "Thank goodness, she's gone," she said as she ran out the door and up toward the garage. "Ray...Ray," she yelled as she ran. Ray and John met her halfway.

"What's wrong?"

"A bat – there's a bat in the store. Hurry! I was afraid it was going to swoop down on Mrs. Fox!"

Ray laughed.

Barbara glared at him. "It's no laughing matter to be working with bats flying around. Well...maybe it isn't flying, but who knows when it will take a notion to. And Mrs. Fox – if she gets word that a bat was hanging on the wall right behind her head...She didn't see it..." Barbara hesitated. "Oh my gosh. That just wouldn't do."

Ray grabbed a big fishing net that was hanging on the wall. She had been told it hung there for the purpose of catching birds that sometimes flew into the store. And now Barbara knew the rest of the story. It also hung there for when bats decided to take their naps inside the store instead of the attic like they were supposed to. Ray covered the bat with the net and flicked it inside. He walked outside with it. The kids ran up to see what was going on. Sarah squealed. The boys hee-hawed.

"Let it go!" Seth yelled.

"No, you never know when they might be carrying a disease," Ray said.

"Carrying a disease?" Barbara echoed. "We're running a store with bats in the attic and they might be carrying a disease? Ray, we can't have this. Make them go away...*now*. I won't work here with bats in the attic." Her heart hadn't stopped racing since she had first caught sight of the ugly thing hanging there. The bat struggled in vain to escape, but the net entangled its wings even more.

"Don't worry. I don't want them in the store either," Ray promised. "I'll block up every hole I can find in the store as soon as we close."

Barbara headed back inside as the kids followed Ray down to the end of the store. Shirley drove up and opened the car door and shouted for the kids to climb in. "Mom, you ought to see what Uncle Ray has," she heard Billy say as they all clamored into the back seat. John climbed into the front seat shaking his head and chuckling.

Ray and Jaime walked back into the store with an empty net as Barbara stood there chewing on her lip and scanning the walls for more bats. "Well, the bat's dead and gone," said Ray as he hung the net back on its nail.

"Yeah, dead and gone," repeated Jaime. "Don't worry, Mom. Dad won't let those old bats hurt you."

"Duck! There's one now!" Ray yelled. Jaime screamed and ran to Barb. Ray laughed. "Ha..ha. Gotcha!"

"Ray, that isn't *funny*," Barbara said.

"I know...I know." Ray rolled his eyes. "I told you I'd take care of it tonight. We'll be closing soon. I'll go out to the garage and find some boards to nail over those holes. Come on, Jaime. Better not stay in here with the bats."

Jaime followed his dad while Barbara stared at Ray as he exited the store.

It was nosy Bertha ringing the wind chimes over the door. "Hey, Barbara - I heard you got bats in your belfry. Ha...ha...ha. Don't worry about it. So do I. They won't bother you if you don't bother them." Bertha lived in a little four-room house right next to the creek that ran behind the store. "At least you don't have to sleep in here. You get to go home at night. Course, at night the bats leave too." She reached over into the box of bananas that sat in front of the counter. "That's when they go out and catch bugs to eat. Daytime they usually just hang around and sleep. 'Course lots of people hang around this here establishment during the daytime, so's you ought not to be prejudice against the bats, huh?" She laughed at her own joke as she tore off three bananas from the bunch and laid them on the counter, throwing the rest back into the box.

"Can I get you anything else?" Barbara pasted a smile on her face. *Thanks for the science lesson, Bertha, and the bruised bananas.*

"Yeah, I just need a loaf of bread."

"How did you know...I mean who told you we have bats?" Barbara stared at Bertha.

"A little birdie. Well, I guess the birdie wasn't so little... bigger than a bat. Ha...ha. You want I should knit you a bonnet to wear in case those bats decide to swoop down and attack - like in that movie, <u>The Birds</u>?"

"Sure," Barbara rolled her eyes. "Make it pink – that's my favorite color."

"Will do," Bertha grinned as she walked out the door, making the wind chimes ring loudly.

Chapter II

The Decision

Ten days had passed and Barbara was still on her feet. The store opened everyday at 8:00 a.m. and closed at 9:00 p.m. She got Jaime ready for school and put him on the bus right in front of the store every morning. He spent his evenings hanging around the store and almost every day his cousins came over to play and eat supper.

No other bats had decided to take a nap hanging from the walls. Barbara hoped Ray had gotten all of the holes plugged. Each morning she ran the register tape and added the total to yesterday's ending cash. Then she subtracted what they had spent out and deposited in the bank. The total left should equal the cash she now had on hand. She called this "checking up." She kept all records in a ledger that they called the 'Day Book'. Each day had a separate page with the payouts and totals of the day's sales – categorized as gas, merchandise, and groceries. Cash and Credit were also separated. She always checked the totals with anticipation – hoping they had made enough sales the day before to cover their expenses. Their payments were high and she realized it would take a lot of business to be able to meet them.

One morning as she was checking up, the phone rang. A man on the other end asked for "Ray Kidd," so Barbara called him to the phone.

"Hello," Ray said. "Oh, yes sir." Ray's posture immediately took on a new stance. He squared his shoulders and raised his eyebrows. He looked at Barbara's questioning gaze as he listened to the man. "Yes sir. I'd be glad to." He continued listening for a bit. "Monday morning will be fine. I'll see you then. Yes sir, I will bring my social security card. Thank you very much." Ray hung the phone up grinning from ear to ear.

"Who was that?" Barbara asked.

Ray picked Barbara up and swung her around. "None other than the C & O Railroad. I'm starting to work for them Monday morning! Can you believe it?"

He sat Barbara down and she stared at him – her jaw dropped open.

Ray didn't seem to notice. "They said I was the most qualified and best applicant they had. I put that application in more than two months ago. I had given up. I never dreamed they would call me after all this time."

Barbara's face grew from disbelief to comprehension. "You're kidding! That was the job you had most hoped for."

"I know! Isn't it great?" Ray swung her around one more time and sat her down.

Suddenly Barbara furrowed her brow and looked down at the floor. *All the good benefits and pay we wanted and couldn't find – now the railroad will provide. We haven't even put our house on the market. We could move back to the country.* Her heart rate went up. *But here we are already committed to the store and the payments. What would Ma and Pa Kidd do if we backed out now?* She sat down on the stool and chewed on her lip.

"What's wrong?" Ray asked.

"Ray, what do we do now? Are we going to keep the store?"

Ray became pensive as he stood silently. Barbara watched his face as she thought about the brick home they had moved from and the serene days they had left behind. Their days now were so hectic, plus they were renting an old house that was not nearly as nice.

Finally Ray spoke. "I don't see how we can just walk away from this commitment. Probably the best thing would be for you to run the store and I'll work the railroad. That will put us ahead. The man said I would be working second shift so I'll help you in the mornings before I leave."

"Ray, I can't run this store by myself and take care of Jaime," Barbara said with tears in her voice.

"Yeah, I know." Ray sighed and started to walk toward the pop cooler. Then he turned around toward Barbara as his face brightened. "Remember when Aunt Pearl offered to help us out in the store?"

"Yeah." Barbara sat down on the stool. "That's right, she did."

"Why don't we give her a call to see if she still wants to help? She could live with us and would be a big help. She said she wouldn't need much pay since she has her Social Security for an income. In fact, she said she could only earn so much. I'd be bringing in an income from the railroad, so we could afford to pay her some."

"Yeah, that would work." Barbara was nodding her head.

13

"She won't work the cash register. She never would when she'd come to help Ma and Pa," Ray said.

Barbara stood again. "That wouldn't be a problem. If she could just help stock, clean and keep meals going, I could work the register." She sat down again. *Ray's right. We can't just walk away. Ma and Pa are counting on the payments from this store to live on and to meet their obligations... It sure would be nice to have some help. I am definitely keeping myself too busy. Jaime needs me, but the customers seem to always be demanding my time... I really do like Aunt Pearl. Things could be right nice if we had some extra income and weren't always worrying about making ends meet. Still...* She let out a long sigh. "Don't you know things would work out like this. I can't believe you get the call we had so been wanting ten days after we take over the store."

"Yeah, I know," Ray answered. "But we can't change the timing. Let's give it a try with me working the railroad and you keeping the store with Aunt Pearl's help. I'll forget about opening the garage right now. You'll see...it'll work."

"Do you really think Aunt Pearl will come?" Barbara asked.

"I think she will. Remember – she was the one that volunteered to help us when she visited Ma and Pa last month. I think she wants a change in her life. Her children are all grown and she lives alone," Ray said as he put his hand on Barbara's shoulder.

Barbara looked up into Ray's face and saw hope in his eyes. "I know. You're right. Might as well call Aunt Pearl and see when she can come. She'll need time to pack and everything. Monday will be here before we know it. I just wish..." Barbara gazed down at her paper work as she fought to hold back the water in her eyes.

Ray lifted her chin and their eyes met as he pulled her into his arms. They stood holding each other – saying nothing.

Chapter III

Aunt Pearl

Jaime stood gazing out the big picture window of their little rental house that sat snugly between the end of the garage and the churchyard. The paved parking lot of the store came up in front of the house, so Jaime and his cousins used the churchyard beside the house to play in. Ray was busy working on the front doorknob with a screwdriver and Barbara was washing the breakfast dishes.

"Mom, how long does it take to get from the big stone to here?"

"Big Stone Gap," Barbara chuckled. "About three hours, I believe. You aren't excited to see Aunt Pearl, are you?"

"Yeah, I can't wait! Last time she came, she cooked us fried chicken, 'member? She sure does know how to cook, don't she?"

Barbara nodded her head. "Doesn't she?" *If Pearl cooks, at least I won't have to try to manage that while I work. We'll eat a lot better.* Barbara started to tell Jaime that it would be a while before Aunt Pearl arrived but was stopped by the sound of a car engine pulling up in front.

"Look! Look! There she is!" Jaime pushed past his dad as he ran outside to meet the dark green Jeep that had pulled up in front.

Aunt Pearl opened the door of the passenger side. Her long legs slid out the side, but Jaime was there before her feet touched the ground. As soon as she stood, he gave her a bear hug around her legs.

She picked him up. "My, how you have grown, you little rascal! What have you been eating?"

"Not too much candy and pop. Mom won't give me too much good stuff." Then he whispered something in Pearl's ear.

She threw back her head and laughed. "Jaime, you *are* a little rascal!"

"Welcome, Aunt Pearl." Barbara hugged her and then stood back and

15

nodded her head. "I like your new hair cut." Aunt Pearl had thick silver hair with a natural wave. It was cut short. She had the same dark brown eyes and complexion as Ray and Jaime and she stood almost six feet tall – another Kidd characteristic.

Ray walked over to the driver's side. Pearl's youngest son, Ken, nodded his head to everybody. Ray slapped him on the back. "Well, son, how was your trip?"

Ken, being only four years younger, grinned at his cousin. "Just fine, old man. How come the store is closed?" he asked as he opened the back of the Jeep and retrieved two pieces of luggage.

"Don't open 'til 9:00 on Sunday mornings. Not many customers before then...everybody sleeps in. Let me help you," Ray said as he took one of the suitcases from Ken. "What time did y'all leave anyhow?"

"About 5:30," Ken said. "Mama was looking forward to coming up and I want to visit and still get back home before too late." He closed the back of the Jeep. "So, we figured we might as well leave early."

"Tell me, how is that old truck you're fixing up coming along?" Ray asked as the two men walked into the house.

Barbara looked at Aunt Pearl and rolled her eyes. "Men and their vehicles," she said. "Let's get you settled." She took Aunt Pearl's arm.

"Yeah, and then you can cook us some fried chicken," Jaime piped.

"Jaime!" Barbara's eyes popped as her mouth flew open.

Aunt Pearl threw back her head and laughed again. "I can see we're going to have a good time, Jaime. It's been a long time since I've had a little boy to take care of. You know mine are all big now."

"I'm not a little boy – I'm big!"

"That you are." Aunt Pearl grinned as her eyes sparkled.

Barbara got up from the table to start the dishes, but the chimes rang out over the door so she started toward the counter. She had already had her supper interrupted a dozen times, but she was getting used to that. "Barney's up front," she said.

"Don't worry about the dishes. I'll get them done," Aunt Pearl called to her.

"Thanks," Barbara called back over her shoulder. Aunt Pearl had fried pork chops, mashed potatoes, cooked green beans, made gravy and homemade biscuits. And now Barbara didn't have to run back and forth to clean the kitchen. It had only been a week, but she hadn't had any trouble getting used to this.

Barney stood just inside the door. "Wanna wittle quart of wine," he said with his head hung down.

"Sorry, Barney, you'll have to walk back there and get it yourself. That's the ABC laws."

"Otay," he said. "I will."

Barbara watched him as he walked down the aisle. He shuffled his feet as he kept his head bent and his hands in his big dirty overcoat. His face showed age beyond his forty-odd years, but his blue eyes were big and held the look of innocence. He sat his "little" quart of wine (a pint) on the counter. "It's cold outside," he said.

"It sure is," said Barbara.

"It sure is," Barney echoed. "I'm gonna go home and stay dere." He reached in his pocket and drew out a handful of change. "Here, you count it."

"Sure," she said as she counted out the $1.66. She put his wine in a paper bag and smiled. "Thank you, Barney. You go home and keep warm now."

"I will," he said as he tucked the wine inside a pocket in his big overcoat. "Tank you too." His voice was almost a whisper as he walked out the door.

Barbara stood there watching him walk up the driveway. He lived with his nephew, Junebug, in the Bottom.

"Dishes are done. Who was that man?" Pearl asked as she walked behind the counter and sat down on a stool.

Ray walked up the aisle from the kitchen. "We call him the Turtle Man," he said.

"Yeah, that's right," said Barbara. "My first memory of Barney was when I was just a young girl. I didn't know Ray and his family then, but we drove past here on our way to visit my grandparents on Sunday afternoons. It was not unusual to see Barney walking beside the road, one pants leg rolled up to his knee, the other pants leg slid down past his shoes. He would be swinging a large mud turtle by its tail. I mean a *live* turtle, two or three feet in diameter!"

"Yeah, the creek down back is full of them," Ray said. "They're also called snapping turtles. Legend has it that if one bites you, it won't turn loose 'til thunder rolls. We used to put sticks at their mouths and watch them grab them. They'd snap those sticks right in two. I've seen them hold on once they get a big stick between their jaws."

"We kids were scared to death of those primitive monsters," Barbara continued, "but there we'd see this strange man walking down the road swinging one of them as if he only had a rope or something in his hand. My dad grew up in these parts and he said they always called him the Turtle Man. He said Barney and his family used to catch the turtles and sell them for wine money. He said some of the locals would buy them and fix them for dinner."

Jaime stood there listening. "Oooh, you ever eat a turtle before, Aunt Pearl?"

"Sure have, Jaime. They're good. Whenever I get one, I boil it up 'til tender and then stick it in the frying pan. Hadn't had one in a long time though."

"Really?" Jaime furrowed his eyebrows and looked at Aunt Pearl. "What do they taste like?"

"They taste a whole lot like chicken," she answered.

"I like chicken." Jaime raised his eyebrows and grinned.

"Well, maybe we'll just have to get Barney to catch you a turtle," Pearl said.

"That's okay." Jaime raised his head and shoulders higher. "When it gets warm, I'll just go catch my own turtle."

"I think not," Barbara said. "Did you forget they bite?"

"Oh, yeah. I don't think I wanna eat a turtle anyhow," he said as he walked over to the candy shelves. "Mom, can I have a Reese cup?"

Barbara looked at the ceiling. "Did you finish your dinner?"

"He sure did." Pearl answered for Jaime.

Barbara shook her head and sighed. "I guess it'll be okay."

The chimes over the door rang. "Hey, everybody. It's me!" It was Ida Boswell. Jaime looked up at her and ran to the office with his candy bar. Ida stood about 6'3" and was big boned. She lived in a little two-room shack at the other end of the Bottom. The dip of snuff she seemed to always have in her mouth was continually running down her chin. Every once in a while she would reach up with the back of her hand and wipe it across her face. Her hair was a dirty grayish blond pulled back with brown streaks of snuff throughout. Today she wore a pair of faded green polyester slacks with a big grayed-white sweatshirt and a man's faded blue work jacket. Her little toes were sticking out of her dirty tennis shoes.

"I just passed Barney," she said in her boisterous way. "Bet he got some wine, huh? He wouldn't tell me. He owes me three dollars already. I'm not givin' him anymore money. Not lessen he pays me back when the first gits here. Blame me?" Ida paused and looked around as she wiped the drool from the corner of her mouth with the back of her hand. The question had been rhetorical and Ida didn't seem to expect an answer. "Oh, yeah, Barbara, how 'bout puttin' up that statue there and savin' it 'til I git my check. I been eyein' it and I done decided that's what I'm gettin' soon as my money gits here…That mommy and her baby sure is purty, don' ya think so?"

"Yes, it is Idy. That's the baby Jesus and Mary," Barbara said.

"Really? Well…I'll be switched. I didn't know that. I special want it now. Don't you let anybody else git it, you hear me, Barbara?"

"Sure, but I need you to pay one dollar to lay it away," Barbara said. She had seen Ida change her mind and Ma Kidd lose a sale because of it. She figured if Ida had something invested in it, she wouldn't change her mind so easily.

"What!?! Betty never made me pay a dollar." Ida pulled her change purse from her pocket and retrieved a dollar bill. She slapped in onto the counter.

Barbara raised her eyebrows and smiled as she handed Ida her receipt. "I'll take a dollar off when you pick it up."

"Why didn't ya say so? That makes it dif-frent. Now give me a Big G Snuff and I've gotta have me some cough drops. Oh, and here…put this cake on there too."

"Idy, you know Granny doesn't want you to have that cake. You've got sugar and it's bad for you."

"Granny ain't my mommy. I'll git what I durn well want. Tain't for me noways." She turned her face upward. "Sides, it ain't none of nobody's bizness what I git."

Barb shook her head and chewed on her bottom lip. Granny Johnson and Ida were sister-in-laws and both were now widows. Granny lived a few houses from Ida and looked after here. Barbara sighed and added the cake to her bill. "You have a good day now, Idy."

"I will, missy. You do the same. See y'all tomorrey."

Aunt Pearl didn't say anything as she stood there watching Ida walk up the driveway. Jaime flew out of the office and stood next to Pearl. "She stinks, don't she, Aunt Pearl – like dead fish and snuff mixed together."

"Jaime!" Barbara frowned.

Jaime looked at his mom and then again at Aunt Pearl. "You see her

19

hair? She has snuff plumb up in it! And she has holes in her britches. And it looked like she didn't have no underpants on!" Jaime scrunched his nose and grinned as he wiped his mouth with his sleeve.

"Jaime, hush!" Barbara scolded. "Idy doesn't know any better and she has so little. Don't you be making fun of her." Her face softened as she continued. "Besides, who just wiped chocolate on his sleeve?"

"Uh-oh," Jaime said as he looked down at his arm.

"Come on you wascally wabbit," Aunt Pearl teased. "I'll clean it for you."

Chapter IV

Rudolph Pays a Visit

Three weeks had passed now and Ma and Barbara were in the store and talking about Christmas. "You need to go on a buying trip and stock up the showcases before the first of the month gets here," Ma said.

"How should we go about doing that?" Barbara sprayed glass cleaner on the counter and rubbed it clean.

"If you want I'll go with you and help." Ma picked up a display of cigarette lighters for Barbara to clean under.

"Sure, we want you to go. I know nothing about a wholesale shopping trip." It had been a long three months that Barbara had worked in the store (two training and one as a new owner). Just to get away for a day and to eat at a restaurant sounded so good. Never mind the work it might entail. She figured it couldn't be any harder than what she was doing from day to day.

"The best place to buy gifts to sell is at Shull's Pottery in Fancy Gap. You'll also need to buy your produce. You'll need oranges, tangerines, apples and nuts besides the regular stuff. There's a place call Horton's Produce just up the road from Shull's for that. We can do it all in one day and Pearl and Shirley could mind the store."

Ray walked in during the middle of the conversation. "Let's plan it for Monday. I work this Saturday, but I'm off on Sunday and Monday. We'll put Jaime on the school bus and leave early."

"Shirley said she could use some spending money for Christmas. I'll call her and ask her to keep the store," Barbara said.

"Monday will be fine with me," Ma said.

It was dark Monday by the time the pickup truck pulled up in front of the store. Aunt Pearl had a hot supper ready and Jaime was sitting at the butcher block table looking at a sheet of paper with different color blocks on it. Barbara walked in with a box of tomatoes, followed by Ray with a box of bananas.

"Where is everybody?" Ray asked Shirley.

"Pearl and Jaime are in the kitchen and I sent the kids home with John. How was your trip?" Shirley asked.

"Fine," Ray said as he turned to see Jaime running to the front of the store.

"Hey, those are bananas," Jaime said as Ray pulled the lid from the box. "Aunt Pearl said y'all were going after Christmas presents for the store."

"Don't worry," Ma arched her eyebrows and grinned at Jaime. "There's a truckload of stuff yet to unload."

"I'll help." Jaime ran toward the door.

"Oh no." Ray grabbed Jaime's shirtsleeve. "The boxes are too heavy for you. You can open and close the door for us as we bring them in."

Jaime looked up at his dad as his face lit up. "Okay, I'll be the door opener. Aunt Pearl," he yelled. "We have a truck to unload."

"Ain't y'all going to eat first?" Aunt Pearl asked.

"No, we had a big lunch and we need to get the truck unloaded first. We'll eat after we finish," Ray said.

"Well, I'm going home and make sure the kids get their homework done." Shirley took her coat from the peg it was hanging on. "See y'all tomorrow."

"I'm going home too. Have fun unpacking all those boxes." Ma left them to their work.

Jaime asked a question each time Barbara walked through the door as they unloaded the truck.

"How many more days 'til Christmas?"

"Let's see. Thirty-one, I believe."

"Did you bring me anything?"

"Yes, a coloring book and some crayons."

"I wish I could have gone with you."

"Well, little helper, next time you can. Mawmaw tells us we still need to go to King's Wholesale in Bristol, Tennessee to restock the handkerchiefs, underwear, and things like that for the customers to buy. We'll go Saturday when school is out."

"Oh boy! Where did y'all eat lunch?"

"We found this great little restaurant called Libby Hill Seafood across the state line in Mt. Airy, North Carolina. It was *sooo* good."

"Why didn't you go to Pizza Hut or McDonald's?"

Barbara laughed and bent down to Eskimo kiss his nose. "We saved that for when you get to go. Speaking of food, I'm hungry. Let's go eat. That's the last of the boxes. We can unpack some after we eat."

"I already ate," Jaime said. "Can I have an ice cream?"

Barbara looked around. "Pearl?"

"He ate good and had a candy bar for dessert," Pearl answered.

Barbara looked at Jaime. "Yeah, but Mom, I'm hungry and I don't want any more supper."

"Have you finished your homework?" Barbara said.

"Yeah, we just had to study our colors." Jaime looked at his mom hopefully.

"Wouldn't you rather have one of those juicy oranges or a banana?" Barbara looked hopefully at Jaime.

"No."

"Okay, go ahead and get you an ice cream," she sighed.

Ray and Pearl grinned at each other.

The next morning Mrs. Fox was in bright and early. "Whatcha' got in those boxes?"

"We're getting ready to unpack them now. They're things to sell for Christmas presents," Pearl answered her.

Barbara sat at the adding machine behind the counter. "Barbara?" Mrs. Fox walked up to the counter. "Shouldn't you be helping Pearl here?"

"I'm figuring prices," Barbara said.

"Well, remember we're just poor folks here. Don't get carried away." Mrs. Fox turned back to the boxes. Barbara looked at her back and made a face.

"Whatcha' laughin' at Pearl?" Mrs. Fox looked at her suspiciously.

"Nothing. Just thinking of something I saw not long ago."

"Well, I need me a baby doll for my grandbaby. She's going' on three. Did y'all get any size 40 briefs? I need them for Harry. He's gettin' bigger around ever time I look at 'im. I got me four grandkids in all. 'Course, three of 'em are boys. I'll hafta figure somethin' out for them. I'll bring a list when I come next Thursday with my social security check to cash."

"We're going Saturday to buy clothing items, Mrs. Fox," Barbara said. "These boxes are full of toys and what-nots."

"That's good…long as you git 'em before Christmas. Hey, Pearl, how about fixin' me up a pound of bologny and two pounds of that hamburger. When did y'all git the meats in? I reckon they're fresh, huh?"

"They are…and so will be the clothes when we get them in." Pearl turned to walk back to the kitchen as she rolled her eyes.

"Huh?" Mrs. Fox looked at Barbara as realization showed on her face. "Oh, yeah. That Pearl's a crackerjack, ain't she Barbara? Now that's funny. Fresh clothes."

Christmas Eve finally arrived. Barbara had posted a big sign in the window a week ahead of time: CLOSED CHRISTMAS DAY…CLOSING AT 6:00 P.M. ON CHRISTMAS EVE. She made a habit of telling all of the regulars that they would be closed. Everybody was in agreement that it was the thing to do. Every Christmas Eve they had dinner at Ma and Pa's and opened presents. The family would be there - totaling about twenty-five. By the time everybody brought in gifts, there were probably close to a hundred or more presents under the tree. Jaime had been over to Mawmaw's and Pawpaw's earlier and seen all the gifts lying on the floor around the tree.

"Mom, how much longer?" Jaime asked for what Barbara thought must be the hundredth time.

"Jaime, it's more than an hour before we get to close and go to Mawmaw's." Barbara sighed as she put a loaf of bread in a bag for Ethan. "Are you sure you have everything you need, Ethan? You know we'll be closed tomorrow."

"Yeah…I know," he answered. "I hope y'all have a good Christmas."

Barbara smiled as she reached around and picked up a bag of chocolate drops. "Ethan, you and Gladys have a Merry Christmas too." She dropped the chocolate drops into the bag with the bread.

"Thanks, Barbara. Gladys will like that candy. We ain't got many teeth left to eat the kind with nuts in them." Ethan grinned his toothless grin. "But we manage, ye know."

Barbara helped him hoist the box up onto his shoulders and handed him the bag with the bread and candy in it. "I'll be seein' y'all after Christmas." He nodded to Jaime as he pushed the door open with his shoulder. "Won't be long now 'til ole Santy gits here, Jaime. Tonight's the night."

"Yeah, I know." Jaime raised his eyebrows as his eyes lit up. "I've been good. We're gonna open presents tonight at Mawmaw and Pawpaw's and tomorrow morning from Santa and tomorrow day at Mawmaw and Pawpaw Warburton's."

"Hey, Jaime, come try out this potato salad I made for Mawmaw's dinner tonight," Pearl called. Jaime took off toward the kitchen.

"See ya, Ethan, and Merry Christmas," Ray said over his shoulder as he walked through the door. He turned toward Barbara. "Where's Jaime?"

"He just went toward the kitchen. Why? What's up?"

Ray just grinned at her – his eyes twinkling. "Jaime! Jaime! Come quick," he yelled. "I saw Rudolph fly over."

Jaime flew to the front of the store. "Rudolph?" he asked.

"Yeah, come outside and I'll show you."

They both went outside and Jaime fairly flew back into the store. "Mom, it *was* Rudolph. I saw his red nose. He landed over behind Flanagan's barn on the mountain. Dad said maybe Santa, Rudolph and the rest of the reindeer are in that barn resting." He grabbed the stool that sat at the end of the counter. "Dad said I could sit outside on the island and watch for them." He turned toward the door.

"Wait, Jaime. You need your coat." Barbara grabbed his coat and toboggan from the peg.

"*Mommm. Hurry.* I'm gonna miss them!"

"Stand still, Jaime. I can't get it zipped."

"I can't wait, Mom," was his anguished reply as he twisted back toward the door. "You're gonna make me miss everything. Dad's waitin' on me. He told me to hurry."

"Go ahead. Tell Dad to zip your coat up." Barbara pulled the toboggan over his ears.

"Okay."

Barbara held the door open for him as he struggled with the stool. "I got the stool, Dad. Are they still up there?"

"I haven't seen them come out yet, Jaime. They must be. Let me help you, son." Ray sat the stool solid on the ground and zipped Jaime's coat. "Now I'll just be in the store. You let me know if you see Rudolph again."

"Don't worry. I will!"

Jaime gazed up at the mountain, keeping his eyes on the barn. Barbara closed the door as Ray walked back inside the store.

"Ray Kidd, what are you doing to that boy?" Aunt Pearl asked.

Ray couldn't hold his laughter any longer. Barbara grinned and chewed her bottom lip as she watched him – her eyes twinkling.

"You know how excited he is. He can't sit still. I was walking across the driveway and saw a plane high in the sky with its red light blinking. First thing I thought of was Rudolph. I figured I'd have no trouble convincing Jaime of it. When the plane flew out of sight, Jaime thought it landed behind Flanagan's barn. I thought about that horse up there and the story grew. This will keep him busy and quiet for awhile."

Barbara and Aunt Pearl laughed. "Ray, I can't believe you sometimes," Barbara chastised him; "to think you would fool your own son that way."

"Oh, Barb, he's having fun and it gives him something to occupy his time."

"Well, I can't argue with that."

The chimes rang out as Fast Eddie walked in the door. "Y'all's boy's out thar sittin' in that grassy place whar ya Ma plants the flowers come spring. Says he's lookin' for Rudolph and Santa." Eddie laughed. "Can ya beat that?"

"Yeah, that's right, Eddie. We think we spotted them flyin' over just a few minutes ago," Ray said as he walked out the door.

"And I thought I was the one with the drinkin' problem," Eddie said. Barbara turned her face away and Aunt Pearl went back to the kitchen. Eddie walked back to the wine cooler.

"Don't forget we're closed tomorrow," Aunt Pearl called back to him.

"I know. That's why I'm here to stock up," he said as he pulled a liter of cheap wine from the cooler. "I better git me two packs of cigarettes this time," he said to Barbara.

Bertha walked in the door and up to the counter. She watched as Barbara rang up the wine and cigarettes. "At this rate, ye ain't gonna live to see forty," Bertha said to Eddie as she looked at the wine sitting on the counter. She turned to Barbara. "What in tarnation is that youngin' and husband of your'n doin' out thar in the middle of the driveway?"

"They're lookin' for Santa and Rudolph, the red-nosed reindeer," Eddie answered her. "They think he's hidin' up thar on the mountain."

Bertha turned around and glared at Eddie. "If I'd wanted a stupid answer I'd have asked you in the first place, Smart-aleck. I was talkin' to Barbara."

Barbara started laughing. She tried to say something, but only managed to shrug her shoulders. She could see Jaime and Ray out on the island. Jaime's face intent as he stared past the roof of the store; and Ray's lit up as he spun his yarn and pointed at the barn.

Jaime hopped off the stool and ran back into the store. "Mom, I saw Rudolph! I saw him for sure. He walked out of that barn and around to the back of it. I gotta go back." He almost collided with his dad who had followed him in.

"Let me know if you see them take off, Jaime."

"I will, Dad."

"Humph. How much for the milk and eggs?" Bertha asked.

"I told ye. Now who you callin' stupid?" Eddie said as he started toward the door. "Merry Christmas everbody. I gotta git home before Rudolph takes off and I'm not home to collect my presents."

"Smart-aleck." Bertha scowled at Eddie as she handed Barbara a five-dollar bill. "Youngins is gonna be youngins, I reckon, but a smart-aleck is another thang."

Barbara waited for the store to clear and looked at Ray. "Well?" she asked.

"He saw Flanagan's pony for a few seconds – just long enough to look like a reindeer in his imagination. I sure hope a plane flies back over soon so he'll come back inside. I'll have him believing Santa is leaving – on his way to take presents to all good little boys and girls. It's getting cold outside."

"Well, you'd better tell him that Santa is starting at the other end of the world so he'll eat at your Mom's, open presents, and get home to bed before Santa gets here."

"Yeah, not a bad idea," he mused as he walked back outside.

Later the older cousins laughed when Jaime told them of Rudolph and Santa's landing, but Susie (Jaime's two-year-old cousin) and Billy wanted to see Flanagan's barn.

Chapter V

The Mess

The week after Christmas Ma and Pa Kidd packed up and decided to take a vacation to Florida. "We don't have to worry this winter about snow, cold weather, keeping fires going at the store," Pa said as he put another box of food in the RV. Just think - sunshine and warm weather. We might just decide to stay there for good."

Jaime's eyes grew wide. "No, Pawpaw."

Pa laughed. "I'm teasing, Jaime. We will probably stay at least a month though. Don't look for us back too soon."

Ma walked out the door with some clothes on a hanger. "I think this is the last of it," she said. We're ready to leave." She bent down and gave Jaime a hug. "You be a good boy while we're gone now."

"I will, Mawmaw."

She hugged Ray and said, "You be a good boy too."

"I will," Ray grinned. "When you get back you won't recognize the store."

"Oh, really?" Ma said.

"What are you planning on doing?" Pa asked.

"I'm going to move the coolers to the other wall and open up the front windows."

"Have fun," Pa said as he climbed up into the cab. He turned to Ma, "Let's go tell Susie bye on our way out." With that they waved good-bye as the RV rolled away.

Ray had worked half of the night moving the coolers from in front of the windows to the opposite wall. That meant that everything had to be taken off of the shelves, the shelves moved over a few feet and then cleaned and restocked. Barbara shook her head in amazement. "Aunt Pearl, look how much brighter the store looks!"

"Boy, we sure do have our work cut out today. Look at this mess." Aunt Pearl shook her head. "I always say, the best way to get a job done is to get it started, but I declare I just don't know where to start!"

Barbara laughed. She looked out over the room before her. Food was stashed in boxes everywhere and the floor had crusty dirt where the shelves and coolers had sat before they had been moved. She heard the door chimes ring out. Looking around she saw Mary Redd standing in the threshold. Mary lived on the other side of the church. She stood only 4'10" tall and had red hair so bright and prominent that everybody called her by her last name. She had worked in the store for Ma and Pa Kidd most of the twenty-two years they had been in business.

"What happened here?" Red said as soon as Barbara's and her eyes met. "I didn't hear about any tornado sweeping through here last night, but it must have."

"No, not a tornado," said Aunt Pearl. "It was Hurricane Ray."

Red laughed. "I never did like it when Gene put those coolers in front of the big windows. This is going to look so much better. Where's Ray anyway? I need him to look at my furnace. It isn't working right."

"Ray worked here yesterday morning," Barbara said, "then second shift on the railroad and got home about midnight and worked until four this morning moving these coolers. I don't think we had better be waking him up."

"Well, put this buttermilk on my bill and I'll come back when he gets up," Red replied.

After she walked out the door, Aunt Pearl threw her hands on her hips. "Ain't she gonna give Ray any time to rest. I tell ye Barb, Gene spoiled her. Every time she wanted something done, he would go fix it for her. Now that him and Betty's gone to Florida for the winter, she expects Ray to do everything for her. She oughta hire some of these ole boys around here to help her. Wouldn't have hurt her to help empty a few of these boxes either!"

"Yeah, I know. Aggravates me too," Barbara said as she started cleaning one of the shelves. "I reckon they have a hard time saying 'no' to her."

Finally about eleven o'clock Ray walked in. "Hey, y'all been working hard! It's really starting to shape up."

"Yeah, well, we didn't have much of a choice. Ever try selling stuff out of boxes? Every time someone comes in looking for something, we're going through boxes trying to find what they want. You should have seen the milk man!" Barbara laughed. "He stopped dead in his tracks and asked Pearl, 'What did y'all do with my milk cooler?' Pearl said to him, 'We're still trying to find it ourselves!'"

Ray laughed. "Tell me, do you like the way I've got the coolers arranged?"

"I sure do," Barbara said, "but more than that I like the sunshine coming in. This all will look so much cleaner and better when we get through."

"Good, now how about something to eat. I've got to leave for work in two hours."

"I'll get it ready for ye," Aunt Pearl said.

As she started back to the kitchen the chimes rang out again. It was Red. They watched as Ray followed her out the door and up to her house. "Dadgum it, Barbara. I knew it! I'll go on and fix his breakfast and pack his bucket. Maybe he won't be too long."

Barbara didn't answer as Mrs. Fox had just walked in the door. "Well, howdy, Barbara. I see Red's done got Ray doing another chore…Good gosh! What happened here? Y'all done tore the place apart. Looks diff'rent. I need me a can of green beans. Now you just tell me whar' I'm gonna find that? How do y'all 'spect a body to find anything anyhow? This is a mess!"

"Yeah, we've been hearing that all morning." Barbara sat a bag of sugar on the shelf. "You just tell me what you want and I'll get it for you. Everything should be in order by this time tomorrow."

"Well, I certainly do hope so. You needed to close the store to do somethin' like this."

"If we had closed the store, how would you be able to get your green beans?" Barbara asked.

"Oh, I'd just knock on the door and you could let me come in since I'm such a good customer. But ye ought to keep most everybody else out, ye know. It's gonna work ye to death tryin' to wait on everbody and do this too. Whar's Pearl at anyways. She should be helpin' ye."

"She's fixing Ray's breakfast and bucket to take to work."

"Oh, well, that's okay. You're lucky ye got her to help. She's a good worker." Mrs. Fox hesitated. "Breakfast? Purty late to be havin' breakfast, ain't it. It'll soon be lunch time."

"After Ray got home about midnight, he worked on this most of the rest of the night and slept in this morning," Barbara said.

30

"Oh, well then, watcha got in the bottom of that box thar'?" she said pointing over to a large open box on the floor.

"Steak sauces," said Barbara.

"No, I don't need no steak sauce. Don't eat steak. Don't have no money to buy steak much. And iffin I did, I wouldn't have the teeth to chew it. What's in the bottom of that box?"

"Um, let's see. Oh, mayonnaise and mustard," Barbara answered.

"Nope, don't need no mayonnaise or mustard. I declare, how's a body supposed to shop out of boxes? I can't even tell what's in the bottoms of half of 'em. Well, I guess I could just get my green beans, and, oh, - some bologny. I'll come back tomorrow. It's an inconvenience, but I reckon a body's gotta do what a body's gotta do. You tell Ray those coolers was good the way they was. Tell Pearl to slice me some thick bologny and I'll be on my way." She walked toward the windows. "Oh, brother, here comes Idy. She gets on my nerves the way she's so loud and laughin' at everthang. Tell Pearl to hurry. One pound will be enough."

Mrs. Fox passed Ida on the way out. "Watch whar ye walk, Idy. They got a mess in thar."

"Lordy, lordy. What a mess!" Ida proclaimed as she stopped at the door. "Y'all open for bizness?"

No, we just leave the door open so everybody can come in and see our "mess," thought Barbara; but instead she said, "Sure, we're open."

Ida walked through the door.

"Just be careful and don't fall over anything," Barbara said.

"Whatcha doin', anyhow?" Ida looked around. "Oh, hi, Pearl. Did you make this mess?"

"No, Hurricane Ray did," Aunt Pearl answered. "Ye shoulda seen it earlier. It was worse."

"Hurricane Ray?" Ida wiped the snuff drool from her mouth with the back of her hand and swallowed.

"Yes, Idy – Pearl's teasing. Ray moved the coolers over against the far wall so the sun could shine through the windows," Barbara said.

"You mean Him-icane Ray," Ida scoffed. "Well, now I'm all for sunshine, but whatcha gonna do when it rains or snows. Somedays the sun don't shine, don'tcha know."

"Yeah, well, we'll settle for just the extra daylight," Barbara quipped.

Ida grinned. "Yeah, well, I need me some Sweet and Low and some cough drops and some instant coffee...and...um...let's see. Oh yeah, a loaf of bread and a can opener...mine broke," Ida said. "And put it on my bill.

I'll be up here the first of the month to git that necklace you got in the showcase. I like that necklace. Granny's gonna take me to the doctor on the first, but I'll be up to pay my bill. Now don't you worry. I'll be here, just a little late."

"I know you will…"

"And I'm a gonna git that necklace. Don't tell Granny I'm getting' it. She thinks I waste too much of my money. By gollys, I say. Whatcha want me to do? Take it with me, I says, but she just stares at me and says nothin'. Nothin' she *can* say." She swallowed again. "It's *my* money, not her-uns, ya know."

"Right," said Barbara. She bagged the groceries as Ida walked up and down the aisles looking in the boxes.

"Here, add this to the bi-ill…," Ida tripped and fell over a box as a can of corn went rolling down the aisle.

Barbara and Pearl both ran to her. They couldn't lift her. "I'll go get Ray," Barbara said, but no sooner had she uttered the words than Ray walked through the door.

"I'm all right. I'm all right." Ida repeated as Ray helped her to her feet. "I jest fell down. Everybody falls down sometime or 'nother."

"You sure you're okay?" Ray asked.

"For pity's sake. Sure, I'm sure. Now let me go afore I hit ye with my can of corn. Whar is my can of corn at?"

"Here it is," Pearl said.

"Thank ya," Ida said as she shook her head. "This place is a mess. I'm goin' home."

"Thank you, Idy. You be careful and have a good day," Barbara smiled.

"I will, Missy. You don't work too hard, ye hear?" She looked around one more time as she went out the door. "Hurry up and git this stuff back on the shelves."

Later that afternoon, Barbara watched as the school bus pulled up outside. Jaime ran into the store waving an envelope. "Mom, we got our report cards. Teacher said I did good." Before he said anything else, he stopped and stared. "What happened?"

"Dad moved the coolers and shelves and we're putting the stuff back on the shelves. Do you like it?" Barbara asked him. "Here let me see your report card."

Barbara opened the envelope as Jaime moved through the boxes. "I'm hungry, Aunt Pearl. You got something to eat?"

"Supper will be ready in a little bit," Pearl answered.

"Jaime, you got all S's on your card. That's real good." Barbara grinned and hugged him.

"What's S mean?" Aunt Pearl asked.

"Well, since he's only in kindergarten they just put S for 'Satisfactory' or N for 'Needs Improvement,'" Barbara answered.

"Hey, you did do good." Pearl hugged Jaime.

"Yeah, I know," Jaime pulled his shoulders back, threw his head up and grinned. "I'll help you empty the boxes, Mom. This place is a mess!"

Barbara laughed as she went to the counter to wait on her next customer that had just come in. Jaime reached in boxes and pulled things out and sat them on the shelves, moving them to and fro trying to display them in what he thought was good order. Presently, Shirley drove up in the driveway and let Seth, Sarah and Billy out of the car. They ran into the store.

"Mom said she would be back in about an hour," Sarah said. She looked around her. "What happened?"

"Uncle Ray moved our shelves and coolers," Barbara said.

"It's a mess," Sarah said in her ten-year-old grown-up voice. "Aunt Barbara, I got straight A's on my report card," she said proudly.

Barbara grinned. "That's good, Sarah. You're a smart girl. I'm proud of you."

"I'm hungry," Billy announced.

"Aunt Pearl's fixin' something," Jaime said. "Let's go see."

"Ugh, brown beans," Billy said as he spied the pot of pintos on the stove. "I don't like brown beans."

"Me neither," said Seth.

"Well, it's what you're getting today," Pearl said as she sighed. "Eat up what ye want and then go out to the churchyard to play or I'll put ye to work."

"I'm not hungry," Billy said.

"Me neither," said Sarah.

"I am," Jaime said.

"I'll eat," chimed in Seth.

"I'm gonna get Mom to get me some potato chips when she gets back," said Billy.

"Eat or empty boxes," Pearl said.

Sarah started emptying a box. Billy sat at the table with a frown and a small bowl of beans. He half-heartedly picked at them. Barbara looked at Aunt Pearl and sighed as she filled up a bowl for herself.

"I know," Aunt Pearl said.

The next morning everything would be back on the shelves and clean. Barbara and Aunt Pearl wouldn't remember their heads touching the pillow as they went to bed that night.

Chapter VI

The Big Snow

Barbara woke to the sound of a rooster crowing – three times. It was the clock radio and she knew it was 6:00 a.m. She loved to listen to WBDY country and western station and she loved to hear that rooster crow every morning. It reminded her of life on Wright's Mountain in West Virginia before they had bought the store. She had loved to walk in the woods with Jaime and teach him about nature as they picked and ate teaberries, strawberries and blackberries. How she loved the solitude and serenity of that life. Now everything seemed fast paced and there was very little solitude. She opened her eyes. The room seemed bright. It wasn't time for the sun to be up. She got out of bed and peeked out the blinds as the National Anthem played.

"Oh, Ray, Jaime, it snowed last night. The ground is covered and the mountain looks like a Christmas card!"

Jaime jumped up and ran to their room. He pulled the blinds aside on the big old window that almost reached to the floor. "Oh, wow, can we build a snowman?"

"Maybe later," Ray said. "Listen, they're giving school closings."

"Mercer County closed, McDowell County closed, Tazewell County closed..." the DJ continued.

"Well, Jaime, looks like you don't have to go to school today. Go on back and lie down. We can get a little extra shut-eye this morning," Ray said.

"Yippee!" Jaime ran back to his room and yelled, "No school in Tazewell County, Aunt Pearl. We get to build a snowman!"

"So much for extra shut-eye," Ray mumbled.

Before 8:00 a.m. they were all four in the store and ready for the day.

The snow kept coming down fast and hard and the driveway was covered. Aunt Pearl fixed a big breakfast of sausage, eggs, homemade biscuits and gravy. Their bellies were full by 9:00 and they had seen only two customers and no delivery trucks.

"I'm going to have to start shoveling that snow or no one will be able to get into the driveway," Ray said.

"I want to shovel," Jaime said.

Ray gathered up four shovels (one snow shovel, three coal shovels) from the basement and garage and they all started shoveling. At 10:30 John and Shirley arrived with Sarah, Seth and Billy. They all took turns shoveling. Even though everyone was having fun, the parking lot seemed enormous. "We really need to hire a snowplow to do this," Ray said. "It's too much snow to shovel by hand and it will take a week to melt if we don't get it off before the cars start packing it down."

"I don't know, Ray," Barbara said. "That will probably cost a fortune. I don't know if we can manage it."

"Well, we can hardly manage shoveling it," Ray retorted. "If this melts and refreezes, it will be ice for a week or more."

"Hey, everybody, how about hot chocolate and popcorn," Aunt Pearl called.

The grownups and kids laid the shovels against the building as they clamored into the store. About noon a pickup truck with a snowplow pulled into the driveway.

"Would you like to have your driveway scraped?" he asked.

"Yes!" Ray answered without hesitation.

Barbara furrowed her eyebrows and rubbed her forehead as she stared at the floor. Ray followed the man outside and Barbara watched as the snowplow pushed the snow out of the driveway with ease. In a matter of twenty minutes the asphalt was peeking through.

When Ray came back inside, the driveway was clean and the truck was gone. "I ought to buy me one of those plows! That's what we need."

"How much?" Barbara asked.

"I don't know. I've never priced them. Probably could get a good used one for a few hundred dollars."

"No, Ray...how much did he charge us for the driveway?"

"Fifteen dollars," Ray grinned.

"You're kidding!" Barbara said.

"Nope, it true. Aren't you glad I let him do it."

"I sure am," Barbara shook her head in disbelief. "I guess we'll have to call him next time it snowsss…" Barbara blinked her eyes as the lights flickered and died.

"Oh no, the lights! That's all we need." Ray groaned. Even though outside was bright, the store seemed dark. Ray manually opened the register by a toggle switch on the bottom. "I guess you'll have to add the purchases in your head or on paper and keep track of the sales on another sheet of paper." Ray looked around. "We need to find some flashlights."

Barbara reached behind the charge books. "Here's one." The phone rang and she answered it. "Hello…Yes, ours are out…I don't know…No, I don't…I hope so…No, I don't know that either." She hung up and looked at the others. "A customer wanted to know if our lights were out, what made them go out, how long would they be out, they hoped it wouldn't be long and wonder if anybody called the power company." She laughed and shook her head. "Wonder why she thought I would know any of that?"

Aunt Pearl chuckled.

"Well, John, lets take the kids and go home. Our lights must be out too," Shirley said.

As they went out, a customer came in. "What happened to the lights?"

"Probably heavy snow on the power lines," Ray answered.

"Well, wonder when they'll get them fixed? You reckon anybody called Appalachian Power?"

"I don't know," Ray answered.

"Wonder how long they'll be out?"

"Hard to tell," Ray answered again.

"Better give me some D size batteries and a couple of candles. I better get about $5.00 in gas."

"The pumps won't work without electricity," Ray said.

"Can't you get the pumps to working?"

"Not without electricity, I can't," Ray said.

"Don't you have a generator or something?"

"I wish I did," Ray sighed.

"But I need some gas."

The phone rang and Barbara picked it up again. "Yes, our lights are out…I don't know…No, I don't…Yes, I suppose we'll stay open until sunset and then we won't be able to see in here. We're already having to use a flashlight…No, it's hard to tell how long…Okay, thanks." The phone rang again just as Barbara hung it up. "Hello, yes, he's here. Hold on a moment. Ray, it's for you."

Ida rang the bells over the door. "Land sakes alive…it's dark in here! I need some candles. You got any candles? I got a flashlight, but it don't work. I put new batteries in it. You think it's the bulb?"

"Let me see, Idy." Aunt Pearl took the flashlight. "We have bulbs. Let me try to fix it."

"Thank ye, Aunt Pearl. Now Barbara where's the candles? Wonder what made the lights go off? A car might have run into a telephone pole. Wonder how long it'll be before they come back on? Did y'all call the power company?"

"No, I should…"

"I tell ye one thing, I'm not payin' my bill if they don't soon get them fixed. I'm glad ole Idy here's got a coal stove. My place is warm and toasty, but I got mighty cold coming up here."

Barbara looked at Ida's feet. She had on a pair of men's galoshes over her ragged tennis shoes. "Here are your candles, Idy."

'And here's your flashlight, - good as new." Pearl grinned.

"Well, I'll be switched! Thank ye, Pearl. I better get me some food so's I won't get hungry. Put this pie on my bill and a loaf of that Sunbeam bread. Oh yeah, I need some bologny to go with it. Slice me about a pound – not too thick – not too thin, Aunt Pearl."

"Idy, you shouldn't be getting this pie. You know what Granny says," Barbara sighed.

"And I know it ain't none of Granny's bizness. Sides, tain't for me noways. Hey, this here's that ole' store-bought bologny. I wanted you to slice me some of the good kind."

"Can't. No electricity for the slicer. Besides, the kind I slice is 'store-bought' bologny, too." Pearl grinned.

"Is not, Pearl!"

"You buy it here in the store, don't you?" Pearl said.

"Oh – you know what I mean," said Ida. "I'll see y'all tomorrey. I don't know how y'all gonna do bizness with no lights." She stood there turning her flashlight off and on. "Thanks again, Pearl." She stood watching out the door, but didn't leave. "I'll tarry here a minute longer. Here comes that snooty Mrs. Fox."

Ray hung up the phone. "Barbara, that was Jeremy over on the hill. He said he got a call from Helen Modena. She's gotten herself in the ditch on the other side of the mountain and needs help. I'll be back as soon as I can."

"What can you do?" Barbara asked.

"I'll take a chain and try to pull her out with my truck."

"Oh, Ray, be careful – that sounds dangerous."

"I'll be okay. Don't worry."

Mrs. Fox walked in the door as Ray was walking out the door. Barbara stood watching him as he climbed into the truck.

The phone rang and Pearl picked it up. "Yes, our lights are out...No, I don't know when they'll get them back on...Yes...No..."

"Whar's Ray goin'?" Mrs. Fox asked Barbara. Without waiting for an answer she asked, "Wonder when they'll get the lights back on? Do ye know what caused 'em to go out? Sorry light company. They need to fix up these lines around here. I ain't even got a candle or flashlight. Looks like they could take better care of the lines with all the money we pay 'em."

"I wouldn't want to be out in this weather – especially up on one of those poles," Barbara said.

"Ain't that the truth?" Ida picked up her bags. "Thanks again, y'all."

"You're welcome."

Barbara walked back behind the counter. "Who cleaned your parkin' lot?" Mrs. Fox asked. "It looks real good. I can't say the same for this floor. Pearl, ye oughta keep a mop in yer hand. That's the only way yer gonna keep it clean in this weather." She looked around. "Whar's the candles at? Oh, yeah and I need some matches. Ye got any matches?"

"Here are your candles," Barbara said.

"How long ye had these candles? Reckon they'll burn okay?"

Barbara smiled as she clinched her teeth. Pearl tapped her foot on the floor and said nothing as she gazed at the ceiling. "I'm sure they'll burn, Mrs. Fox," Barbara said. "I don't think candles have an expiration date."

"Well, we'll see. How much? You ain't raisin' the price 'cause of the lights bein' out, are you?"

"Mrs. Fox! I'll have you know Ray and Barbara don't operate like that!" Aunt Pearl snapped as her brown eyes flashed fire. "Those candles are the same price today as they were yesterday!"

"Well, ye don't hafta get yer dander up, Pearl. I was just inquirin'. I'll see y'all tomorrey."

The telephone rang again. "Yes, Red, our lights have been out about an hour or so...No, I don't know how long...No, Ray had to go help somebody out of the ditch on the other side of Peeled Chestnut...It's hard to tell how long he'll be gone...Yes, it will be dark soon...Okay. Bye."

"What?" Pearl asked.

"She wanted Ray to come out and go up into her attic to find her candles for her. She sounded aggravated because he wasn't here," Barbara answered.

"Good Lord." Aunt Pearl shook her head.

Five minutes later Red walked in the door. "Let me have some candles and a six volt battery. I'm so aggravated. I had a cake in the oven when the lights went out. It was for Ray. He's always so good about helpin' me with things."

Barbara glanced around and caught a look of dismay on Aunt Pearl's face. She tried to hide a grin.

Red continued on. "I hope the lights don't stay off long. My house is getting cold 'cause the fan won't blow on the coal furnace. I'll have to crawl under the quilts pretty soon."

Barbara handed her the battery and candles. "Here you go. You try to keep warm now. I'll tell Ray about his cake…and thanks."

"You're welcome, Barb. Cake's ruined though. Maybe I'll make him a pumpkin pie when the lights come back on. That boy always did like his pumpkin pies. Did he ever tell y'all about him and John settin' me in the produce cooler and wouldn't let me out until I promised to make them each a pumpkin pie?"

"No," said Aunt Pearl.

"Yes," said Barbara.

"Well, anyways, they were both teenagers. What one of those boys didn't think of, the other one did. They were something else." Red turned and almost bumped into her neighbor that lived on the hill behind her. "Oh, hi, Ethan. How are you and Gladys getting along?"

"We're fine, Red," he answered quietly and smiled at her. "See ye later." He turned to Barbara. "Hi, Barbara, how are you."

"I'm fine," Barbara answered.

"And how are you, Aunt Pearl?"

"I'm good too, Ethan. How 'bout you and Gladys. Y'all keepin' warm?"

"Yeah, we're fine. I just need some bread, bologny, snuff and pop," he said. "It's gettin' cold in here. You want I should put some more wood and coal on the farr, Barbara?"

"Oh, yes. That would be great, Ethan. Ray's gone to get somebody out of the ditch and the fan's not working. We're getting pretty cold. Here's the key to the basement."

"Yeah, I guess it's kinda' hard to work in your coats, huh?"

"Yes, it is," said Barbara and Pearl at the same time.

"I'm not too cold," Jaime said as he sat over the heat register with his coat, hat and gloves on. "It's warmer than outside building that snowman."

They all laughed. "I'll be back in a minute," Ethan said.

"Barbara, he is the kindest soul," said Pearl. "There he lives up on the side of that hill in a little three room shack and he comes down here and takes care of us."

"I know, Aunt Pearl. He's my favorite customer."

"Mine too," Pearl said.

They spent the rest of the afternoon answering the telephone and waiting on customers by flashlight - with a pad and pencil.

Finally about 5:30 Ray came back. He looked tired. "Let me fix the fire and then we'd better close. It's getting too dark to see. It's really not safe trying to wait on people in the dark. They can fill their pockets and we can't even see what they're getting. I bet you've sold out of candles and batteries by now."

"Yes, candles are all gone and only a few batteries left. We even sold out of flashlights," said Barb. "I'm ready to go home." Aunt Pearl agreed and Jaime was ready to 'go watch TV'.

"Honey," Aunt Pearl said. "There is no television over at the house. The lights are out there too."

"Oh, no! Well, can I have my own flashlight?" Jaime asked. "Wonder if there will be school tomorrow?"

"I doubt it," Barbara sighed. "Why do you want your own flashlight."

"'Cause it's dark."

"Oooh," said Barbara.

Ray banked the fire for the night as Barbara and Aunt Pearl gathered their belongings and walked outside. Ray slid the key into the lock and said, "Let's go home."

The snow had quit and the black sky was brilliant with a million stars. Barbara watched the steam as she blew her breath into the cold air. The four of them walked up the driveway to their little house next door.

"Ray, why does everybody call here to find out about the electricity? Why would they think we have the answers?" Barbara asked.

"I'm not sure. Maybe because we're a business and they expect us to service whatever needs they have, including the need for information."

"Well, I tell you one thing, it has worn me out."

"Me too," said Pearl.

"Me too," piped Jaime.

"How did it go with you and the rescue mission?" Barbara asked Ray.

"Well, let's put it this way. I pulled her out of the ditch, escorted her six miles back across the mountain to her house, shoveled her driveway by hand so she could get her car parked in it and she didn't even say as much as a 'Thank you'. Maybe she was just too frustrated. All she said was, 'I'm going to bed.'"

"No wonder you look so tired." Barbara hesitated as she looked up at Ray's face in the darkness. "Poor Ray," she said.

Ray let out a deep breath and chuckled as he put his arms around Barbara's shoulders and looked down at her. "I think it should be more like, 'poor all of us'."

"Yeah, all of us," said Jaime.

"What time did the lights come back on?" Barbara asked the next morning as she watched Ray add coal to their little Warm Morning stove.

"About 2:00 a.m. I'm glad we're heating with this stove," Ray said. "I bet a lot of people got cold before the electricity came back on. And I'm glad it was cold enough for y'all to put the milk and meats outside in washtubs and cover them with snow last night, but I'm sure we lost all of the ice cream."

"Yeah, now we have to put everything back," Barbara said.

Ray shook his head. "We'll get it done. Leave Jaime and Pearl sleeping since they announced no school again today. We'll go early to check on the ice cream and put the perishables in the coolers."

"I'm up," Aunt Pearl said as she walked up behind them "I'll be over to start breakfast soon as I get dressed."

Sure enough, the ice cream had melted. "I added it up in my head yesterday," Barbara said. "It's about $400.00 worth."

"Maybe either Flav-O-Rich or our insurance company will pay for it," Ray said.

"I hope so. Boy, what a mess we'll have to clean out of this cooler."

"Yeah," Ray said, "but we'd better get the milk and other stuff uncovered and put back into the coolers before customers start coming in."

As soon as breakfast was over and the coolers were cleaned and restocked, Barbara started making her phone calls. Ray walked in as she was sitting at the adding machine doing her checking up. "Why the downcast look?" he asked.

"Flav-O-Rich said there is no way they can make up all of the ice cream. There are just too many stores that had the same loss. They told me to call Appalachian Power. Appalachian said they are not responsible for these acts of God. They suggested I call the insurance company. I did. They said they had quit covering the loss of food for grocery stores several years ago. They said food is too perishable and easy to lose...too big an expense." She looked up at Ray. "We have to suffer the loss."

"I can't believe it," he said. "It doesn't seem fair."

"I know. I wanted to buy Jaime a new pair of shoes. Have you noticed the ones he's wearing? Now I'll have to wait until you get your payday. I hope the ones he has lasts 'til next month."

"For Pete's sake, Barbara. Buy them anyway. Take the money out of the register."

Barbara stared at Ray, and then dropped her gaze. She laid her papers down; slowly rose and walked back to the kitchen with her shoulders slumped. *He has no idea how hard these bills are to pay.*

Ray walked outside.

Chapter VII

Bobby Darling

January slipped into February and February into March. Barbara was able to restock the ice cream cooler a little at a time. She had to miss restocking a few items here and there so that it would be possible to pay the bills on time. For every item she was unable to stock, she realized it meant lost profit, but she also reckoned that a bad credit rating would be a greater loss. An advertised clearance sale at K-Mart constituted a trip to Bluefield and a new pair of shoes for Jaime.

Since Ray was working second shift as a machinist on the big engines for the railroad, the plan for opening the garage was put on the back burner. He would use the garage for personal repairs and occasionally fixing a few flats and oil changes for customers. Barbara and Aunt Pearl worked hard and managed to do the "manly" work when Ray wasn't there; although, Barbara always felt less stressed when he was there. Sometimes she would awaken in the middle of the night and marvel at the things she had done. Her experience in the business world had always been behind a desk in an accounting department. She had even kept the books for Ma and Pa and that came in handy now. When they had decided to buy the store, she thought she would hate stocking shelves and filling liquid propane bottles on cold wintry days. Well, she still minded filling LP bottles on cold wintry days (especially on dark evenings), but stocking, cleaning and waiting on customers was certainly a different world – a world she was beginning to like.

"A pack of Camels," he said with a heavy mountain drawl. Bobby Darling was a man of few words. He rarely asked for cigarettes since he usually dipped Big G Superior Snuff. He wore the same clothes every day and carried a plastic spoon in his shirt pocket. Barbara supposed it was to dip the fine powdery snuff from the box before putting it in his lower lip. He was severely buck-toothed and the snuff always clung to his teeth. He was about 5'6", and had jet-black hair and dark brown eyes.

As Barbara turned to get the pack of cigarettes, she heard him say, "My woman left me." She turned back and looked at him. There was a clean imprint of a spoon above his shirt pocket, but no spoon today. He looked distressed. He had been in the store many times with his "woman." She looked to be in her fifties; he was in his late twenties. She was overweight, gray haired and toothless – and the boss.

He repeated, "Yeah, my woman left me. Had me take her down to North Caroliner to visit her kin. Then after I got her thar, she let her dag-gone mother and kids talk her into stayin'. Sent me home. Says she's not comin' back. I'd of never took her down thar if I'd a knowed what she was goin' to do. Well, she ain't a gonna have me to look after her no more. No sir, she ain't a gonna have me to do fer her. And if she thinks I'm a gonna take her back, she's got another think a comin'. No sir, she done lost me fer good."

Barbara stood there with the cigarettes in her hand staring at him. "I'm sorry, Bobby," she said. "Maybe she'll be back."

"No sir. I don't care if she does come back. I can cook and do fer myself. I don't need no woman to look after me. I was good to her. NO sir, I ain't gonna take her back. Do ya blame me?"

"Well…no. I don't guess so."

"Dag-gone right." He looked Barbara in the eye, paid for his cigarettes, turned around and walked out the door. "Dag-gone right," he repeated.

Aunt Pearl started laughing. Barbara joined her. "He'd take her back in a heartbeat," Pearl said. "I've never heard him talk so much."

"Yeah, I was thinking the same thing," Barbara said. "He's never said more than a short sentence to me and there he stood baring his soul. I didn't know what to say. My insides were churning. I could hardly keep from laughing and at the same time I felt sorry for him."

Ray walked in the door and found them giggling. "What?"

They both took turns telling the story, trying to mimic his words and accent. "I almost dropped the cigarettes when I heard him drawl, 'My wo-man left me'," Barbara laughed. "There was a lot of 'woe' in his 'wo-man'."

Ray laughed with them. He shook his head. "Poor Bobby," he said, "but I'm hungry. Let's get something to eat." As they ate, Ray sat staring at the other end of the store. "I've been thinking. I could tear down that wall between the store and feed room. We could turn it into a place to put the pop and make more room in the store. All those big windows would make it even brighter in here. It wouldn't take too much to do it. I've got a good payday coming this week."

"Hey, I like that idea," Barbara mused. "We hardly ever sell a bag of feed – besides I hate the way it smells and it only serves to draw the mice and rats from the creek down back."

"Yeah, and besides, half the time we sell a bag, they expect us to carry it and put it in their truck or car," Aunt Pearl said. "I won't miss that part of it."

"Me either," Barbara said.

"Okay, that settles it," Ray said. "I'll leave early for work and stop by Lowe's to pick up some supplies that I'll need. I'll need to build a step up to the room from this main part of the store. That will be no problem." Ray stopped and looked at Barbara. "I've also been thinking that I'm going to close off part of it for an office for you…big enough for a cot for Jaime's naps or in case some of us need to lie down."

Barbara lifted her eyebrows and grinned.

Barbara awoke to an empty bed. She looked at the clock radio. It was 3:00 a.m. *Where could Ray be? He's never been past 1:00 getting home.* She eased out of bed, tiptoed through Jaime's room and went upstairs (the bedrooms were in the basement). *Maybe he came home and was watching TV and fell asleep in the chair.* The living room was quiet and dark. She looked out the window on the side to the store. There she saw the lights on and through the big windows could see Ray tearing down the wall between the feed room and the main part of the store. "I don't believe this," she muttered. She stood watching a few minutes and finally shook her head as she descended the stairs to go back to bed.

The next morning she found Ray lying beside her – gently snoring. She grinned, planted a kiss on his forehead and eased herself out of bed. By 8:00 a.m. she had put Jaime on the school bus and she and Aunt Pearl were looking at the mess.

"Well, at least he got the big stuff up and it's not as big as the last 'mess' we had," Pearl said. "Might as well get started cleaning up."

By the time Ray had gotten up, they had the floor cleaned, the few bags of feed stacked in the back corner and Pearl was washing the windows.

"Hi, Ethan," Ray said as he walked in the door.

46

"Hi, Ray," Ethan nodded toward Ray's project. "It sure does look good. Barbara was just tellin' me how much she loved seein' that sunshine come in those big windows. It'll make a whole lot more room in here fer you'uns."

"Yeah, it will," Ray said. "We plan to move all of the pop up there and move the chips over to where the pop is. That'll open up this space around the counter here and everything won't be so crowded. I think Pearl's jumping the gun cleaning windows since I still have a lot to do before it's finished. What do you think?"

"Well, maybe I'll just finish by dusting everything down and clean when the project is finished." Pearl stepped down from the stepladder she was on.

Ethan nodded. Barbara put his groceries in a box. Ethan preferred his groceries packed that way instead of paper bags. They were easier to carry (up on his shoulder) and he could use the box in his stove to start the fires or use as fuel when coal and wood ran low.

"Let me drive you home," Ray said.

"Nah, I'll be okay," Ethan said. "Thank ye, anyways."

Ethan lived about 1/3 mile up the mountain in a little three-room shack. He walked back and forth two or three times a day. He was in his sixties and had been a customer of the store since the day its doors had opened in June of 1960. He had never worked a steady job, but he was not lazy. He was willing to help anytime anyone needed him. He was usually tinkering at something. Ray had asked him to tend the furnace fire when the store opened and bank it at night on the days he was working. Ethan did, and he even checked in more often on cold days to make sure it was still warm enough for Aunt Pearl and Barbara. Ray would pay him a little every so often, and Ethan was thankful to get it. He was almost always dirty and wore old clothing. They had no running water; he carried it from a wet spring that ran out of the mountain just above his house. Some people might have regarded him as worthless, but Barbara called him a "diamond in the rough."

Ray ate his breakfast and started back to work on the new room by measuring the sheetrock dimensions. He walked up to the garage to cut the first sheet just as Bobby Darling pulled into the driveway in his El Camino. Bobby had taken a truck camper topper and cut it to fit on his car. The windows revealed it piled full of junk and clothing.

"Hey, Bobby," Ray yelled. "Could you come up here for a minute?"

"Sure thang," said Bobby. "Whatcha doin'?"

"I'm trying to make a little more room in the store. How about holding the other end of this piece of sheetrock while I cut it…"

"Sure," Bobby said.

"What's been going on with you? How have you been?" Ray asked.

"Not too good. My woman left me."

Ray listened to his story and sympathized as if it was the first time he had heard it. "Well, Bobby, why don't you go to the welfare office and get you a woman?"

Bobby gasped. "What!?! Ain't no welfare office gonna give me a woman!"

"Why not?" Ray asked. "You need a woman to do your cooking and cleaning, don't you?"

"Well…yeah."

"They give you a check every month, food stamps, a medical card, heating and other assistance, don't they?"

"Well, yes sir, they surely do," Bobby answered as he studied Ray's face.

Ray nodded his head. "Well, it's like this – when somebody's left without anybody to take care of them, they have to hire somebody to do their cooking and cleaning."

Bobby cocked his head sideways and with a look of wondering asked, "You kiddin' me, right?"

"No sir," said Ray. "Now you just think about it. You don't have a job and they have to take care of you. Right?"

"Well sir, I reckon that's true enough." Bobby slowly nodded his head.

"Now, what you have to do is go to the office and ask for a woman. They'll surely give you the runaround, so you'll need to stick up for yourself. Be firm. Walk into that office and demand that you need a woman and you won't leave there until they give you a woman."

Bobby's eyes were wide. "Well, I'll be dogged," he said. "I never knew that. I just might have to go over to that welfare office and see about that thang. You sure you know what you're talkin' about, Ray?"

"Sure, I'm sure. Just you remember, you have to stick to your guns."

Bobby stood looking up at Ray and nodding his head up and down. Finally he said, "Thank ye, Ray." He turned and walked a little taller as he trotted down to the store. With a new air of confidence he said to Barbara, "Give me a Big G."

As he strutted out to his car, Pearl remarked, "Looks like he got over his wo-man soon enough."

"Sure does," Barbara agreed.

Saturday morning dawned with the sun shining bright and the birds singing. "Won't be long now 'til we see the robins," Aunt Pearl commented.

"Smell the air. It smells like spring," Barbara said. "Listen to the cardinals. They sound like they'll be glad to have their cousins back soon."

"They got cousins?" Jaime's interest was piqued.

Aunt Pearl laughed.

"Sure, Jaime," Barbara said. The robins are the redbirds' cousins."

"Cousins...like me and Billy?"

"Sort of...just like that." Barbara patted his back.

"Oh," said Jaime. He stood in the driveway and took an exaggerated breath of air. "Mom, will Mawmaw and Pawpaw be coming home soon? When they called, they said they were coming home in the spring."

"I don't know exactly when, but you're right, son. After they bought that piece of land with a mobile home, they decided to stay the winter... but, winter is almost over."

"I would think it would be soon since it is already getting hot in Florida," Aunt Pearl said.

After a big breakfast, Ray went straight to work on the 'pop room' as they had begun to call it. Later he walked outside for a break with a Pepsi in his hand. He stood outside leaning up against Charlie Fuller's car, talking and watching traffic go by.

"How's your room coming along, Ray?" he asked.

"Pretty good...pretty good. I'll have it ready to paint by this time next week."

"Oh brother...there goes that Bobby Darling in his silly El Camino." Charlie shook his head and muttered something that Ray didn't understand. "He couldn't stuff another sock in the back of that wagon." He stopped and stared at Ray for a moment. "You wouldn't believe what he did to me yesterday."

"Hard to tell with Bobby," Ray said.

"Well, I'll tell you. He came down to the house and says, 'Hey, Charlie, I'll give ya five dollars iffen you'll take me to the welfare office.' Sounded good to me so I told him I would."

"Why didn't he drive himself?" Ray asked.

"He can't take that old thing anywhere near a town…no sticker, tags run out…hard to tell what all he'd get a ticket for. Have ya heard the story about Clarabelle leaving him?"

"Oh, yeah; he told us all about that. But what did he do to you?"

"Well sir, it's like this. All he talked about all the way over there was about his woman, Clarabelle, leaving him. I didn't make any connection to it maybe being the reason he was going to the welfare office. I just figured he needed to sign up or renew something. Anyway, when we got there, I walked in with him and sat down in the waiting room, but he just kept going. Next thing I knew, he'd walked back into one of those cubicles and slammed his fist down on some young girl's desk and yelled, 'I need a woman and I ain't leavin' here 'til y'all give me a woman!'"

"Oh, no…you've got to be kidding," Ray laughed as he shook his head. "It's too good to be true. What did they do?"

"Well sir, that poor girl was shaking. I was afraid we were both going to jail, the way that her supervisor ran over to Bobby; but he just led him over to his desk and talked to him awhile. Then they commenced to filling out some paper work. Bobby said on the way home that he thought they were going to get him someone to come in and clean for him. I'll tell you one thing…I'll never take him anywhere again."

"No?" Ray's face was quivering.

"NO," said Charlie. He stood there a moment looking hard at Ray – then said, "Now where do you think he got such a notion?"

Ray stood there – shaking his head in disbelief – a half smile on his face – owning up to nothing.

Chapter VIII

Isaac

The short breath of spring had faded. The air was crisp, yet heavy with the smell of smoke. The store and every house in the Bottom burned coal and wood for heat. The snow fell hard and fast and traffic was light. "I hope this is our last snow this season," Pearl said.

"Me too," Barbara answered. "I'm glad spring snows are short lived."

"It's not spring yet. We still like a few days being there." Pearl grinned.

"You know what I mean, Aunt Pearl. It sure felt like spring last week." Barbara lifted the Day Book (a record of their daily transactions) from the counter and slid it into a shelf under the counter. "Business sure is slow on days like this. We've only taken in about twenty-five dollars all morning."

"Well, at least that's twenty-five dollars you didn't have before," Pearl said.

"No, it's not, Aunt Pearl." Ray stomped the snow from his feet on the rug. "We have to make at least enough money to pay the day's expenses. We'll go in the hole big time today."

"Oh, I never thought of it that way," Pearl said.

"Most people don't," Barbara said. "Most of the customers give you a dollar and think that you get to keep the whole dollar, but in this business you only average keeping a penny or two of every dollar. If business isn't good, you can go in the red real fast."

"Yeah, I guess so." Pearl nodded her head thoughtfully. The wind chimes rang out as the March wind gusted through the open door. Barbara and Pearl sat on stools over the heat register that was behind the counter – trying to keep warm.

"Hey, Isaac," Pearl said.

"Fine, Pearl, and how are you?" Isaac always answered 'fine' to a greeting instead of hello. He walked over to the pop cooler and chip rack. Then he walked over and sat a bottle of Sunkist orange pop and a bag of peanuts on the counter. "And how are you doing Miss Barbara Ann?"

"I'm fine, thank you," Barbara grinned up at him. Isaac was about 6'4" tall, in his mid sixties with dark, slightly graying hair and dark chocolate brown eyes that revealed a mind of intelligence and a soul of patience and wisdom – a real southern gentle-man. He handed Barbara a five. She took Isaac's money without even telling him how much it was. As was his almost daily ritual, he poured the peanuts into the bottle of orange pop and walked to the door looking out onto the porch. There sat two old metal swing-back chairs that had been painted bright yellow. Pearl and Barbara secretly called them the men's gossiping chairs. If the weather permitted, you would find Ray and Isaac sitting in those chairs, talking, nodding, and laughing as they watched traffic go by.

"Ray, our chairs are full of snow." Isaac grinned as Ray walked up the aisle from the kitchen.

"Yeah, reckon we'll have to loaf inside today, Isaac," Ray laughed. "At least you can. I have to leave early for work today. It takes over an hour to drive it on good days. It'll probably take a lot longer today."

Ray picked up his bucket and told them all goodbye.

"You be careful," Barbara and Aunt Pearl said in unison.

"Always," Ray answered. "You watch over the girls, Isaac. I'm gone."

A shiver from the cold air sent Barbara and Pearl crowding over the heat register again. Isaac picked up a stool and his peanut filled orange pop and came behind the counter to sit. Very few people ventured behind the counter, but Isaac was an exception.

"Hey, Isaac, you want to hear a good one?" asked Pearl.

"Sure 'nough," said Isaac.

"Now, this really happened," Pearl stressed. "It's not just a joke. My niece works with this guy at the big office." (The 'big office' was the main employer of the region, Consolidated Coal Company). "He came in to work last Monday and told her about his weekend."

"Okay, go ahead – tell it." Isaac nodded his head and grinned.

Barbara sat there watching them – her head cocked slightly - biting one side of her lip. She had already heard the story and was wondering how Aunt Pearl was going to tell it. *This might become a little sensitive.*

"Well, here goes." Pearl plunged ahead with a deep breath and a giggle.

"This guy – like I was sayin' – he works at the big office. He said he went home Friday evening from work and his wife told him that their cat had died. They live in an apartment in Princeton and didn't have a place to bury it." Pearl lowered her voice and spoke slowly as she deliberately leaned toward Isaac – "It was a solid black cat."

"Uh-huh." Isaac didn't blink as he nodded his head.

"Well, sir, so anyways, the man tells his wife he guessed they'd have to put it in a garbage bag and take it to the landfill; being as they didn't have a place to bury it. 'Okay,' she said. 'I'm going to the Mercer Mall tomorrow. Guess I'll drop it off on my way since I drive right by there.' So he puts the cat that they had wrapped in the garbage bag down in a shoppin' bag – you know the kind with the handles?" Pearl took a breath and Isaac nodded his head.

"Well, anyways, the next morning, lo and behold she got to talkin' to her girlfriend and they drove right by the turnoff for the landfill. I reckon she forgot the cat was back there 'cause he said later on they came out of the mall with their packages and opened up the trunk of the car and there sat that shoppin' bag with the dead cat. They took the bag out and sit it on the roof of the car while they put their new bags in the trunk. One of them says they're hungry so they decide to go back into the mall and grab a bite to eat before they leave. About halfway across the parkin' lot they remember the cat was left on the roof of the car. They turned around to go back and put it in the trunk when, lo and behold, a big black woman was standing next to their car looking at the bag. She looked around, grabbed the shoppin' bag and scooted on off."

Isaac laughed. "Yeah, that is a good one, Pearl."

"No, wait, I'm not through yet. It gets better." Pearl took another deep breath and chuckled. "Well, they're glad to be rid of the cat. It didn't bother them any that it was stolen. They just laughed and laughed all the way into the mall. Well, the two women go into Hardees and order them some lunch and sit down to eat. About the time they get their sandwiches open, who walks up to the counter but that cat thief with the shoppin' bag. They look at each other – flabbergasted, of course. The woman walks up to the counter, orders a Big Deluxe, large fries and a Dr. Pepper and sits down. But before she opens her sandwich, she decides to see what goody she has stolen, uh, - I mean acquired."

Isaac chuckled.

Pearl continued. "The two friends sit back watching the whole ordeal as the woman fumbles around in the bag, unfolding the garbage bag inside of it. They watch as her eyes grow big. She squeals and passes out – fell out of her seat – right there in Hardees. Isaac, she was black and the cat was too!" Pearl lowered her voice and leaned toward Isaac. "Is it true that blacks are superstitious about black cats?"

"I reckon maybe some," he said.

"Yeah, well, so are some whites." Pearl sat back up and continued, "Anyway, everybody gathers around and the manager yells for a clerk to call the Rescue Squad. They give the woman some ammonia to sniff. She comes to for a second, opens her eyes and spots the bag and faints again. Pretty soon the Rescue Squad is there. They put the woman on the stretcher, lays her pocketbook at her side...and you know what the best part is, Isaac?"

"No, tell me."

The manager says, 'Wait! Here's her package and they put the shopping bag on the other side, right next to her stomach, and roll her away. Now what do you wonder happened when she came to in the ambulance with that bag sitting right up there with her?" Pearl fairly screamed with delight.

All three of them were hysterical by now. Isaac was laughing so hard he almost fell off the stool. Barbara was wiping tears from her eyes.

"Now that is what I call poetic justice," Isaac said.

Everything got real quiet, then Isaac snickered and hysteria started over again. Mrs. Fox walked in. She stopped and stared. They quieted down again as Barbara said hello to her.

"Humph." was all she said and walked back toward the meat cooler that sat in front of the kitchen. "Pearl, I need me some of this hamburger ye got back here."

"Coming," Pearl said.

"Well, I guess I'd better be gettin' myself on home. It sure was good visitin' with y'all today," Isaac said.

Barbara looked up into his warm brown eyes. She tried to figure out if he had gotten his feelings hurt, but couldn't tell. "It sure was, Isaac. I'm glad Ray wasn't here and Aunt Pearl and I could visit with you ourselves for a change."

"Yeah, it was fun," Isaac grinned. "I'll be glad when Gene gets back from Florida. I miss him. Us retired fellers gotta stick together."

"Jaime's ready for his Mawmaw and Pawpaw to come home too. I'm sure they're glad they're not here in this snowstorm though."

"Speaking of Jaime, where is he?"

"Building a snowman in the churchyard with Billy."

"Oh, for the young days." Isaac chuckled. "See you later."

"You be careful going home, Isaac."

"Thanks, I'll do that."

Mrs. Fox laid her hamburger on the counter. "When did y'all git this in?" she asked as she checked the dates on the milk and cheese.

"Yesterday."

"Okay, ring me up," she said frostily.

"Do you want me to put it on your bill?"

"No, I said 'ring me up,' didn't I?"

"Oh, sorry," Barbara said. After she gave Mrs. Fox her change, she said thank you and gave her a wavering smile.

"You're welcome, I guess," Mrs. Fox said as she picked up her package and turned on her heel to walk out the door.

After she left, Pearl told Barbara that Mrs. Fox had told her back at the meat cooler that she "didn't think it was right the way you let that colored man have the run of the store."

"Run of the store? He was just sitting behind the counter with us!" Barbara hesitated. "What did you say to her?"

"I told her it was okay – that you were color blind."

Barbara laughed. "Good for you, Aunt Pearl."

Chapter IX

Dr. Hobo

Jaime's room was right next to Barbara and Ray's and had no door between them. The house was old and had no hallways. Their only privacy was a curtain hanging in the doorway. They were in bed already when she heard Jaime say, "Mom."

"What, Jaime," she answered.

"We're supposed to dress up for school tomorrow."

Barbara sighed. "What do you mean 'dress up for school tomorrow'?"

'Teacher said we should dress up like somebody. I want to dress up like a doctor."

"Jaime, its 10:30 at night. You are supposed to be asleep and now you tell me you need a costume for tomorrow. There is no way I can make you a doctor's outfit by morning."

"But we're supposed to..."

"I know, son. Go to sleep. I'll try to think of something. ..Why didn't you tell me earlier?"

"I forgot."

Barbara sighed again. She heard Aunt Pearl's laughter from her room which sat on the other side of Jaime's. "Things sure haven't changed much since I was raisin' my younguns. You might not get to dress up, Jaime."

"But, Aunt Pearl, we're supposed to."

Barbara could hear the despair in his voice. "Jaime, go to sleep. We'll figure out something in the morning."

"Good!" Jaime blew out his breath and added, "Mom's gonna get me something, Aunt Pearl."

"Uh-huh," Aunt Pearl said.

The sound of rain on the windowsill woke Barbara. She jumped out of bed. *I wanted to get up early to work on a costume for Jaime. Now I'll barely have time to get him ready.* "Jaime, get up," she said as she started searching through his chest-of-drawers. She pulled out a pair of bibbed overalls, slamming one drawer and opening another.

"What are you doing?" Aunt Pearl stood in the doorway watching Barbara.

"I'm looking for Jaime's plaid shirt...you know, the red and blue one." She sat on the edge of Jaime's bed and bit her lip. "Actually, the only plaid flannel shirt he has...Jaime, get up." She pulled the covers from him and ran her finger along his foot.

He jerked his foot and yawned. "I'm fixin' to get up."

"Now just what kind of 'fixin' does a youngun have to do to get up," Aunt Pearl grinned. "I think I know where his shirt is. I'll be right back." With that Pearl disappeared into the bathroom. A few seconds later she reappeared with the shirt in question. "Here it is."

"In the dirty clothes hamper?" Barbara put her hands on her hips and shook her head. "Dad-gummit! I need that shirt for his costume."

"What kind of costume?" Pearl asked.

"The only thing I could come up with is a hobo," Barbara said. "But now his only 'hobo-looking' shirt is dirty."

"Barbara," Aunt Pearl chortled, "isn't that the way a hobo is supposed to look. I mean, dirty-like?"

"Well, yeah, but we don't want to send Jaime to school looking dirty."

"What's a hobo?" Jaime asked as he looked from his Mom to Aunt Pearl.

"Barbara," Aunt Pearl continued, "it's all you've got and it's dress-up day."

"Yeah, you're right. Here let me have it and I'll press it real quick." She reached for the shirt.

Aunt Pearl jerked it back.

"What's a hobo?" Jaime asked again.

Barbara gave Aunt Pearl a surprised look as she dropped her hand.

"You can't iron it. It won't look authentic!"

"Mommm, what's a hobo?"

"It's someone from the old days who would hop on trains and get a free ride," Barbara answered.

"All right!" Jaime started hopping around the room on one foot.

"See…I can hop real good. Dad works on the trains and I can hop on them."

"Speaking of Dad, you need to keep your voice down, Jaime. He didn't get in until 1:00 this morning." She looked over at Aunt Pearl who was buttoning the shirt on Jaime.

"Here, little hobo, put your legs into these here overalls." Pearl looked up just in time to see Barbara emerge from her bedroom with a red bandanna in hand. She reached out and took it from her. "Good. Here you go, Jaime, let's stick this in your back pocket."

Jaime pulled on his socks and reached for his tennis shoes. "NO!" Barbara said a little too loud.

"Shhh." Aunt Pearl put her finger to her lips. "You'll wake Ray."

"Yeah, Mom, you told me not to wake Dad."

"Sorry," Barbara whispered. "You need your brogans. Let's go find them." As they made their way to the living room, Barbara's face fell. "Oh, no, look how muddy they are."

Pearl grabbed the boots and said. "Uh – remember – a hobo."

"Oh yeah." Barbara stood looking down at Jaime. "Quit that hopping, Jaime. A hobo doesn't go around hopping. He just hops one time up onto the train." She grinned and shook her head. "You look like a little hobo. Let's eat breakfast before the bus gets here."

"Billy said he was gonna be a doctor. I wanted to be a doctor too." He looked down at himself and shrugged his shoulders.

"Oh, Jaime, this will be better," said Aunt Pearl. "Probably no one else will be dressed like you."

"Yeah, this is much more funner."

"More fun," said Barbara.

After a quick breakfast of Cheerios, Aunt Pearl walked over to the warm morning stove that sat across from the door. "Jaime's costume looks real good, but what he needs to complete it is a stick."

"A stick!?" Barbara looked at her as if she'd lost her mind.

Aunt Pearl was rummaging through the wood box that sat next to the stove. "Yes, we'll take the bandana and tie it to the end with something stuffed in it. He can carry it across his shoulder."

"I don't know about the stick," Barbara said. "He might poke somebody's eye out on the bus."

"No, I won't," Jaime said.

"It doesn't matter. There's the bus going up to turn around now. We don't have time for the stick," Barbara said as she stuffed the bandana back into his pocket. "Hurry, Jaime. You don't want to miss it."

"Wait." Aunt Pearl grabbed Jaime's arm as she leaned over the coal bucket that sat next to the Warm Morning. She started smudging his cheekbones and forehead with coal dust. Barbara stood with her mouth open. Jaime wriggled lose and headed out the door. They heaved a sigh of relief as he jumped up on the bus and the doors closed behind him.

"That was a real good idea you had for the hobo, Barbara."

"Yeah, well, it's the only thing I could think of." Barbara stopped and put her hands on her hips. "Coal dirt?"

"Makes him look real authentic." Pearl cocked her head and grinned with a face full of self-satisfaction.

Barbara shook her head. "Thank goodness Ray bought him those overalls last summer. They were too big then and still are a little; but I'm glad I remembered them." Barbara shook her head again. "I just can't believe he waited until the middle of the night to tell me."

"Hey, girl, he's only in kindergarten. You've got a lot of years ahead of you to find out how many things he'll forget, and you'll scramble every time to try to come up with whatever he needs," Aunt Pearl said.

Barbara sighed as they walked along the driveway to the store. She put the keys into the lock and snickered. "Coal dirt. I never thought I'd send my son to school looking like he did this morning."

Pearl broke out in giggles. "Nothing like starting the work day with a good laugh."

As they opened the doors, Barbara noticed the roof was dripping rain again. Her shoulders sagged. "I wish Ray could find the leaks. He's been up on that roof patching half-dozen times. All of that snow melting has just made it ten times worse."

"Yeah, well, let's get to soppin' and moppin'. Aunt Pearl said.

Barbara laughed in spite of herself.

The rain stopped a little after lunch. "Tomorrow's Saturday. I'll try to climb back up there on the roof and patch some more," Ray said. " It's too wet right now and I have to leave for work in an hour. I'm getting so sick of this. As soon as summer gets here, I'm going to hire some help and put on a new roof."

"Hallelujah," said Aunt Pearl even though she knew summer was a couple of months away. "Ray, you should have seen Jaime this morning. Barbara dressed him up as a hobo for school."

"A hobo? I heard all the commotion. Why a hobo?"

Barbara shook her head. "He told me about 10:30 last night that he had to dress up for school today. He said he wanted to be a doctor, but I knew that would be impossible. I put those overalls on him that you bought last year. He was cute until Pearl smudged coal dirt on his face."

"Oh, Barb, it's like Halloween," Pearl said. "All the kids will be dressing crazy. I wanted to fix him a stick with his belongings in a handkerchief on the end…like you see in the funny papers – but Barbara wouldn't let me."

"I'd like to have seen him in those overalls," Ray said. "I'll be gone to work when he comes in so why don't you take a picture of him for me. Is something special going on at school?"

It's 'dress-up day' is all Jaime said. I noticed other kids on the bus had on costumes," Barbara said.

"Know what? You could have just let him go to bed dirty last night in the clothes he wore all day yesterday, get him up this morning and sent him just like he was. Would have saved you two a lot of trouble."

"Oh, Ray." Barbara rolled her eyes.

"It's true." Aunt Pearl grinned.

Barbara tapped Ray on the chest with the candy order form she was holding. "Know what to you? He had already been bathed and in bed two hours before he even let me know that today was 'dress-up' day."

Ray laughed and grabbed her hand as he bent and kissed her nose. "I've got to get to work. See y'all later."

That afternoon Barbara watched the bus pull up onto the parking lot and the doors slide open. The kids filed off one by one and soon Jaime burst through the doors making the chimes ring loudly. "Look at my paper I got today." He handed an eight-by-ten certificate to Barbara.

"Hey! Way to go, Jaime. What is it for?"

"Everybody that dressed up today got one," he grinned.

Barbara's smile faded as she read. "OH, NO!" She sat down on a stool behind the counter and put her head in her hands.

"What's wrong?" Pearl asked.

Barbara moaned as she handed the certificate to Aunt Pearl. "It says: 'FOR PARTICIPATION IN CAREER DAY'." Aunt Pearl started laughing.

Barbara raised her head. "Jaime, why didn't you tell us it was Career Day?"

"I don't know," was his only reply.

Pearl laughed harder.

"Well, I bet those teachers think I'm a good one." A look of dismay crossed Barbara's face. "A hobo, I can't believe we dressed him as a hobo."

"Teacher said I was a farmer," Jaime said.

"A farmer?" Barbara stared at Jaime. "You didn't tell her you were a hobo?"

"No, she just looked at me and said I was a farmer."

"Really?" Barbara looked at Aunt Pearl.

Jaime looked up at Barbara and raised his eyebrows. "I would have told her, but I didn't 'member that word - hobo. I told her Dad worked on the railroad when she said I was a farmer, but she just looked at me and said that I had something on my face and she washed the dirt off. It's okay, Mom. I liked being a farmer too."

Barbara grabbed Jaime to her and hugged him close as she laughed heartily. "It's a wonder she didn't call you a coal miner."

"Thank goodness we didn't have time to fix up that stick," Aunt Pearl chortled.

Chapter X

Porky

"They're here! They're here!" Jaime burst through the doors of the store, ringing the wind chimes with force.

"Who's here?" Barbara and Pearl asked together.

"Mawmaw and Pawpaw! They just went by in the Winnebago blowing the horn."

"Jaime, I believe if that were Mawmaw and Pawpaw they would have stopped. They wouldn't drive on by," Barbara said.

"No, it's true." Ray walked in behind Jaime. "I bet they've gone up to see Susie first."

"I wouldn't doubt it," Pearl said. "They're crazy about her."

Susie was the youngest of Jaime's cousins – about to turn three years old. Before they had left for Florida for the winter, Ma and Pa Kidd were always taking Susie with them to different places – from McDonald's to weekend camping trips.

An hour later they were back at the store with Susie in arms. Jaime ran up to give them a big hug.

"How was your winter?" Ray asked.

"Great!" Pa answered as he ruffled Jaime's hair and smiled. "The place we found and bought is near Uncle Alsup. It's just a trailer, but we've already started working on it. We poured a patio a couple of weeks ago."

"It's real pretty where we bought," Ma said.

"Yes, it is. It backs up against a National Audubon Park and has a lagoon running next to it. There are a lot of birds and other wildlife. Know what, Jaime?"

"What, Pawpaw?"

"There are alligators in the lagoon!"

"Alligators? Can I go back with you and see them?"

"Me too. I wanna see the ow-a-guators," Susie said.

They all laughed. "We'll see," said Pawpaw. "We won't be going back until the fall. It's much too hot down there right now. We didn't miss these snowfalls y'all have been having though."

"Guess what, Pawpaw? Aunt Pearl's fixin' you some pork chops," said Jaime.

"That's right," said Pearl. "Come on back to the kitchen and y'all can finish telling us about your winter in Florida."

About a week later Barbara noticed Pa sitting in the grass in his front yard. Their brick house sat across the road and faced the store. He was chewing on a blade of grass and watching the store. *He looks wistful. I wonder what he's thinking. Maybe he regrets selling us the store.* She got busy with customers and didn't notice how long he sat there, but the image didn't leave her head all day. Later when he came to the store she didn't ask him any of the questions that were on her mind.

The next morning Ma came over to the store for some groceries. "Pa's not feeling well," she said. "I may have to take him to the hospital."

"What's wrong?" Barbara asked.

"I don't know, but he fell on a shovel when we were working on the patio in Florida. The handle jammed into his stomach and that's where he is hurting. I'm wondering if it did something to him."

"Maybe," Barbara said.

"He's stubborn. I tried to get him to go to the doctor when he was in Florida and he wouldn't. I guess when he gets bad enough he'll give up and let me take him." She picked up a can of chicken noodle soup. "I'm going to fix him some soup. Maybe this will be easy to digest and make him feel better. Soup will be good on a cold day like today."

"Cold? Sure don't feel cold to us," Pearl said.

"It's cold up here compared to what we got used to in Florida," Ma said.

"I guess so, but the weatherman said it's going to get up to sixty degrees today," Barbara said. "The robins are back, the tulips are starting to bloom and it won't be long until we'll be cutting grass."

"Sixty is nothing like eighty or more," Ma chuckled.

"No, I guess not," Pearl agreed. "Soup is probably an excellent idea. Maybe I'll fix us some good ole vegetable soup tomorrow. I hear it's going to rain."

"Reckon you two can handle the weather and the menus while I take a break?" Barbara asked.

"Well, I reckon we might," Ma said.

Barbara headed toward the office. She flipped on the office light and headed toward the inner room that Ray had partitioned off. It held shelves for their extra supplies and a cot, and then a step up to the bathroom. A movement caught the corner of her eye. She turned around, stared at the cot for a second and then let out a big scream. Back to the front of the store she went running and met Aunt Pearl, Ma and Red (who had just come in).

"What is it?" Aunt Pearl asked.

Barbara's eyes were wide as she yelled, "A pig is in the office!"

"What?" the three women said in unison.

"A pig!"

"A live pig?"

"Yes, a live pig!"

They all began to laugh. "It's the truth! Go back there and see for yourselves."

"This job has gotten to you," Ma said. "There's no way a pig is in that office."

"It's lying on the bed with a towel over it. It peeked out at me as I was walking through to the bathroom."

They all laughed harder. "Really, Barb." Red slapped her knees as she laughed.

"I'm going to get Ray. Think what you want," Barbara said over her shoulder as she ran out the door.

"Let's go see what it is," said Pearl.

"Probably one of the kid's stuffed animals. I noticed them playing in there on the rainy days last week," said Ma. "I'm going back over to the house and see about Gene. Try to feed him some of this soup."

"Okay, Betty. We'll see you later. Tell Gene hello and holler if ye need me," said Pearl. She looked over at Red. "Well, I'll tell ye one thing. I think we would have noticed if a pig had walked through the door."

"Yes, I imagine we would have. "Scuse me ma'am, but I'd like to order one bucket full of hog slop, oink – oink." Red slapped her knees again as she mimicked a pig.

"Well, let's go see what spooked her. It's a wonder she hadn't wet on herself, she was so excited." Aunt Pearl laughed.

Ray walked in the door with Barbara behind him just as Pearl and Red disappeared into the office. They almost knocked him over coming back out as he started into the office. "There's a pig in there...sure enough a pig lying under a towel...just like Barbara said!" Red exclaimed.

"How did a pig get in the office?" Ray asked.

"I have no idea," Barbara said. She walked behind Ray as he walked into the office. "See," said Barbara. "How did he get under that towel, anyway?"

"Probably rooted his way under there," Ray said. "He sure does look like he's satisfied there, doesn't he."

"Well, I'll be blamed if I ever let Jaime take a nap there anymore. The mattress is probably filthy now. How in the world....?" Barb's voice trailed off as she looked around the room. "There's not even a window in here, much less a door to the outside."

"Who around here has pigs anyway?" Pearl asked. "Only animals besides cats and dogs I know of belong to Flanagan's up on the mountain. And all they have is a horse and some chickens."

"True, except maybe the Jacksons who live at the end of the road across from the store. They have all those kids and I heard him say a while back that he was thinking about buying a couple of pigs to raise." said Ray. "I'm going to take a walk up there and see if it belongs to him."

"Hey, come back here," Barbara said as he started out the office door. "You can't just leave the pig in here."

"Whar's everbody at?" she heard Ida yelling from the front of the store. "This is the gall-darnest place to git waited on I ever saw."

"Coming," Barbara yelled back. She turned around to Ray. "Take the pig with you and don't let anybody see it."

"What?" Ray laughed. "I can't exactly hide it in my shirt pocket."

"Well...think of something. We don't want everybody thinking we allow pigs in the store," Barbara said.

"Why don't we leave it here 'til Jaime gets home from school? He'd love playing with it," Ray grinned.

"Are you nuts?"

"Whar is everybody..."

"Coming, Idy." Barbara walked out of the office and smiled at Ida.

"Whatcha doin' in thar. The customers is out here," Ida said.

Pearl chortled. "Yeah. Her and Ray were just figuring out the cheapest way to supply the meat cooler."

"Pearl!" Barbara said.

"Speaking of meat cooler, I need me some bologny and some meat fer supper," Idy said.

"Sure thing," said Pearl. "Bologny coming right up; how about some real, real fresh pork chops?"

"Sounds good. Barbara hand me one of them Big G's...What are you laughing about?"

"Oh, Pearl's funny."

"Hello, Idy," Ray said.

Barbara rolled her eyes and gritted her teeth. Ida turned around. "Hi, Ray..." She turned toward Barbara. "Did you see that? Ray had a pig under his arm. Good looking little thang. Y'all going to start raisin' pigs?"

"No, Idy. I don't know whose pig that is."

"Hmmmm. Me neither. Put this honey bun on my bill too."

"Idy..."

"I don't want to hear it. It's not for me."

"Okay...well...then..." Barbara said as she reached for Ida's charge account book.

Ray came back a few minutes later minus one pig. "It did belong to Teddy Jackson. Said it must have gotten out of the pen and slipped down this way. I've got it figured out how he got into the office."

"How?" Pearl and Barbara asked.

"The garage doors have been open all morning and the bathroom in there is open. It must have wandered into the garage, gotten spooked or curious and squeezed through that big plumbing hole between the bathroom in the garage and the bathroom in the office. Then when it got in there, there was probably too much activity out here in the store, plus the office was dark and cool, so it found its way to the bed and got comfortable."

"Makes sense," Pearl said.

"Pearl...there's nothing about a pig on the cot in the office that makes sense. I know it didn't come through here," Barbara said. "We may have had bats and birds and even mice, but we've never had a pig in the store before."

"At least not the un-human kind," Pearl said.

Ray laughed and walked to the door followed by Barbara.

"Look across the road," she said. "Isaac is helping Pa fix up the flower beds. They sure are good friends, aren't they?"

"Yeah, they are," Ray said.

Pearl walked over to them. "The soup must have made him feel better."

"Why? Who's been sick? Pa or Isaac?" Ray asked.

"You sure miss a lot what with that crazy shift you work," said Aunt Pearl. "Your mom said your Pa was sick yesterday and this morning. She believes he hurt himself while he was in Florida and won't go to the doctor to have it checked out."

"Well, Isaac always perks him up," Ray said. "I'll go tell them about Porky. That'll sure cheer him up."

Chapter XI

Troubles

The rain was pounding against the window. Barbara didn't want to get up as she lay in bed listening to the rooster crow and then the Star Spangled Banner playing on the radio. She needed five more minutes. *We'll be sitting out buckets and dealing with the leaks again today. At least the rain will bring on the greening of the mountains faster. Spring may be here but it's still a good way from being green…except for the creek willows. They're looking beautiful and green.* She stretched and yawned. *Rainy days make me lazy.* She slowly laid the covers back and sat on the edge of the bed. If only she could sleep in with Ray. She tiptoed into Jaime's room and kissed him on the forehead.

"Time to get up, Sleepyhead."

"Okay," Jaime murmured as he rolled over but didn't open his eyes. She shuffled to the bathroom to get ready. By the time she came out, Jaime was dressed and waiting his turn for the bathroom. Barbara smiled. One thing about Jaime, he was easy to get up. He hadn't missed a day of kindergarten yet.

Barbara unlocked the glass doors to the store as Pearl buttoned the sleeves on Jaime's shirt. As she walked through the door, Pearl heard her moan. "Oh, Aunt Pearl, a new leak has sprung and it's over the counter. Look at it…a mess! How am I going to wait on customers with water dripping between me and them?"

"It'll be okay. Let me get us some breakfast made before Jaime's bus gets here." Aunt Pearl said as her half smile betrayed the look of forlorn in her eyes.

"I guess." Barbara shook her head. She grabbed paper towels and started blotting up the water from the counter. She found an empty bubble-gum bucket to catch the leak.

Barbara looked up as the chimes rang. "Hi, Ethan."

"Hi, Barbara. Give me the keys and I'll go down to the basement an' build y'all a wood farr. It's chilly outside. Looks like a new leak, huh?"

"Afraid so." Barbara said. Ethan held the door open for Bertha.

"Hey Barbara – uh-oh. Looks like ya gotcha a new leak. I hate rainy days. My place is a-leakin' like crazy too. Looks like Ray could get up there and fix y'all's."

"He's tried and tried," Barbara defended Ray. "He says the water travels from where it lands and comes out at a different place in the store. It's hard for him to find where they are coming from. As soon as the weather gets warm and sunny, he's going to put us on a new roof."

"Well, good." Bertha moved the bubble gum bucket and sat a carton of eggs on the counter. A drop of water splattered her hand. "Durn it… ooh, sorry Barb. I guess you had that thar to catch the leaks."

Barbara smiled and nodded her head as she moved the bucket back into place. "That'll be eighty-three cents."

"Wait a minute. I ain't finished. Sheesh. Give a body time to thank of what she needs."

"Oh, sorry," Barbara said. She looked around Bertha as a new face walked through the door. He was dressed in a three piece grey pin-striped suit. "May I help you?"

"Yes, I need a pack of Rolaids and a cup of coffee, please." He looked at the bucket collecting the leak but said nothing.

"Cream or sugar?" Barbara asked.

"No, black will be fine. How much?"

"The coffee is free, the Rolaids are sixty-nine cents," Barbara said.

"Thank you," he said as he glanced at the bucket and back at her. He counted out the exact change and handed it to Barbara.

"Thank you. Have a good day," Barbara said as he left.

"You too," he said as he looked back at her and the bucket one more time.

Daggone it! I hate looks of pity. "You ready yet, Bertha?"

"I guess so. I can't 'member what else I was supposed to git. Wonder who that feller was? I ain't never seed him in this neck of the woods. Have you? Prob-ly some big shot from the coal company."

"Or maybe he's a new teacher or somebody visiting the school," Barbara said.

"Yeah, well, maybe so. See ya later...when I thank of what else I need." She turned to leave. "Oh, hi, Ray. I almost bumped into ya. Don't be sneakin' up on a body like that. Hey, you better be gittin' that roof fixed. I almost had me a shower while I was a-gittin' waited on...and it ain't even Saterdey." Bertha laughed.

Ray looked at the bucket. "Oh no," he moaned. Bertha fairly skipped out the door.

"Ray, this is embarrassing – trying to wait on people with water dripping and splattering," Barbara said.

"Well, I'm doing the best I can. What do you expect?" Ray snapped. "Nosy Bertha," he added.

"Don't take it out on her. You know how she is; and I know you're doing your best," Barbara snapped back. "It's just so frustrating."

Ray clamped his mouth shut and fixed his eyes on his wife. He turned, shook his head and walked back to the kitchen to get some breakfast.

Barbara stared after him. *I hate it when he walks away. Wish I wasn't stuck behind this counter so much.* Ethan handed her the keys. "Barbara, put this loaf of bread on my ticket. I'll be back later to check on the farr."

"Thanks, Ethan," Barbara answered as the bucket sounded *ker-plunk* again. She hung the keys on the peg, looked up at the ceiling, took a deep breath and wiped away a tear. She squared her shoulders as she headed back toward the kitchen. She was hungry – leak or no leak.

The rain let up around noon and Barbara let out a sigh of relief. "I'm glad the rain's gone."

"Me too," said Pearl. "You know things could always be worse."

"Yeah...I know. This is so frustrating to Ray. He's trying to work on the railroad and keep all of this going here." She moved the bucket from the counter and looked up as Ray walked in the door.

"Hey babes," he said with a sigh and a warm look in his eyes.

"Hey, yourself." She knew he was apologizing for the morning episode and she was apologizing back.

"I'm leaving for work early so I can stop by Lowe's and get some more roof patch." He bent down and gave her a quick kiss. "Hope it dries up enough before Saturday. I can't wait 'til it gets warm enough to put on a new roof."

"I know. You be careful."

"Always," he said.

An ambulance pulled up in Ma and Pa's driveway about an hour after Ray had left for work. "I'll go see what is going on," Aunt Pearl said. She passed Mrs. Fox on the way out.

"What's goin' on?" Mrs. Fox looked at Barbara.

"I'm not sure. Aunt Pearl has gone to check. Pa has been feeling really bad lately." They stood in the glass doors watching across the road and waiting. It seemed to take forever and for once Mrs. Fox didn't talk much. Finally the EMTs rolled the gurney out the door. Sure enough, Pa was its occupant. Barbara sighed as she slowly walked back behind the counter.

"Now you let me know iffin thar's anythin' I can do to hep you'uns out. Y'all been good to me...Gene and Betty's been good to me."

"Thank you," Barbara said.

The chimes rang out as Pearl walked back into the store. "The pain finally got so bad, he let Betty call the ambulance. Maybe now he'll get something done for himself."

"Yeah, they'll fix him up," Mrs. Fox said. "You can count on that. Won't be long 'til he'll be his old self again. Now don't you'uns be a-worryin'. Ever-thang'll be jest fine."

"Betty said she'd let us know something soon as she can. She called Mary Ann at work to meet them there."

"Whose Mary Ann?" Mrs. Fox asked.

"Ray's older sister," Barbara said. "She lives in Bluefield. She'll probably beat the ambulance there."

"Oh yeah. See, ever-thang's under control." Mrs. Fox smiled. "How 'bout slicing me up a couple pounds of bologny, Pearl."

A little after dark, Mary Ann brought Betty home. Barbara was behind the counter as usual waiting on customers. Word had spread through the bottom and the rest of the neighborhood about the ambulance. They had been trying to answer questions without really knowing what was going on all evening.

"I'll go see what the news is," Pearl said. Pearl had refused to learn the cash register. Even though she was a big help in so many ways, Barbara was still always the one who waited on the customers unless Ray happened to be there. *I hate always being stuck back here, always getting news secondhand.*

Pearl seemed to be gone forever. Finally she came back across the road. "They kept him. The doctor thinks it's his stomach again. They've already taken out forty percent of it, because of ulcers, a couple of years ago. I hope they don't have to take out anymore. Tomorrow they're going to start running tests and decide what to do."

"Well, I'm glad he's finally going to get some help," Barbara sighed.

"Me too," added Jaime.

Chapter XII

The Little Leprechaun

"Barbara, wake up," Aunt Pearl whispered. Barbara didn't budge. It was 11:00 p.m. and Pearl had heard the door open upstairs. Ray always came home well after midnight. "Barbara!" she whispered louder. "Wake up! Somebody's come in upstairs."

Barbara slept on. Pearl went to the doorway of Barbara's room and whispered as loud as she could without shouting. "Barbara, wake up! I hear footsteps upstairs." Barbara turned over in bed, but still didn't awake. Pearl turned around and looked at Jaime who was also sound asleep. "Oh, no!" she said. "They're coming down the stairs!" She ran over to the wood box and grabbed a big stick of firewood. She perched herself at the bottom of the steps with the firewood raised into the air.

"Aunt Pearl, put down that stick of wood," Ray said.

"Ray! You scared me half to death." Pearl lowered the stick. "What are you doing home so soon? And how did you know I was holding a stick of wood?"

"I got off early." Ray held his hand over his mouth to muffle his laughter. "You were silhouetted on the wall by the streetlight and I could hear you whispering the whole time." He gasped and laughed a little more. "If I were a burglar, I'd have known your every move."

"You rascal. Next time, announce yourself. You like to have given me a heart attack."

"Didn't know I had to announce myself in my own house," Ray said. "You were going to hit me with that stick of wood, weren't you Pearl?"

"'Course I was," Pearl hissed. "It's the only thing I could think of. Barbara sure wasn't any help. I don't believe you could wake her with a stick of dynamite. You could expect it out of Jaime, but you'd think Barbara would wake up."

"When Barbara's head hits the pillow, she's gone for the night," he whispered. "Go to bed, Aunt Pearl." Ray grinned as he walked toward his bedroom.

"Ray, they took your Pa to the hospital this afternoon and kept him to do some tests."

"Well, that's good. Maybe now they'll fix him up and he'll be better."

"Yeah."

"Goodnight, Aunt Pearl."

"Goodnight, Ray."

"A lot of good you were last night," Aunt Pearl grinned as she watched the school bus pull out. She and Barbara waved back to Jaime and Billy as they waved through the bus windows.

"What do you mean?" Barbara slid the key into the lock.

"I mean someone came into the house in the middle of the night and you slept through it all. I had to defend us by myself!"

Barbara left the key hanging in the lock and turned around to face Pearl. "We had an intruder? What happened? Why didn't you wake me? What did he do?"

"Well, he told me to put down the stick I was aimin' to hit him with and go back to bed."

"What? What in the world are you talking about, Aunt Pearl?"

Pearl cackled. "Never mind, you sleepyhead. If you can't wake up and help a body defend your family, you don't need to know anything."

"Come on, Aunt Pearl. I can't help it if I sleep soundly. I always have. Now did or did not somebody break into our house last night?" Barbara's eyes lit up. "It was Ray, I bet."

"It was near around 11:00 as I recall…too early for Ray to be coming home."

"Well…who was it? What did you do?"

"Well, I grabbed me a piece of that firewood and was ready to let him have it. Good thing I didn't have to use it."

"Somebody we knew, huh?"

"Well," Pearl grinned. "I guess you could say we knew the rascal."

"*Whooooo* was it? It was Ray, wasn't it?"

"Like I said, it was too early for Ray."

"Then who?"

"Can't say."

"Pearl...never mind. I give up. Ray or Jaime will tell me later." Barbara pushed the door open and entered the store.

"Jaime takes after his mama, I'm afraid. He slept through the whole thing. And why do you think Ray would know anything?" Pearl grinned and went back to the kitchen – leaving Barbara standing there with her mouth open.

She started to follow Aunt Pearl when the chimes rang out. She turned and walked back up to the counter. *Never mind, I won't give her the satisfaction. I wonder what in the world happened...* "Can I help you, Junebug?"

"Yes'm. Jest need a pack of Winstons today."

"Hidy, hidy; it's me, 'ole Idy! Hey, whar's ever-body at?"

Barbara was behind the shelves at the cooler making a list of items to order for next week's grocery truck. Pearl was in the kitchen making sandwiches for lunch. "Hey, Idy, we're here," Barbara answered as she walked toward the counter. "How are you doing?"

"I'm fine. Boys I tell ya, it's like spring outside. Makes a body feel like goin' barefoot." Pearl walked up the aisle and grinned as she looked at Ida's little toes sticking out of her tennis shoes. Barbara suppressed her giggle. "How's Mr. Kidd doin'?" she asked.

"They kept him in the hospital. They're doing tests but he's hanging in there," Aunt Pearl said. "How are you doing, Idy?"

"Well sir, I just told ya I was doin' fine. Don't ya listen to anything, Pearl? I'm in a good mood. Don't be a rufflin' my feathers today."

"Yes ma'am," Pearl saluted and Barbara laughed out loud. "What can I do for you, Idy?"

"Well, sir, how about gittin' me one of those fryers. I'm gonna cook today. Yes sir, no junk for me today. I'm gonna fry up some chicken and make me some gravy. I might even make me some biscuits. How 'bout that?"

"Ummm. Sounds good," Barbara said.

"Here put this buttermilk on my bill. I'm comin' up here on the first and git me that pit-cher of Jesus and the sheep. I like that pit-cher. Somebody else can have that old Elvis thang. Why in the name of goose bumps would anybody want a pit-cher like that?"

"Well, a lot of people liked Elvis. He was such a good singer. I like him," Barbara said.

"You mean you'd like a pit-cher of Elvis a-hangin' in yer livin' room?" Ida asked.

"Well...no, I'm not *that* much into him, but I do like to hear his music. Don't you like his music, Idy?"

"No sir, I ain't got me no hankerin' fer any of that fool rock & roll stuff. I like my blue grass. Now that's real music. You ought not be a-hankerin' after Elvis, Barbara. You're a married woman!"

"I'm not!" Barbara said.

"You're not a married woman?"

"Yes, I'm married; and no, I'm not hankering after Elvis!"

"Yeah, well why did ye buy that pit-cher and sit it in yer store, huh?"

"To sell."

"Yeah, sure," Ida said. She cackled and wiped her mouth with the back of her hand. Barbara watched as Ida walked down the aisle surveying the shelves. She picked up a jar of pickled eggs, sat them on the counter and walked over to the candy case. "Here," she said as she laid down a roll of cough drops and a Milky Way.

"I thought you weren't going to eat any junk today," Pearl said.

"And I told you not to be rufflin' my feathers!" Ida shot back. She looked at Barbara who was standing behind the counter looking back at her.

"I'm not saying anything." Barbara grinned and threw up her hands. She started adding up her groceries. "Is this all you want, Idy?"

"Yeah, I guess so. Boy it's warm in here." Ida took her sweater off and threw it across her arm.

Barbara looked up to hand her a copy of the charges. "Oh, Idy, what a pretty pin!" It was a little mouse dressed up as a leprechaun holding a shamrock. The pin was green and white and made of plastic.

"You like it? Ida asked.

"I sure do – very much," Barbara said. "I've never seen one like that before. It's cute."

With one swoop Ida reached up and took the pin off of her dress and handed it to Barbara.

"Here, you can have it." Her smile was wide as she reached out her hand to Barbara.

"Oh, no. I didn't mean I wanted it, Idy. It's your pin. Put it back on your dress."

"No. You said you liked it. I'm givin' it to ya. Don't cha really like it?" Ida asked with a vexed look on her face.

"Sure I do. But I don't want to take your pin away from you," Barbara answered.

"Yer not. I'm a-givin' it to ya. I want ya to have it...from me to you." Ida pushed the pin across the counter. She grinned from ear to ear as Barbara took it and pinned the little leprechaun mouse onto her shirt.

"Thank you, Idy." She swallowed hard as she bagged Ida's groceries and handed her the paper bag. She looked into Ida's blue eyes and Ida smiled back.

"Idy says 'You're welcome.'" She grinned and nodded her head at Barbara as she wadded the bag up under her arm and pushed the door open. "I'll see y'all tomorrey."

Aunt Pearl cleared her throat. "Well, now, if that don't beat all."

"Yeah," Barbara whispered as she fingered the little pin.

Chapter XIII

Tears

The tests were in. Pa Kidd was going to have to have exploratory surgery. His white count was elevated. Antibiotics were doing no good. Dr. White explained the x-rays showed something, maybe infection, in his digestive tract. Ma worried because they had no insurance. Because it was so high and they were so close to being old enough for Medicare, Pa had dropped their insurance when he sold the store to Barbara and Ray. He was sixty-four years old, less than two months shy of being covered by Medicare; but according to the doctor, the operation could not wait. Ray had three sisters and one brother. They all decided to wait with their mother while their father was in surgery. Aunt Pearl was Pa's youngest sister. She wanted to be with them, so Barbara stayed and kept the store alone. The morning dragged by. Isaac called, but she had no news.

Ethan came in to get a pound of bologna and a loaf of bread. He decided he would build a wood fire for Barbara. It was a gray overcast day in April with clouds threatening. The air had dampness in it. "Knockin' the chill out of the air will make it seem less dreary, Barbara," Ethan smiled. "Things will be okay."

The majority of the customers that came in were asking about Gene, but Barbara had nothing she could tell them. About 3:30 the school bus ran. Billy, Seth and Sarah got off at the store with Jaime.

"How's Pawpaw?" Sarah and Seth asked.

"I haven't heard anything yet. Maybe the doctor had to start surgery late."

"Why don't they call and let us know something?" Sarah asked.

"Because it is long distance and the hospital doesn't allow them to call."

"Why don't we call them?" Seth asked.

"I don't know exactly where to call in the hospital, so we'll just have to wait," Barbara said.

"Mom, what's wrong with Pawpaw?" Jaime asked.

"That's what the doctors are trying to find out, honey." Barbara tried to smile but her eyes held only concern. "You kids go on outside and play. They'll all be back soon."

"Can't we have a snack first?" Billy asked.

"Yes. All of you can get one thing and something to drink. If they don't get back soon, I'll fix us some sandwiches," Barbara promised. They all headed for the candy case and the pop machine and out the door they ran. "Must be afraid I'll put them to work," Barbara mused.

Granny Johnson came in about 4:30 p.m. "Has Idy been up here gittin' sweets agin?"

"Granny, she's always getting sugary snacks, but she always claims it's not for her."

"Well, it durn shore is for her. I told ye, Barbara, not to let her have that stuff."

"Granny, I try. But I can't stand here and argue with Idy in front of the other customers, making them wait. Like I said, she always tells us it's not for her."

"Well, you'll jist hafta tell 'er she can't have 'em. It's for 'er own good, ye know."

"Yes, I know and I also know we can't control what Idy does. Maybe you should come up here with her each time."

"Heck, I can't control 'er neither. Look at me. Don't weigh much more than a wet dishrag. How do ye expect me to control 'er? All I'm askin' ye to do is try."

Barbara took a deep breath. "We do try, Granny."

"Ye seem a little testy today. Somethin' wrong?"

"They're operating on Pa today and I haven't heard anything yet."

"Oh, sorry Barbara. I plumb forgot about that. Now don't you be a worryin' your pretty little head. He'll be all right. Whar's ever-body at, anyways?"

"They're up at the hospital."

"The whole family – even Pearl?"

"Yes."

"Well, you put this loaf of bread and a bottle of aspirin on my bill. Ever-thin' will be all right. I'll see ye tomorrey."

Barbara put her bread and aspirins in a bag and Granny started out the door, but Jaime and Billy almost ran over her as she was leaving. "Boys, slow down!" Barbara cried out.

"Durn younguns! Watch whar you're goin'." Granny added.

"Mom, guess what!" Jaime didn't wait for her to guess. "Red's cat had kittens. Can I have one?"

"I don't know…"

"They're so cute. You ought to see them. She's got four boy kittens and two girl kittens. Red held them up and looked at the bottom of their feet."

"Why did she do that?" Barbara asked.

"That's the way she tells if they're a boy or a girl."

"Yeah," said Billy. "We watched her. She'd hold one up in the air and look at it and say, 'That one's a boy.' Then she'd hold another one up and say, 'That one's a girl.' She kept holdin' them up and lookin' at their feet. She *knows.*" Jaime nodded his head in agreement.

Barbara started laughing. She couldn't stop. Jaime and Billy looked at her and then shrugged their shoulders at each other. Then they started snickering. Pretty soon they were all three hysterical. Ray and Pearl walked in the door.

Barbara looked at them and sobered up instantly. She could see the strain in their faces. *I hope that's only tiredness I'm seeing.*

"Hi, Dad. How is Pawpaw?" Jaime was the first to speak.

"He's still sleeping and pretty sick right now, son."

"When's he comin' home?" Billy asked.

"I don't know," Ray said. "You boys go on out and play."

"Okay. Red has kittens – four boys and two girls," Jaime said. "Mom said I might can have one. Come on, Billy, let's go see if she'll let us hold them. You ought to see them, Dad. They're so cute."

"Aren't you hungry?" Barbara asked.

"No, Red fixed us some egg salad sandwiches. We don't need to eat."

"Yeah, and some chocolate brownies too." Billy grinned as they headed back outside. They almost knocked over a stranger that was coming in the door.

"Boys, slow down," Ray shouted. "Sorry, sir," he added to the man.

"I understand," the customer said. "I raised a couple of boys myself."

One customer after another came through the doors and all Barbara got to learn from Ray was that it was serious and he'd tell her all about it later. She saw Aunt Pearl wipe a tear from her eye as she headed back to the kitchen.

John and Shirley came in. "Where are the kids?" Shirley asked.

"They're up at Red's," Barbara answered. "She's got a new crop of kittens."

"I'll go get them," John said.

"Tell Jaime to come home too," Barbara said. She looked at Shirley. "Pa's bad, huh? Customers keep coming in and Ray or Pearl can't tell me much." About that time another customer walked in.

"It's cancer. I'll talk to you tomorrow," Shirley whispered. "Ray and Pearl will fill you in."

Barbara felt as if she'd been punched in the stomach.

About 8:00 p.m. things slowed down and Aunt Pearl took Jaime home to see that he got his bath and ready for bed. "Tell me Ray, how bad is it?"

"The doctor met us in the waiting area after the operation. He said he is pretty sure Pa has pancreatic cancer. He only gives him five or six months to live."

"What do you mean 'pretty sure'?" Barbara asked.

"He said there is so much scar tissue from his previous surgeries. The pancreas is so small and hidden behind the scar tissue that he cannot be definite; but he says all of the symptoms lead to cancer."

"Does Pa know?"

"No, and Ma doesn't want anyone to tell him. She says he will be better off not knowing."

"Okay." Barbara let out a heavy sigh. "What do we tell everybody that has been asking about him?"

"Why don't we just tell them that he came through the surgery okay and will be home in a couple of weeks," said Ray. "At least that's what we can tell them for right now."

As they turned off the lights and locked the door, Barbara and Ray's shoulders were sagging. "I'm going to go over and check on Ma before I come home," Ray said. "I'll be there in a little bit."

"Sure," Barbara said. She walked into the house and went immediately downstairs to check on Jaime. He had already fallen asleep. She stooped over to kiss him and wiped away the tear that had fallen onto his cheek from her face.

Pa was in the hospital most of April. Ma would go up and spend every day with him. She would come home at night with her shoulders sagging and her footsteps heavy. Besides worrying about his health, she was worried about the high hospital bill that they had no insurance to cover. Everyone was relieved when Pa got well enough for the doctor to release him to come home.

"You know," said Ma, "they never could get a biopsy to come back positive for cancer. I believe the doctor may have made a mistake. He might be all right. You can tell he is much better now than those first two weeks."

"Really?" said Barbara. "I hope the doctor is mistaken too."

"I don't know," Ma sighed as she seemed to change her mind. "He didn't sound encouraging when he told us this. He says this happens sometimes. They have to draw the specimen from the right place and the doctor said that was hard to do."

Barbara looked at her and wanted to hug her, but she dared not. She knew Ma was not a person to show her feelings, and a sympathetic gesture might embarrass her or make her break down. She was sure that Ma did not want that to happen. Ma had learned to be tough and Barbara was sure she wanted to keep that reputation, even if it was sometimes a façade. Ma looked at Barbara as if to say, 'that's enough. Let's change the subject.'

"Have you and Ray thought about making a trip to get the plants and flowers. You really need them by the first of May. If you don't, customers will buy them elsewhere when they get their checks and you'll lose the sales. You'll need to buy hanging baskets and some flowering shrubs. People buy them for Mother's Day presents," Ma said.

"Can you go with us?" Barbara asked.

"No, I'd better not this time. Pa feels some better, but he is too weak to leave alone for very long. Go to B & B's in Cana and then to Harold's Nursery in Mt. Airy, N.C. It's just across the state line on Route 52. I always find the best ones there. You handpick the prettiest and healthiest ones. Look at the stems and make sure that they're fat because the spindly ones won't last very long."

Barbara wasn't too disappointed that Ma wasn't going. She couldn't remember the last time she and Ray had any time alone. Now they would have a whole day and a good sit down meal in a restaurant.

Ma brought her back to the present. "I've been thinking. Pa turns sixty-five on June 5th. I'm going to give him a big birthday party. We'll set up tables on the carport and invite everyone. It'll be as grand as the party we had for him when he turned fifty-five. Remember? He loved that party.

I'm going to go home and call Mary Ann. She'll help me." She smiled as she walked back across the road to take care of her husband.

Barbara watched her until she went into her door. Moods seemed to be swinging like a pendulum...too often for comfort. She sighed and walked back behind the counter. It felt safe there.

Chapter XIV

The Reverend

Barbara lay in bed listening to the birds sing. The rooster hadn't crowed yet, but she was wide awake. Today was May 1st – check day. That meant a busy day and hard work. It also meant a lot of customers would be paying their bills, making it possible for her to make the store payment on time. Some of them would be coming in earlier than usual to cash their checks. She smiled as she got out of bed and tiptoed to the window. Just as she suspected, the day promised to be glorious. The creek willows and many other trees were fully leafed, Bertha's tulips were blooming and the mountain was greening up nicely. The radio clicked on and the rooster crowed. Ray turned over in the bed, but never opened his eyes. She dressed and went to get Jaime up. As she bent down to kiss his forehead, he opened his eyes and grinned.

"Today's library day, Mom. I get to check out a new book. Where's my old one?"

"You left in on the counter at the store. I put it in the rack with the paper bags. Jaime, you are going to have to be more careful," Barbara said to him.

"Yeah," he answered absentmindedly. "I saw one last week about monkeys. I think I'll get that one today, Mom. Will you read it to me tonight?"

"Probably. You'd better get up and get ready now. You need to get to the store early enough to get your book and eat breakfast."

Pearl walked into the room. "If you're talkin' about his library book, I found it in the paper bags at the store. I brought it home last night. Jaime, ye shouldn't be leavin' the school's library books among the paper bags."

"I didn't – Mom did."

Aunt Pearl shot Barbara a quizzical look. "Don't ask," Barbara said.

Aunt Pearl and Barbara walked across the driveway to the store as Jaime ran ahead and waited at the door. "Mom, Miss Bryant said we get to go to the park in Bluefield and play on the swings and ride the train. We're going to have a picnic and everything. You have to sign a paper so I can go."

"Did she give you a paper to bring home for me to sign?" Barbara slid the key into the lock.

"Yeah, I have it in my backpack."

"The backpack you left lying on the counter?" Barbara said as she opened the door and spotted it.

"There it is! Let me get it out." Jaime rummaged through his papers. "Here it is. We have to bring it back today."

Barbara read the wrinkled paper and signed the permission slip. "You'll be going next Friday," she told Jaime as she slid the permission slip into his backpack along with the library book. "Don't let me forget to pack you a lunch."

"Okay," Jaime ran back to the kitchen as the wind chimes rang out on the door.

It was Barney. "Wanna *big* quart of wine," he grinned, as he started walking back toward the wine cooler.

Something is different about Barney. I guess maybe he looks different without that big dirty overcoat on. She reached under the counter for the book that held the sheets for her daily ritual of checking up. It had the payments written down that they had paid to the vendors the day before, along with places to record the breakdown of the sales and a summary of the money taken in and spent out. If everything balanced with the money she had on hand, then it meant a lack of mistakes on her part – or at least only a few minor ones. She laid the book on the counter and glanced up the aisle at Barney. He was high stepping instead of shuffling his feet as he usually did when he walked. He reached into the wine cooler and got his "big" quart (a liter) of wine and turned around and saw Barbara watching him.

He grinned and started walking back down the aisle. As he picked up one foot, he would slightly shake it before setting it back down. Then he would do the same with the other foot. Barbara turned her head away trying to contain her laughter. The 'turtle man' was sporting a new pair of boots. They were brown and black checkerboard and the laces were dangling instead of being tied. His pants legs were tucked down in the boots.

"It's a boot-it-ful day, ain't it." Barney grinned.

"It sure is," Barbara smiled back as Barney handed her his welfare check. I need a pen so I can sign my name."

"Here you go." Barbara handed him a pen and turned the check over as she laid it on the counter. Barney marked a big X on the back. Barbara took it and wrote 'his mark' and 'Barbara Kidd'. She motioned to Aunt Pearl as she spotted her walking up the aisle. Pearl witnessed Barbara's signature and Barney's mark with her own signature.

"Wait, I wanna hunk of cheese and some quackers," Barney said as he high-stepped it back down the aisle to the cooler that had the cheese in it.

Pearl's eyes got big as she looked down at Barney's boots. Jaime ran up the aisle and spotted them about that time. "Wow! I like your new boots, Barney," Jaime said.

"Tank you." Barney grinned.

"Bus," Aunt Pearl blurted out as she picked up Jaime's book bag and scooted him out the door. She headed back toward the kitchen without looking back. Barbara watched her, grinning the whole time. Aunt Pearl stood behind the meat cooler on tip toes watching Barney.

Barbara rang up his purchases and gave him the change out of his check. "Thank you, Barney," she said.

"Tank you too, Miss Barber. I gotta go up to that other store now and pay fer my new boots. I got dem yesterday and theys waitin' fer der money. I see ye later." Barney walked to the door with his new gait. Pearl hurried back up front and together she and Barbara stood in the doorway watching Barney strut through the driveway.

"Look at the way he's walking, Aunt Pearl. I've never seen him proud like that."

"Where in tarnation do ye think he found them?" Pearl asked.

"I think at the new consignment shop that sets around the curve. I've never seen anything like them." Barbara was laughing so hard tears were rolling down her cheeks.

Pearl was no better. "I tell ye, I had to run back to the kitchen when I saw those boots. Jaime didn't make the matter any better when he stood there admiring them. If they were red and black, a body could play checkers on them."

"Uh-oh. There's Idy. Look at her standing there with her hand out. I bet Barney owes her money again," Barbara said.

"No doubt." Pearl wiped her eyes with her apron as she headed back to the kitchen. "Want me to bring you a plate up here?"

"Not until Idy leaves," Barbara said.

"Hidy. ever-body!" Ida walked in the door as she pulled her check out of her pocket.

"Hi, Idy," Pearl and Barbara answered her at the same time.

"What y'all laughin' 'bout?"

"Oh, just a good day to be alive," Pearl answered.

"Yeah, it 'tis. I got my money from Barney. I might as well save it back," she said as she crammed the ten-dollar bill into her pocket. "He'll be down at my place afore the month's half over, askin' to borrey it back. He done got him some snazzy new boots. Y'all see 'em."

"Sure did," Pearl said.

"His money won't last long this time. He thinks he's so smart. Clothes ain't ever-thang, ya know." Ida rolled her eyes heavenward. "Git my bill out, and let me pay it. I need to borrey your pen."

Barbara handed her the pen as she watched Ida slowly pen her signature. Even though she was illiterate, someone had taught her to sign her name. She handed the check to Barbara and turned around and walked back to the showcase. "Hey, Pearl. How about gittin' me that bluebird. I been spyin' it since y'all got it in here."

"It's a music box," Pearl said as she wound it up for Ida to hear.

"Oh boy. That's some purty music." Ida smiled. "I'll take it. I changed my mind about the pit-cher. What's that song it's playin' anyhow?" She walked back toward the counter.

"I think it's called *Zip-pe-de-doo-dah,*" Barbara said. She marked Ida's charge tickets paid and handed them to her with her change.

"Here. Take out enough for this music box," she said. Pearl wrapped it up as Barbara rang up the sale and gave her the change back. "Now let me git my other stuff and you can put in on my new bill. I gotta hurry. Granny's waitin' on me to take me to the doctor's. I ain't ate no sugary stuff. He'll pro-bly be pleased as punch with me." She grinned and looked around at Pearl. "Give me a big box of Big G. I need a dip now, but Granny will be mad iffin I take it afore I git back from the doctor's. He makes me go home and clean up iffin I don't come in already clean. He's high-faluttin', ya know."

"Yeah, those doctors are like that." Barbara grinned. "I hope you have a good check-up, Idy."

"Here put this pie on my bill."

"Idy…," Barbara started.

"Don't worry. It's for after my check up. See y'all tomorrey," she said as she walked out the door.

"Tomorrey," Aunt Pearl nodded back. She looked back at Barbara. "Clean as a whistle. Tomorrow she'll be wearin' snuff in her hair again."

Barbara laughed as she walked back to the kitchen. "Yeah, did you notice she slipped? She forgot to say the pie was for somebody else. I reckon breakfast has gotten cold, but I'm hungry."

Ma came over to the store about mid morning. "Pa's sick today. He couldn't eat breakfast. He said he'd try some chicken noodle soup." Her shoulders sagged as she sighed. "Put this on my bill," she told Barbara and walked back across the road.

"She's got a long road ahead of her," Pearl said. "I know. I've been down it."

"You have?" Barbara asked.

Yes, my husband, Lyle, died of lung cancer. It was hard nursing him and watching him struggle."

"I didn't know," Barbara said.

"No, that was before you married Ray. He's been gone nigh on to fifteen years now. His cancer was in his lungs. Back then nobody knew smokin' was bad for ye. If people had to watch a loved one struggle for every breath the way I had to, you'd never sell another pack of cigarettes," Pearl said.

"That would be okay with me," Barbara answered. "Neither Ray nor I could ever stand the smell of cigarettes. If only people knew how bad they sometimes smelled to us non-smokers, they'd be embarrassed. I'm glad I never started, and I hope Jaime never bends to that peer pressure. It gives me a sad feeling whenever a young person comes in and buys a pack."

"Yeah, I know. They're wastin' their money and their health at the same time." Pearl sighed as she stared at the brick house across the road. "It's a shame; course Gene's not got lung cancer, but it's still cancer." She walked back to the kitchen as another customer walked through the doors.

"Hi," he said as he extended his hand. "You must be Barbara. I'm Reverend John Bowles."

"Oh, yes! I'm glad to meet you. We kept missing each other at the hospital. Ma Kidd has talked so kindly of you. You have really been a comfort to both Ma and Pa while he was in the hospital."

"How is he feeling now that he's back home?" The Reverend looked across the street.

"You just missed Ma. She said Pa couldn't eat breakfast. She's going to try to heat him up some soup."

"Hi, Preacher," Pearl said.

He turned around. "Oh, hi, Pearl. It's good to see you again."

"Yeah, especially since it's not at the hospital," Pearl said.

"I agree. I was just thinking about visiting with Gene and Betty. I was wondering if it would be a good time to go see them."

"I'll call over and ask," Barbara said as she picked up the telephone.

"Isn't it a beautiful day," Pearl said.

"Yes, it is. Psalms 118:24 says 'let us rejoice and be glad in it'," Reverend Bowles answered.

Barbara hung up the phone. "Ma said to tell you to come on over, Reverend."

"Okay, thank you – and please call me John."

"Thanks, I will," Barbara smiled and turned to a customer that was waiting.

"I'll walk ye across," Pearl said. "I'll be back in a minute, Barbara."

Barbara kept waiting on her customers. Pearl came back within a few minutes. "Sorry, Barbara, I forgot about it being check day. I wasn't thinking when I left you alone."

"That's okay, Aunt Pearl. I do need you to slice a pound of ham for Ethan. I already sliced his bologna, but customers kept coming and I couldn't get back there to slice the ham."

"Sure, I'll have it for you in just a bit. You want it sliced thin as usual, Ethan?"

"Yes, and take yer time," Ethan said. "I've still got some more stuff to get."

"Here, Aunt Pearl, you need to witness Ethan's check. He already signed his mark and I've already signed it."

"Sure." Pearl signed the check and went back to the meat counter to slice his ham. "Ethan, we got in some of those big, hot wieners you and Gladys like," she said.

"Good. Give me about eight of them," Ethan answered.

Barbara marked his bill paid and gave him his change from his check. He put several items on the counter as she added and put them in a box for him. "This box is getting heavy, Ethan. You want I should have Ray bring it up to you when he comes in."

"Nah, I'll be okay. I've carried heavier boxes than this. Just start me a new bill," he said. Barbara added the ham and hot wieners to the total and gave Ethan a copy of the ticket. She watched as he walked up the hill with his little dog, Benji, following him.

"You know, Aunt Pearl, it's been a long time since we went to church. There was a time we went every Sunday. Then we got lazy and now that we bought the store, we never go. It may cause a little bit of hardship, but I think we should close on Sunday mornings and open up after church. I'm going to talk to Ray about it."

"I agree,' Aunt Pearl said. "That's the worst part about this store, is the way it ties us down. We don't do much business on Sunday mornings anyway."

"That's right. Most people are sleeping in or at church. I feel guilty not taking Jaime. I never intended when God blessed us with him to be neglecting his spiritual needs."

"That's true. The Bible tells us to bring up our children in the way of the Lord and when they grow up they'll remember it," said Pearl. "Says that somewhere in Proverbs, I believe."

"Reverend John seems to practice what the Bible tells us," said Barbara. "Ma said he visited Pa all the time while he was in the hospital, but the preacher from the church they're going to came very little."

"You want to go to Preacher Bowles' church come Sunday?" Pearl asked.

"Yes, let's plan to do that," Barbara said. She stared across the road at Ma and Pa's brick house while she thought of how she would approach Ray about closing the store on Sunday mornings.

Chapter XV

Closed on Sundays

"I don't know, Barbara," Ray shook his head. "The customers expect us to be here on Sunday mornings."

"So? We can put a big sign on the door. They'll understand, Ray. No one could fault us for closing the store for a few hours to go to church. You like Preacher John. You said so yourself. Besides, Jaime needs that influence in his life. Just last week he was witness to Fast Eddie lying drunk at the end of the store. I don't want him to grow up with only those kinds of memories."

"You're right. I realize that, but..." He looked at Barbara. "Okay, if it means so much to you, we'll give it a try. Put a sign up today saying that we'll be closed until 12:30 on Sundays so the customers will have plenty of warning."

Barbara grabbed his face and pulled it down to her as she smiled into his eyes. "Thanks, honey," she said as she gave him a kiss.

"Don't thank me," Ray grinned. "You're the one always trying to get the bills paid. You may change your mind after a while."

"Ray Kidd, I'll get the bills paid, but some things are more important than money."

"I know that. I just wasn't sure you did." Ray chortled as he picked up his bucket and gave her a peck on the cheek. "See you tonight. I've got to get to work."

"What do you mean 'closed on Sundays'?" Bertha asked.

"Closed on Sunday *mornings*" Barbara corrected. "We want to go to church. We'll be open by 12:30."

"Well, okay. But ye need to help me remember to get my stuff the day before," Bertha said.

"We'll only be closed for the morning," Aunt Pearl said.

"Well, that's about the time I'll pro-bly need somethin'. I guess it'll be okay. After all, a body's got the right to worship, I guess."

"That's what we're a-thinkin'," Pearl answered.

It was a warm day and they had decided to open the front door. Granny Johnson walked in. "I need me some bread and a pound of bologny." She directed her request at Pearl.

"Comin' up," Pearl said as she walked back to the kitchen.

"Hey, Granny, they're gonna start closin' on Sundays," Bertha said.

"Why?" Granny asked.

"No, we're not closing all day on Sunday. Just the mornings so we can start going to church," Barbara said.

"Can't y'all take turns a goin' and leave somebody here to run the store?"

"No, we all want to go," Barbara said. "We'll be here for anything you need right after church."

"Well, I bet it won't work. You'll see. People will start complainin', ya know."

"Yeah, that's right," Bertha chimed in. "I don't know how we're ever gonna get used to this. What does Gene think about it?"

"I don't know what Pa will think about it. He doesn't know yet," Barbara said.

"Well, don't ye think ye ought to be a-tellin' him?" Granny said. "After all, he did own this store forever. Why I 'member when he built it. Ray was just a kid. He was raised in this store. He oughta know better than this. Gene and Betty didn't raise him to be lazy ye know. I didn't like Gene buildin' this thing right in front of me. But he did it anyways. I let him know how mad it made me, but he just kept right on buildin'. He warn't a bit considerate of me and mine. Here I was trying to raise my children and lookin' at the back of this big ole store buildin'. Warn't easy, I tell ye. But I managed. I learnt to depend on it. Now here comes the young whipper-snappers and starts shuttin' it down when they feel like it."

"She's right, ye know," said Bertha. " Us'uns down in the Bottom don't have no cars or trucks to run to Bluefield. We depend on this here store."

Barbara looked them both in the eyes – one at a time. "I'm sorry, Granny, and I'm sorry to you, Bertha; but I want to raise Jaime in the church. You'll manage."

They looked down at the floor. Bertha was the first to speak. "She's right, Granny. I wish I'd raised mine in the church. Maybe then they wouldn't be out in the world a drinkin' and done forgot about me."

Granny gave a half-hearted laugh. "Sure, we was just a-funnin' ye, Barbara. No need to get yer dander up."

Barbara knew they hadn't been 'funnin', but she also knew they'd be okay with it after they got used to it.

"Here's your bologny, Granny." Pearl laid the package of meat on the counter.

"Well, ye better wrap me up one of those fryers too, Pearl. I might forget my Sunday dinner stuff, so I'll jest git it while I'm here."

"Good idea." Barbara smiled at her.

Jaime jumped off the school bus and ran inside. "Mom, we had the best time *ever* at the park in Bluefield. They have a kid's train and we all rode it. It went all over the park and the engineer – that's the man who drives the train – he wore a cap like Dad's and he had a bandana handkerchief around his neck. I told him my dad works on trains. He said he'd give me a call if he ever needs his worked on."

"Sounds like you had a real good day, Jaime."

"Yeah, and he wore overalls like mine, too. I told him next year I'm gonna be a engineer for dress up day at school."

"*An* engineer," Barbara said.

"Huh? That's what I said. You think Dad would let me borrow his cap, or maybe he could buy me one like his?"

"Maybe," said Barbara.

"I wish you could have gone, Mom. Lots of kids' moms went."

"I know. I'm sorry I couldn't go, Jaime. Maybe next time."

"It's okay. A whole lot of the moms had to work like you do. I still had fun."

"Guess what, Jaime. We're going to start going to Sunday school," Barbara said.

"Like we used to when we lived up in the woods on the mountain?"

"Yes, but we'll go to another church. We're going to Preacher John's church."

"Really? Kirsten and Matthew ride the school bus with me. They're nice."

"Do they go to his church?" Barbara asked.

"Mom, they're his *kids*."

"Oh, *excuse* me," Barbara chuckled.

"That's okay. You didn't know," Jaime said. "I'm hungry. Can I have a ice cream?"

"*An* ice cream," Barbara said.

"Okay, thanks!" Jaime ran over to the ice cream cooler.

"I didn't say you could have an ice cream, Jaime," Barbara said.

"Yes you did," Jaime said.

"Sounded that way to me," Aunt Pearl said.

"Okay, but you'd better eat your supper," Barbara said.

"I will," he said as he unwrapped a Brown Mule.

Shirley walked in with Billy and Seth. "I thought I'd leave the boys here while I take Sarah shopping," she said. "John said he'd be here after work to pick them up."

"I want a ice cream," Billy said.

"Me too," Seth piped in.

"No. Pearl will have supper ready pretty soon. You don't need to spoil your appetite," Shirley said.

"But Jaime has one." Billy looked at Jaime and then his mom.

"Go ahead. Put in on my bill, Barbara." Shirley shook her head. "Y'all be good and your daddy will pick you up in a couple of hours. And don't be going over to Mawmaw and Pawpaw's. He's not feeling good today," she said as she walked out the door.

"Get on up to the churchyard, boys." Aunt Pearl shooed them with her hand. "It's too pretty a day to be spendin' inside."

They ran out the door and up the driveway. Barbara laughed as she watched them. "At least they can play outside now," she said.

"I better go open up another pack of pork chops. Looks like we'll have three more hungry mouths for dinner – time John comes to pick them up."

"Yeah." Barbara sighed.

Sunday morning Jaime was out of bed before anyone else. "Hey, Mom," he whispered. "Ain't ya gonna get up. We don't want to miss Sunday school. I told Kirsten and Matthew I was coming. They're probably waiting for me."

Barbara opened her eyes and found Jaime almost nose to nose with her. "No, they're not there yet, Jaime. We have a couple of hours before Sunday school starts. Go back to bed."

He left the room and Barbara heard him talking in Aunt Pearl's room.

She heard her laugh out loud. *Might as well get up.* She met Jaime and Aunt Pearl in the kitchen. Aunt Pearl was still in her housecoat and getting the sausage and eggs out of the refrigerator.

"Feels good to sleep in a little late, doesn't it?" Barbara grinned at Aunt Pearl.

"Yeah, it does," Aunt Pearl agreed. "But it's good we have a second little alarm clock." She looked at Jaime and grinned.

Jaime didn't notice as he was getting the orange juice out of the refrigerator. He sat the carton on the counter. "Let's hurry," he said as he climbed up on a stool near the cabinet with glasses. "You want me to go wake Dad up?"

"Don't worry, Jaime, we have plenty of time. Let Dad sleep until we get breakfast ready. He was called in to work last night and didn't get to bed until the wee hours of the morning."

"Okay," he said. Barbara grabbed the orange juice carton just as he was starting to tip it over to fill his glass.

"Easy, Jaime. That carton's too heavy for you to handle."

"Mommm."

Barbara shot him a look that made him sit down.

"Patience is a virtue, Jaime," Aunt Pearl said.

Jaime looked at his Mom. Barbara answered his questioning gaze. "Patience is waiting quietly for something to happen and virtue is… ummm…a good thing."

"Well, I would think it is a good thing to get to Sunday school on time," Jaime said.

Aunt Pearl threw back her head and cackled. Barbara turned her head so Jaime couldn't see her face. "I guess we'd better get this breakfast done up and start gettin' ready for church," Aunt Pearl said.

"Right," said Barbara. Jaime smiled and took a drink of his juice.

"Ray, I can't believe you fell asleep in church," Barbara said.

"It was so warm and I was so tired. At least I went," Ray defended himself.

"Yeah, I know, but wonder what the preacher thought," she answered.

"Dad, I heard you sleepin' from where I was sittin'," Jaime piped.

"How can you hear somebody sleeping?" Ray grumbled.

Pearl laughed. "We could hear you breathin' heavy behind us. I knew you were somewhere in dreamland."

"I'll explain the next time the preacher comes in the store that I had to work last…"Ray gasped as they rounded the curve just before sight of the store. "Look, the parking lot is full. We'd better hurry." He parked the car and they all hastened to the door.

"Whar y'all been?" Idy asked.

"Church," Barbara answered.

"Church? I thought maybe somebody died or somethin'."

"We put a notice on the door last Thursday and tried to let everybody know," Ray said.

"Well, nobody let me know and I was up here ever-day. I been sittin' out thar on that bench for a hour or better. Ye should've seen the people pull up and drive off. I bet thar was at least half a dozen – not countin' these that waited fer ye."

"Sorry, Idy." Barbara tried to soothe her.

"Well, jest don't let it be a habit."

"We're going to close every Sunday morning and open up right after church," Barbara said.

Ida's mouth flew open. "Well, I'll jest tell ye one thing – Gene Kidd never closed on Sunday mornings."

"Well, *I'm not* Gene Kidd," Ray retorted.

"Humph, guess not," Ida shot back.

Ray shook his head and walked outside. Barbara tried to hide the smile as she realized that Ida had just determined their future store hours. Ray was tired of being compared to his father. From now on they *would* be closed on Sunday mornings.

Chapter XVI

A New Home

The Memorial Day weekend had passed, and June was fast approaching. School would soon be out and Barbara knew that meant kids running in and out of the store all day long. On the plus side, she would get to sleep longer in the mornings.

"The plants are selling slower now. Most everybody has already planted their gardens and flower beds. Let's sell what we can at regular price through the third of June and then put them on sale at half-price. I think I'll let Jaime give his teacher one of those hanging baskets we have left. She'll probably like that," Barbara said.

"I'm sure she would," Pearl agreed. "Maybe if the deal goes through on the house across the road, you could hang the others on the front porch."

"It will go through. I'm sure of that Aunt Pearl. I'm so excited; I fall asleep at night thinking about it. It was hard emotionally to sell our home over on Wright's Mountain in West Virginia. It was just so hard when we first moved here to let it go. I regret that I talked Ray into keeping it just in case we couldn't make a go of the business. The sad part is that we have not spent one night in it since November because it's too far to drive after the store closes – almost an hour, you know. Paying rent here plus making house payments on a house we can't live in is ridiculous."

"Have you got a buyer?" Pearl asked.

"Yes, my brother is buying it. At least we'll get to visit it now and then."

Pearl grinned. "I know the little white one is not as nice as your brick on the mountain, but it's better than the one we're in now."

"I know…but I miss the serenity of that home in the woods. I got to spend so much time doing things with Jaime. Ray and our neighbor would have been tilling up the garden spot and we'd spend the evenings planting rows of vegetables in about a half acre of bottom land we shared. In about three weeks, Jaime and I would go strawberry picking with my friend and neighbor. Life is so different than it used to be."

"Well, the house across the road will be nice," Aunt Pearl said. "You'll see."

"True. At least we'll have more room and *doors* on our bedrooms that we don't have now. The yard is what makes me excited. It's so big and green. The apple and walnut trees really make it pretty...the prettiest in the neighborhood...don't you think?"

"I sure do." Pearl smiled.

"And Jaime will have a real place to play. He won't have to use the churchyard for a playground."

"That's right," Aunt Pearl said as they stared across the road at the pretty one-story white frame house with the big green yard. They both let out a happy sigh as the chimes rang out over the door. They looked at each other and laughed. "You owe me a coke," Aunt Pearl said.

"Go get it," Barbara grinned as she walked behind the counter to ring up Junebug's candy bar.

The telephone rang and Aunt Pearl answered it. "Barbara it's for you – the bank," she whispered with her hand over the receiver.

"Thanks, Junebug. Come back." Barbara took the phone. Her eyes lit up as she nodded her head. "Yes, Mr. Akers. We can come and sign the papers in the morning. Nine o'clock will be fine."

She hung up the phone and started dancing around the counter. "We can start packing now, Aunt Pearl. We sign the papers for the house tomorrow."

Pearl grabbed Barbara's hands and started dancing with her. "Well, I guess we'll have to wait until we get home tonight before we can pack. Better call Shirley and see if she can come out to work the counter while y'all go to the bank."

"I'll do that right now!"

Barbara and Pearl started packing and cleaning a little each day. Ray spent the mornings moving a load of furniture each day in his pickup truck from Wright's Mountain to their new home. When Monday came, they moved the sparse furniture and boxes from the rental house and spent the first night in their new home. Jaime played in the yard all evening.

"Dad, can I make me a clubhouse in that shed out back?" he asked Ray.

"Well…I think you could. I've got enough room in the garage at the store for my stuff."

"I'm starting me a club. Everybody has to pay five cents for dues and our uniforms are going to be a red shirt and blue jeans. I'm the President and Billy is the Vice President."

"Oh, really?" Ray grinned. "How did you decide what kind of uniform you guys would have?"

"I looked in my chest-of-drawers. That's what I already have."

"Oh, I see. What if Billy and the others don't have a red shirt?"

"I guess their moms will have to buy them one."

"I see." Ray laughed. "How would you like a tire swing in that big bean tree that sits down next to the driveway?"

"Oh, boy! Like up on the mountain?" Jaime asked

Ray nodded.

"Here comes Billy now. I'll go tell him. Thanks, Dad."

Ray hugged Barbara as they watched Jaime run to meet Shirley's car. "I think next year, I'll help him build a tree house in that big tree. Don't you think he would love that?"

"I do," Barbara smiled. It seemed so good to have all of their furniture back and a big yard. It felt especially nice to live in a house that belonged to them. It felt like home, and unpacking boxes with Aunt Pearl's help seemed more like fun than work.

Barbara woke up the next morning listening to the birds singing in the trees outside. They had quit using the radio alarm since they had gotten used to waking up the same time every morning. She walked out on the porch and looked up at the mountain. She could see it so much better from this side of the road…she didn't have to look straight up. It was beautiful. *June 1st and I never would have imagined last month we would be here. I think I love it here!* Ray had gotten up and joined her. "Ray, Peeled Chestnut Mountain is even more beautiful from here."

"That's right," Ray said in his imitation of John Wayne in <u>Rooster Cogburn.</u>

Barbara laughed and jabbed his side. "Silly!"

He yawned and grinned at her. "I may as well go to the store with you this morning. I got a good night's sleep last night. Let's go over early and let Pearl get Jaime ready for school."

"Sounds good to me. It will be busy today."

"Yeah, today is 'give-away day' as Bertha calls it." Ray laughed.

"You know, that irritates me when she says that."

"I know...since it's our taxes they're giving away." Ray slipped the key into the lock.

"Well, I kinda like Bertha...guess she doesn't know any better."

"I guess, but some of these people could be working and paying taxes with us, don't you think?" Ray said.

"Some of them, yes...some of them, no. But whatever, I wouldn't change places with them for anything."

"Well, you got me there. Here comes Henry and Charlie Bob. They'll want their checks cashed. Better get the register set up."

Henry and Charlie Bob were brothers. They lived about one-half mile from the store across the state line in West Virginia, but were raised in the Bottom. They were both bachelors in their forties and alcoholics. They usually made a trip to the store every day. Both were illiterate. Henry was shy, but Charlie Bob was not.

"Howdy, Ray. Didn't think you'd be open this early. Thought we'd be sittin' out here on the bench for a while." Charlie Bob laughed and held out his hand to shake Ray's. "Wanted to be the first ones in line to get our checks cashed."

"Last month we had to come back three times afore y'all had 'nough to cash them," Henry said in his soft voice.

"Well, y'all come on in. I guess Barbara's got everything turned on by now."

"Hey, Barbara. We want to cash our checks. Reckon ya got enough money?" Charlie Bob said. "We're gonna get a big wine and some cigarettes." He laughed again. Charlie Bob laughed after almost every statement.

"Yeah, go ahead and sign the back of your check." Barbara handed Charlie Bob a pen. He made his X on the back. Henry was looking over his shoulder.

"What are you doing?" he asked his brother.

"What does it look like I'm doing? I'm signing my check." Charlie Bob straightened up and looked at his brother as if he'd asked the silliest question.

"Oh, no, you don't. That's my signature!"

"What do you mean, it's your signature. I've been using that mark all my life!"

Henry pushed Charlie Bob on the shoulder. "You thief! I had that mark first. You can't be using my mark."

"It's the same one I've been using all along." He pushed Henry back.

"I don't care if it is the same one. I'm the oldest and I had that mark first. I was using that before you ever even started gettin' a check…and don't you dare be pushin' on me!" Charlie Bob was ready to throw a punch when Ray stopped him.

"Hold it, guys. You can't be fighting in this store. What's the matter?"

"He stole my signature!"

"No, I didn't!"

"Hold it; let's see what you're talking about." Ray picked up Charlie Bob's check and looked at the X on the back.

"See! That's my signature," Henry said.

Ray started laughing. He passed the check to Barbara. She had been standing behind the counter watching the near fight in amazement. When she saw the back of the check, she started smiling.

"Oh, guys, it's perfectly okay. You can use the same mark. When I sign it, I will witness your signature with my name and also write your name next to your mark, and Ray will sign his name as a second witness. It's really okay that you use the same mark."

"It is?" Henry looked at her with doubt written all over his face.

"Yes, I am sure. We do it all the time."

"Have you noticed before that Charlie Bob was using my mark?"

"Yes, I noticed, but I knew it didn't matter so I didn't say anything."

"Well…" Charlie Bob leaned over to Henry and said, "I guess it's 'cause we're brothers."

"Yeah, maybe so." Henry's face relaxed.

"'Sides, what does it matter. We're gettin' the money." Charlie Bob laughed.

"Dummy, don't ya know if the government saw the same signature on both our checks, they might stop sending them!"

"Never thought of it that way," Charlie Bob said.

"I promise you, I wouldn't cash them if there was going to be any trouble. I don't want to go to jail," Barbara said.

"Well, I guess you know more than we do about cashing checks, but I still say Charlie Bob ought to get his own mark." Henry scratched the stubble on his face.

"No, then it might 'cause trouble since you see he's been using that mark for years." Barbara patted Henry's hand. "I promise you, it'll be okay."

"Yeah, Barbara wouldn't dare tell you a lie."

"No, I guess not," Henry said.

"Like I told ye, the government knows we're brothers. We got the same last name."

"Oh, now I see!" Henry smiled, shook his head and turned his check over to the back. "Let me have that pen, brother."

"Aunt Pearl, you should have seen 'Barbara, the diplomat,' with the Taylor brothers earlier this morning. I didn't know she could think so fast on her feet." Ray laughed.

"What happened?" Pearl asked.

When Ray told her the story, she thought he was pulling her leg. "Don't tell me that happened. I don't believe you, you rascal."

"Ask them the next time they come up here if they use the same signature."

Pearl rolled her eyes and walked back to the kitchen. "No wonder Jaime is so full of himself. He gets it honest."

That night after prayers Barbara tucked Jaime into bed and gave him a big hug and kiss. "Guess what? Saturday Mawmaw is having a big birthday party for Pawpaw."

"I know," Jaime whispered. "She told me and Billy all about it. I don't think Pawpaw knows. He was in the bed sleeping. He sleeps a lot. Mrs. Bryant said next year we don't have to take naps in school. We'll be big then."

Barbara pushed back his hair as she kissed his forehead. "I know Pawpaw sleeps a lot, but that's what people do when they're real sick."

"Mawmaw told us we couldn't come over and play 'til he got better. She said he couldn't stand the noise. We weren't hollering hardly any. We were just playing."

"I know, Jaime, but Pawpaw needs to sleep to heal. Just a little bit of noise might wake him up. You and Billy have this yard to play in now. Don't go over to Mawmaw's until she asks you to come over. Okay?"

"Okay, I won't, but Billy might."

"Maybe he won't if you remind him Pawpaw is too sick for company."

"Mommm. We're not company. He's our Pawpaw."

"Jaime, go to sleep and do as I say."

"All right, but first I have to do something." Jaime slipped out of bed and knelt down with his hands crossed under his chin. "Dear God, I forgot. Please bless Pawpaw and make him better." He started to get up and then knelt back down. "And help him not to hear us play. Amen."

Barbara smiled as she gazed at her five-year-old. *My prayers should be so simple and full of faith.*

Chapter XVII

The Party

"Would you look at that sky? Paint me a couple of cumulus here and there and it would look like a picture. I declare it looks like a good day for a party."

"Yeah, Aunt Pearl. It does." Jaime's face lit up. "Mom, can I go over to Mawmaw's and help her get ready for Pawpaw's birthday?"

"No, Jaime, you need to stay away until time for the party. Mawmaw is going to be very busy. She has already asked Aunt Pearl to come and help her set the tables."

"Tables? She just said she was gonna paint a picture. Are you gonna give Pawpaw a picture for his birthday?"

"No, Jaime, I think I have changed my mind about the picture." Aunt Pearl laughed. "I'm going to help Mawmaw cook and get ready."

"I can carry stuff and help. Mom, please?"

"Barbara, I can take him with me. He's so antsy you'll never get a customer waited on if he does stay with you."

"Okay, you twisted my arm." Barbara's green eyes twinkled as she looked at Jaime's hopeful brown ones. "Go ahead Jaime, but stay out of the grown-ups' way. Okay?"

"Okay, Mom." Jaime took Pearl's hand and started pulling her toward the door.

"We're gone." Aunt Pearl called over her shoulder.

"What in tarnation is goin' on over at Gene and Betty's?" Granny Johnson asked as she swung the door open.

"Today is Pa's sixty-fifth birthday and Ma is having a party for him."

Ray had just walked in the door behind her. "We got all the tables set up." He nodded to Barbara.

"Well, y'all sure must be expectin' a lot of people. The whole carport is full of tables."

"Yeah, probably will be a lot. She's been cooking for days and had the rest of the family cooking as well. Ought to be enough food for everybody. You come on over about 1:00 and get yourself a plate and tell him 'Happy Birthday,' Granny."

"I don't know, Ray. I didn't get a invite and 'sides I don't even have a present to give him."

"Well, you don't need either one. Ma didn't send out invitations and he doesn't need presents."

"Well, in that case I'll think about it. Meantime, I need me a pound of that good bologny sliced. Whar's Pearl?"

"She's helping Ma. I'll slice it for you." Ray started back toward the kitchen.

"Thick...I like it thick, don't I, Barbara." Granny turned to face Barbara at the counter.

"Consider it done," Ray said over his shoulder.

"Are y'all gonna close for the party?" Granny asked Barbara.

"No. Shirley is going to come and watch the counter while I go over for a while. Aunt Gladys and Uncle Hubert are in from Indiana and Aunt Annie is on her way in from Ashburn, Virginia. It should be a good time."

"Who are they?" Granny rubbed her chin as she stared across the road.

"Uncle Hubert is Pa's brother and Aunt Annie is his sister," Barbara said as she took the charge book from the rack and wrote Granny's name and the date on the ticket.

"Oh, yeah. I'm pretty sure I met them before. They have a bunch of kids and they all used to come in the summers from Indiana and there'd be all kinds of doins goin' on. How's Gene today anyway? Is he in any shape for a party?"

"Not really, but he seems pleased about it. It was supposed to be a surprise, but between the grandkids and the relatives visiting, the surprise fell to the wayside a couple of days ago."

"He knew something was up." Ray laid the pound of bologna on the counter.

Granny chuckled. "No, you never could keep anything from him. He don't have no more education than I do, but he sure is a smart man. I'll hand him that."

"Yeah, guess that's true," Ray smiled. "He only stayed in school through the fourth grade, but yet he ran a successful business for more than thirty years."

"Ray, I 'member when he built this store. That was just in 1960. How do ye get thirty-some years?"

"Granny, he had a store over the mountain in Anawalt. He opened it in 1950 and ran it until about 1961. For a few years Ma and Pa had three stores: here in Pocahontas, Virginia, one in Anawalt, West Virginia, and one for a while in Bluefield, Virginia. It just got too much to handle so they sold the other two and kept only this one."

"Oh, yeah. I remember them talkin' about Anawalt, especially. I thought you was a-talkin' about here – in Pocy – that he was in bizness more than thirty years. People from Anawalt still come across that mountain to shop here. I'd hear them talkin' old times when I'd come in to shop."

"That's right." Ray said in his John Wayne tone.

Rooster Cogburn again. Barbara grinned.

"Now I get to catch up on old times with the friends I had growing up in Anawalt." Ray started bagging Granny's groceries as Barbara wrote them down on her charge book.

"Getting back to Pa's education," Barbara said, "I tell you he always amazed me when he would figure the prices when stocking the groceries every week. I could never understand what he was doing. He didn't use division. He would only use multiplication to figure it up. Somehow he would take the total price of the case and the number it held and sit on that stool with paper and pencil scribbling figures as fast as a hound dog chasing a rabbit. He would always come up with the same answer I did." She shook her head slowly as if she were still trying to come up with his equation.

"Here's the way I figure it," Ray said. "Some people's intelligence exceeds their education – and well, other people's education exceeds their intelligence."

"Well, yer talkin' over my head now. Put the rest of this stuff on my bill. I better get back to the house if I'm a gonna make it to the party."

"Sure," Barbara smiled as she finished bagging the groceries. "I'll see you after while."

"Now, I didn't say I was comin' fer sure. Is Chuggles invited too?"

"Of course," Barbara said. Chuggles was the nickname given to

Granny's sister-in-law that lived with her. Even though she was about fifty years old, she was childlike and could not speak plainly. She was always chattering up a storm with a smile on her face. The general public could not understand her most of the time – especially if she was excited. Her bright attitude and innocence endeared her to almost everyone she met.

Granny turned back around as she started out the door. "I see Idy comin' down the driveway. Don't you let her have no sweets now."

Barbara sighed. "I'll try, Granny."

"Hi, Idy," Granny said as she walked out the door.

"Bye, yerself," Idy hooted. "Hey, Barb, what's a goin' on across the road? They's got tables and chars everwhars in your Mama's porch and yard."

"She fixing a birthday dinner for Pa. We have lots of kin folk in for his sixty-fifth birthday."

"Really? I tell yer one thang. Betty's a mighty good cook. She was always fixin' vittles back thar in that kitchen, just like Pearl does now. Is Pearl over thar helpin' her? Pearl's a real good cook too, huh?"

"Yes, she is." A half-smile crept over Barbara's face as she watched Idy smear the drool from her mouth across her chin and up the side of her face.

"They havin' any cakes or pies that ye know of?"

"Well, I'm sure there will be. I tell you what, Idy, would you like for me to sneak over there and fix you a plate?"

"Now, that would be right nice, but I wouldn't want you to go to no trouble for little 'ole Idy here."

"Won't be any trouble at all." Barbara looked up at Ray. "I'll be right back."

He grinned and nodded at her. "I'll hold the fort down."

"I know it's early, but I need to fix Idy a plate," Barbara breathed as she rushed into the kitchen.

"O-kay. Now who is Idy?" Aunt Gladys laughed at Barbara's urgency. She was patting out hamburgers for the grill.

"Believe me," Aunt Pearl interjected. "We want Barb to take her a plate. You don't want Idy over here while people are trying to eat."

"Is that the big woman I saw walking down the driveway a few minutes ago?"

"That's right, Aunt Gladys."

"Poor thing. Let me help you fix her a plate. Then I imagine we'll be better off on both sides of the road." Aunt Gladys was already washing her hands as Pearl walked outside to get a paper plate from one of the tables.

"Make that a dessert plate too, Aunt Pearl. That's the main thing that she's looking forward to."

"Uh-oh." Aunt Pearl rested her hand on the plates.

"I know. Granny just passed her in the driveway. It was the last thing she said to me."

"I'm in the dark," Aunt Gladys said.

"She's a diabetic and Granny helps take care of her. She doesn't want us to let her have any sweets," Barbara said.

"That sounds reasonable."

"Well, Aunt Gladys, that's one of those things that works on paper only. It is so hard to stop her from buying sweets. She gets so angry and always, *always,* says it's for somebody else," Barbara answered.

"Phsaw! Let her have a little piece of cake now and then," Red walked up with a big piece of her homemade chocolate cake on a plate.

"I don't know, Red. Maybe we should cut that in half."

"Let her live a little, Barbara." Red shook her head as she started wrapping the cake up.

"How about this," Aunt Gladys said. "We'll give her a small piece of Red's cake and then fix her a small dish of this fruit salad."

"That sounds good. I better hurry," Barbara said. "Looks like the driveway at the store is filling up with cars. Ray will have his hands full."

"Call if you need me," Aunt Pearl said as Barbara went out the door balancing a regular plate, a dessert plate and a small bowl of fruit.

"Thanks, but I think we'll be okay." Barbara hurried down the sidewalk and across the road.

Ida had seen her coming and met her outside. She looked at the dessert. "You got kind of stingy with the cake, huh?"

"Well, there is a lot of family over there to feed, but we fixed you up a fruit cup for dessert too."

"Fruit? Fruit ain't dessert. It's – it's – well, it's fruits, what it is. But I guess I like it too. Anyways, there's plenty on the other plate. I won't be goin' hungry. That's fer durn tootin' sure. Thanks, Barbara and tell Betty thanks, too. Oh, and tell Gene ole Idy says 'Happy Birthday'. Tell him he's a youngun' yet."

Barbara laughed and started to walk back into the store just as she heard, "Mom, help me across the road." She turned and Jaime was standing on the other side. He wasn't allowed to cross by himself. Barbara walked back to the edge of the road and watched for traffic. "Run," she said as he raced across the road.

"Guess what, Mom? We're going to have hamburgers and hot dogs and chips and potato salad and turkey and macaroni salad and beans and cakes and cookies and pop and..."

"And, and, and! Slow down, Jaime. I know. I was just over there. There sure is a lot of food, huh?"

"Yeah. Mawmaw said she needs some ice and some napkins. She said Billy would be here in a little while. I helped Aunt Pearl put the plates and forks and knives and stuff on one of the tables. I held the shed door open while Dad got the tables and chairs out and set them up. I've been helping a lot."

"Good for you, Jaime. I'll ask Dad to bring the ice and you can take these napkins. Let me help you back across the road. I'll be over after while when Shirley comes over to relieve me."

Ray walked up to her as he finished with the last customer. He leaned into her ear. "Boy, I'm sure glad you thought to take Idy a plate. I was getting kind of nervous there for a bit."

Barbara laughed. "I know. You could tell she wanted in on it all right."

"Mom, help me back across the road. Here comes Susie!" Jaime took off running to meet her.

"Jaime, take the napkins into Mawmaw first," Barbara yelled to him.

"Okay, Barbara, it's your turn to eat. You wouldn't believe the people that are over there!"

"Oh yes, I would, Shirley. Look at the cars. They're lined up in the churchyard and both driveways."

"Guess what. Barney showed up. I guess he saw all the people and wanted something to eat."

"Is he drunk?"

"About half. John, Ray and Uncle Hubert are talking to him while Aunt Pearl and Aunt Gladys are fixing him a plate. Uncle Hubert is getting a kick out of this."

"Oh, brother!" Barbara rolled her eyes and burst out laughing. "I don't want to miss this. Thanks, Shirley. I'll be back in a little while."

Ray was handing the plate to Barney as Barbara walked up. "Tank you, Way. I do appweciate this food. You a dood man."

"That's right...Hey, why don't you tell some of these guys here about me being such a good man, Barney? I try to tell them, but they just don't believe it."

"Oh, yeah. We know what a good man you are, Ray. Good for pulling pranks, good for causing trouble, good for...uh..." John hesitated.

"Good for nothing?" Uncle Hubert added.

"Yeah, that's it," John laughed.

"Hey, watcha-your-tongue," Ray grinned.

"No, he not dood-fer-nutin'," Barney said earnestly.

"It's okay, Barney. We're just picking on Ray. You enjoy your dinner." John took him by the arm and started leading him down the driveway.

"Oh, otay. I will. You get you sumpin' to eat, Barbie." Barney smiled at her. "There's lot of dood food."

"Thanks, I will." Barbara smiled at him as she hugged Uncle Hubert. "Where's Pa?"

"He's sitting in the back yard," Uncle Hubert answered. "He's getting pretty tired, but I think he's enjoying himself. I know you must be hungry by now. Go fill yourself a plate."

"Thanks. I will, but I want to wish Pa a happy birthday first." Barbara passed up the food tables and headed toward the back yard. Pa was sitting in a chair talking to one of his cousins. *He looks so frail. He must have lost thirty or forty pounds.* "Hey, Pa. Happy Birthday!"

He smiled up at Barbara. "Thanks. Me and Rose was just talking 'bout the good ole days."

"Yes, we did have some good times." Rose smiled at Barbara. "And how are you doing in that store? It's a lot of work, isn't it?"

"Yes, it really is – especially with Ray working on the railroad. I don't know what we would do without Aunt Pearl."

"Me either," Jaime chimed in.

Barbara laughed. "Well, just where did you come from, young man. Are you having a good time?"

"Yeah, me and Billy and Susie and Renae are playin' hide and seek. Mom, can Renae spend the night? She hardly ever gets to come down. Aunt Peggy said it would be okay."

"I suppose so." Barbara glanced around at the people. *There must be sixty or seventy people here!*

"Thanks, Mom." Jaime raced off with his cousin, Renae. She lived in Bluefield and didn't come to see them very often. She was six, and since she was a girl and she and Jaime didn't get to spend much time together, they played together real well – no fighting.

"Hey, girl. Shouldn't you be getting a plate loaded before you have to go back over to the store?" Barbara turned around to see Aunt Annie walking up to her.

"Yeah, I guess I should. I'm starving," Barbara said. "How was your trip down here?"

"Good. We got here about an hour ago. Tim let me out and had to go search for a place to park. I think he parked over at your house. He'll probably spend the night with you guys, anyway."

"Fine with us. Ray always enjoys spending time with Tim."

"Don't know how much time he'll get to spend with him – way that store ties y'all down and him working on the railroad too. I always told Gene and Betty that you couldn't give me that store."

"Yeah, I can remember you saying that a few times. Fact is, tomorrow is Sunday and we started waiting until after church to open. Ray isn't working this weekend either, so he will get to spend time with Tim."

"Well, now that's good. We'll be leaving in the early afternoon. Tim and I both have to work Monday."

"Good, you can go to church with us," Barbara said as she put some potato salad on her plate.

"Be sure to get some of that strawberry shortcake," Ray whispered. "I'm going to sneak some of it over to the house. I already wrapped me up the turkey legs."

Barbara grinned as she pictured Ray sitting in front of the TV gnawing on the turkey leg. Ma would always wrap up the neck and legs from the turkey every Thanksgiving, Christmas and Easter. It had almost become tradition. Barbara realized Ray was talking to her. "Huh?"

"I said I would go over and help Shirley so you can eat and visit. Tim is staying with us tonight."

"Yeah, Aunt Annie already told me so."

"Is that okay?"

"Sure, he'll be good company."

"Enjoy," Ray said over his shoulder as he walked away.

"Yeah, well, you enjoy your work over there," Barbara threw back at him.

"Sure thaang," he shot back.

She laughed and looked around to find her a seat to sit down and eat.

The day had been long and they were all tired. "Let's go over to Ma's before we go home tonight," Ray said as he turned the key in the lock.

"Fine with me. We need to gather up Pearl and Jaime anyway." Barbara breathed in the new night air and looked up at the star-filled sky. "It turned out to be real good weather for the party, didn't it?"

"Yeah, it did." Ray slipped his arm around her waist as they started across the road. "Where are you going to put Tim tonight?"

"Oh, gee. I just remembered. Jaime asked Renae to spend the night. I guess we will have a house full. We could put Tim in Jaime's bed and fix pallets on the living room floor for Jaime and Renae. We'll tell them that they're camping out. That will make it fun for them."

"They have fun anyway. I just hope they don't stay awake giggling half the night."

"One word from you and I dare say they'll quieten down."

Ray gave Barbara a 'Who me?' look as he pushed the front door open to the family room. Jaime and Renae were sitting on the floor watching a cartoon. They glanced up and then back to the television. "You ready to go home kids?"

"Almost. Wait 'til this goes off, okay, Dad?"

"Okay, son." They walked on into the kitchen where everybody sat around the table, including Pa who looked washed out. They all greeted Barbara and Ray.

"Do you guys want something to eat?" Ma asked.

"Maybe some dessert," Ray said. "Any banana pudding left?"

"No, but there's some coconut cake. I don't know what happened to the strawberry shortcake." Ma grinned as she unveiled the coconut cake.

"Yummm. Coconut cake will be just fine," Barbara said.

"Where's Aunt Annie?" Ray asked.

"She went home with Mary Ann," Aunt Gladys answered. "We're staying here tonight and the rest of the week. "If anybody else had shown up, your parents would have had to put them on the floor."

Ray laughed. "Or in the back of the produce truck. Remember that's where all the boys would have to sleep when y'all came down to visit in the summer."

"Those were the good ole days," Uncle Hubert said. "Too bad all you guys had to grow up on us."

"Well...most of them grew up," Barbara said as she grinned at Ray.

"Watcha you mouf," Ray teased as he grinned back.

Barbara sat down next to Pa. "So, how was your big birthday?" she asked. "There sure were a lot of people here, huh? Makes you know how much they care for you."

He half-smiled and looked over at Barbara. "I was thinking about that today when everybody was here. I was watching them eating, laughing, having a good time. But then I also thought of something else too."

"What's that?" Barbara asked as she tilted her head and gave him a serious look.

He looked her in the eyes and quietly said. "Most of them have never invited us to their home for dinner, even though we have invited them many times throughout the years to our dinners and get-togethers."

Barbara didn't know what to say.

Chapter XVIII

The Zoo

Barbara propped the door open with a river rock that sat just inside the door for that purpose. Aunt Pearl pulled her hair away from her neck and fanned her face with a paper advertisement. "Maybe some air will help."

"What air? I don't believe there's any stirring. Too bad we can't turn on that air conditioner sitting in the window back in the kitchen," Pearl said.

"I agree, but Pa warned me that he had to turn that air conditioner off as soon as he received his first electric bill last summer. It took the whole month's profit to run it. This store has no insulation and with these high ceilings it didn't help much anyway. This store definitely was not built with air conditioning in mind."

"Well, I've made it through fifty-two years without air conditioning. I guess I can make it another summer." Pearl sighed as she stood in the doorway.

"One good thing, though, Ray said that Saturday he is going to take the air conditioner out of the window here and put it over to the house. At least we'll have some coolness over there."

"Good," Aunt Pearl grinned. "Now all we need to do is find some time to spend at home."

Barbara shook her head and walked behind the counter as Red walked in the door.

"Sure is hot today." Red laid a paper plate wrapped in aluminum foil on the counter. "Thought y'all might like some of this chocolate cake left over from Bingo last night."

"Thanks, Red." Barbara pulled the foil back and licked her lips. "I'm tempted to eat this for breakfast!"

"Well, you better save some for Ray and Jaime. Jaime was over to the house while I was baking it yesterday afternoon. I promised him a piece of it. I doubt he'll forget it either."

"He's still sleeping in. Ray will bring him over when he gets up. Meantime, we'd better hide it back or he will want it for breakfast."

"Red, I don't see how you can bake on such hot days," Pearl said.

Red grinned and rocked her four-foot ten-inch – ninety-six pound frame in a sideways motion and tapped her red hair. "Ah, I'm used to it Pearl. It's all in your mind."

"Well, I wish my mind would quit making this sweat run down my neck," Pearl said as she pulled a Kleenex from its box and wiped her neck again.

"Wonder if Ray would have time to dig me a couple of post holes today?" Red looked at Barbara.

I guess we're going to pay for this chocolate cake. Barbara smiled hoping to hide her thoughts. "Don't know. Guess you'll have to ask Ray when he gets up. He's working this evening, though."

"Shucks. Won't take him but a few minutes. I'm extending my fence along the side next to that empty store building next door. That place has rats. I saw them come up from the creek and I bet it's full of snakes."

"Ain't no fence gonna keep a rat or a snake away." Pearl shook her head.

"Well, I reckon I know that, Pearl. I just want to put a definite border between me and that old building. I wish Mr. Smith would either fix it up and rent it or tear it down. Put this buttermilk and baking powder on my bill. I used the last up when I was baking yesterday. I gotta go. Tell Ray I already have some posthole diggers."

"Okay," Barbara didn't look up as she wrote the items down on Red's charge book and turned around to put it back in the tray that held the customers' books. Red was out the door before she turned back around.

"I tell ye what. That woman can move," Aunt Pearl said. " How old is she anyway?"

"She won't tell anybody. But I do know this. Her kids had a big fiftieth wedding anniversary party for her and her husband back in 1974. Ray and I went. It was really nice. She says she got married when she was thirteen. So let's see. 1982, minus 1974 is eight, plus fifty, plus thirteen. That would make her about seventy-one. Right?" Barbara grinned.

"Tickles you, don't it? Figuring up her age, I mean."

"Yeah. Wouldn't you think she would realize that people can add? What's the big deal anyway? She ought to be glad she's lived so long."

"Well, that's easy to say when you're young, Barb. Maybe you'll feel the same way when you get old."

"Maybe, but she really gets angry when people ask her how old she is. She flares up and tells them it's none of their business."

"Well, I tell ye one thing. She sure don't move like she's seventy-one. That's probably why she's so skinny. She's downright hyper, if you ask me."

"Yeah, I hope I have that much energy when I get that old."

Jaime burst through the door about an hour later with his Dad behind him. "I'm hungry, Aunt Pearl."

"Ye oughta be, you little sleepy-head." Pearl lightly smacked his rear and turned him toward the kitchen. I kept the gravy and biscuits warm for you guys."

"Wow! A hot breakfast on a hot morning. How did we rate this?" Ray grinned.

"I guess 'cause I'm just a kind-hearted kind of girl." Pearl put her hand on her hip and tossed her head.

Ray laughed as he followed her down the aisle toward the kitchen. Barbara folded the checkbook and grinned. *Might as well join 'em...let them know I'm still here and all that stuff.*

As Barbara appeared at the doorway Jaime jumped up from the table. "Hey, Mom, Red said the kittens are ready to give away. Please, please, please let me have one." Jaime had been asking Barbara for weeks if he could have one. He'd already picked one out and was trying to think of a name.

"I've been thinking, Ray. Do you think Bear will tolerate a kitten? You know how he hates cats." Bear was their big black Belgium Shepherd and was a year older than Jaime.

"Well, I guess we could show him the kitten and forbid him to harass it. It might work." Ray looked at Jaime. "You do realize that you will have to feed it and make sure it stays away from Bear. He might eat it."

"*Daad!* Bear wouldn't eat a kitten."

"Oh, I'm afraid he might. It is the natural instinct of a dog to do away with the cats in this world. Bear minds pretty well, so we can give it a try, but you'll have to remember that they will be natural enemies." Ray lowered his head and looked through his long eyelashes at Jaime trying to emphasize the gravity of the idea of having a cat in the same family with a six-year-old dog that had not been raised with a feline.

"Don't worry, Dad. I'll make Bear and the kitten be friends."

"Ye can't *make* them be friends, Jaime." Aunt Pearl shook her head.

"Yes I can 'cause Miss Bryant said I was good at making friends."

The serious mood broke as everybody except Jaime laughed.

"Hey, I almost forgot, Ray," Barbara sighed. "Red wants you to dig her some postholes."

"Postholes? What for?" Ray asked.

"She's going to put a fence around her yard."

"A fence? That's a lot of postholes to dig!" Ray put his fork down. "I'll go talk to her. Sheesss!"

"Well, she said she has the posthole diggers," Pearl offered.

"Yeah, I know all about those posthole diggers. They're mine! I let Pa borrow them over a year ago and somehow he let Red borrow them and I haven't seen them since." He hesitated. "Maybe this will be a good way to get them back."

"Or you could just ask for them – direct-like," Barbara said.

"Yeah, I will. I'll go give her about an hour's labor before I go to work; but if it takes more than that, she'll have to find somebody else. This weekend I have two guys coming to help me start the roof for the store. If we're not careful, summer will get away from us and it won't be done."

About an hour and a half later, Ray came stomping through the door.

"What's wrong?" Barbara asked.

"A handle broke on the posthole diggers and Red wants me to buy her a new set!"

"What?" Barbara gasped. "Those are yours, Ray, and besides even if they weren't, you're out there giving her free labor. Surely, you're not going to do it, are you?"

"I told her they were mine and she got real hot. Said they were not – that Gene had given her those posthole diggers before he went to Florida."

"Did you maybe try to explain that they weren't 'Gene's' to give away?"

"Sort of, but she said, 'Oh no, if that's what I thought then I needed to go talk to Gene.'"

"Pa is too sick to be worried about such a thing."

"Don't you think I know that. I'm going to buy her a set, but that will be the last thing I do for her!" Ray's face was red with anger as well as the hot sun.

"Ray, we can't afford to buy her those diggers when they're not even hers to begin…" Barbara stopped as Mrs. Fox walked through the door.

"Y'all a arguin'?" she asked.

Ray gave her a sideways glance and looked back at Barbara. "I'm going home and get ready for work." With that he walked out the door.

"Shucks, he don't hafta take his bad mood out on me. After all I'm a good customer to y'all. I didn't do nothin' to him."

"No, I know, Mrs. Fox." Barbara sighed. "It's just been a rough morning and a hot one to boot."

"Boy, ya got that one right. I come for some buttermilk. Don't reckon it's soured in this weather, do ye?"

Pearl walked up the aisle with a broom in one hand and a cold glass of water in the other. "'Scuse me, Mrs. Fox, but I kinda thought that was the whole idée about buttermilk?" She laughed.

Mrs. Fox frowned at her as Barbara stood back grinning and waiting for the fireworks. "Ye know what I mean, Pearl."

Pearl dropped her head and walked past her. Then she looked over at Barbara and rolled her eyes with a big grin on her face.

Barbara dropped her eyes trying not to laugh. "It's okay, Mrs. Fox. The milkman makes sure the dates are good and the cooler hasn't broken down. I think the buttermilk will be okay."

"Thank you, Barbara. At least somebody around here is civil to me. A body just can't be too kerful, ye know. All this hot weather and stuff goin' bad. Happens in even the best stores, much less one like this."

Pearl stopped dead in her tracks as Mrs. Fox made her way toward the milk cooler. She turned and stuck her tongue out at Mrs. Fox's back.

Barbara laughed. Mrs. Fox turned around. "What?" she asked.

"Oh, nothing, Mrs. Fox. I was just thinking about something Jaime said the other day."

Mrs. Fox gave her a dubious look, but reached into the cooler to get her buttermilk. She held it up to check the date as she walked back down the aisle. "Well, its got a week on it," she said as she sat it on the counter. "I guess I'll have it drunk up afore then. Let's see. Might as well get a bag of flour while I'm here. How long's it been sittin'on the shelf?"

"Two or three weeks, I think," Barbara said. "It'll be okay."

"Well, iffen I see any bugs, I'll be right back up here. I gotta ad-mit that y'all been doing purty good on this freshness stuff. But a body can't be too kerful – like I said."

"I know. Anything else, Mrs. Fox?" Barbara asked.

"Nah, that'll do it today. Just put it on my bill. Reckon how much I owe y'all right now. Will ye add it up?"

"Sure," Barbara moved toward the adding machine. As she added, Mrs. Fox walked over to Pearl.

"One thang I gotta say for ye, Pearl. Ye keep this here store looking mighty clean."

"Thank ye," Pearl smiled.

"It's $96.74," Barbara said.

"Good, Lord. How did it git to be so much. I reckon I *am* a good customer. You just tell sourpuss Ray that!"

"He's tired and upset, Mrs. Fox. Just pay him no mind." Barbara said as she put the book back into the box.

"Humph!" Pearl shook her head.

"I know. I'm just a foolin'," Mrs. Fox grinned. "Ole Ray's been purty good to me all in all, I reckon. See y'all later." With that she walked out the door.

"Barbara, she makes me so mad. How do you stand there and be nice to her? You even smile at her."

"Ah, Aunt Pearl. You just have to think about the money she's spending. It just goes with the territory. I can smile all the way to the bank, as they say. Besides she doesn't realize that she's aggravating us."

Pearl grinned and shook her head. "I guess when you put it that way…"

Ray walked back in the door a few minutes later. "I'm going to leave a little bit early for work and pick up those posthole diggers for Red. Where's Jaime?"

"Over to Mr. Webb's. Oh, Ray…We can't afford to do that. It's just not right. She…"

Barbara stopped in mid sentence when she caught Ray's lips pressed together and a glare in his eye. She knew she might as well give up. He had set his mind to buying them. "Well, will you go out to the bank and get us some change before you leave?"

"Sure, how much do you want?"

Barbara handed him the bank bag. "I already have the bills in there with a note for the teller."

"Okay, I'll be back in a few minutes."

"Ray, your lunch is in the refrigerator in the back." Pearl turned to Barbara. "I think I'll mosey on over to the house and clean it up a bit since we're not too busy."

"Okay, Aunt Pearl."

With that Barbara found herself alone. She picked up the Want Book and started down the aisle to write down an order for the wholesaler. A few minutes later Ida walked in the door.

"Hidy, Barb. Hot 'nuff for ya yet?"

"Pretty much, I think so." Barbara walked back to the front of the store. "How about you...are you surviving this heat okay?"

"Okay, I reckon. I...EEEEEEEH!"

"What?" Barbara screamed.

"A snake. Look!"

Barbara saw the snake and screamed louder and longer than Ida had.

"Give me a hoe! I'll kill it for ya!" Ida yelled.

Barbara started to the hardware section, when the snake slithered under one of the shelves.

"Never mind," Ida said. "Can't use a hoe under thar."

"What's going on?" Junebug had walked in unnoticed to Barbara.

"A snake is under the shelf there," she pointed to the potato chip rack.

"I'll get him. Ya got any bug spray," Junebug offered.

"Bug spray?" Barbara stared at Junebug. "What'll that do?"

"Well, it might put him to sleep or chase him out of there, one or the other."

Barbara handed him a can of ant and roach spray; and then she backed up to and hopped up on the counter - sitting with her legs dangling. *Where is Ray? He talks forever when he goes to town!*

She watched Junebug as he got down on his hands and knees and peered under the shelf. "I think I see him!" Junebug started spraying under the shelf. The snake slithered out the other side and across the aisle to the paper supply shelves.

"Oh, no!" Barbara jumped down and moved to the phone. "It went up under those shelves and now it's cornered! I'm going to call Ray!" Her hands shook as she dialed the bank's number. "Hello, Jane, is Ray still out there? Tell him to hurry back. It's an emergency!" With that she slammed the phone down and scooted back over to the counter – ready to jump onto it if necessary.

The bank was only a mile away. Ray was back within two minutes. He ran into the store looking around. "What's wrong?"

"Ooooh, Ray, there's a snake under the paper towel shelf," Barbara's voice shook.

"A snake? I thought you were being robbed or something."

"I sprayed this stuff up under there, but I think it's just making him mad." Junebug stood there holding the can of spray.

"It was jest a little garter snake," Ida said. "Not anything for Barbara to git so all fired upset about."

Ray stood there assessing the situation and started grinning. "Well, now how did a snake find its way into our store? It would have had to crawl across that hot asphalt in the driveway."

"Who cares? Get it!" Barbara cried out.

"Yeah, never mind. It's here so I'll have to take care of it. Thank you, Junebug." He reached over and took the can of spray from him and sat it on the counter.

Barbara, Ida and Junebug stood still moving their eyes from Ray to the paper shelves.

Jaime burst through the door. "Mom, look what Mr. Webb gave me..." His voice trailed as he looked at the adults.

"Jaime, you go back to Mr. Webb's for a while," Barbara said as evenly as she could.

"Why?"

"Oh, Barb, it's just a garter snake. Jaime will be okay." Ray reached for the 'bat net' as Barbara secretly called it. He got down on his hands and knees and looked under the shelves. "Give me a flashlight...Jaime get back over there with your Mom."

Barbara reached for the light and handed it to Ida, who handed it to Junebug, who handed it to Ray.

Ray turned the light on and laid it on the floor to shine under the shelf. Then he pushed the long handle of the net up under the shelf. In a minute or two (seemed like fifteen to Barbara) he pulled the net back out with the snake wrapped around the handle. Everybody backed up as he made his way to the door.

"Sheesh," Ida backed farther away. "So much to do over a little garter snake."

"Well, everythang's okay now," Junebug said. "Here's my $5.00 for the gas I got. See y'all later."

"Thanks," Barbara said.

"Can I go outside and see what Dad did with the snake?" Jaime asked.

"I don't know. Better wait," Barbara said.

"Where's Aunt Pearl?" Jaime looked around the store.

"She's over at the house."

"Can I go over and tell her about the snake?"

"Yeah, go ahead, Jaime, but you steer clear of Dad and that snake and watch where you're going. Get Junebug to help you across the road."

"Okay, Mom," he called as he ran out the door.

"Barb, I was a noticin' that purty flower pot you got sittin' outside. How much is it anyways?" Ida wiped the drool from her mouth as she spoke. "Barbara?"

"Huh?' Barbara said as she sat down on the stool behind the counter.

"I said, how much is that flower po..."

"Snake's gone," Ray walked back in the door and over to the nail to hang the net up.

"Did ye kill him?" Ida squared her shoulders.

"No, I just took him down to the creek and let him go."

"What!" Barbara jumped up.

"Good boy, Ray. They help eat up the rats down thar."

"What?" Barbara said again.

"Better watch. You're going to swallow a fly with your mouth open like that, Barb." Ray laughed. "I don't know if that little garter snake will eat a rat, but they're not poisonous and will eat the mice...maybe someday a rat."

"Yeah, he's right, Barb. How much is that flower..."

"I don't like snakes, Ray. Especially snakes that decide to come in the store. Only good snake is a dead snake!"

"Never mind," said Ida. Ain't got no money 'til the first anyhow." She walked out the door.

"Barbara I doubt if we'll ever have another snake come into the store. That was just a fluke. This is becoming a regular zoo, huh? Don't worry. I grew up here and that's the first time I ever remember seeing a snake anywhere near here."

"Well, it just better be the last time." Barbara sat back down.

"What did Idy, want?" Ray asked. "She left here empty handed."

"Dogged, if I know." Barbara shrugged her shoulders and looked back over to the paper towel shelf.

"Well, I've got to get to work. I'll see you tonight." Ray gave her a quick hug and out the door he went.

Ethan walked in about that time. She sighed with relief and smiled. "Hi, Ethan."

"Hey, Barbara." He walked down the aisle to the meat counter. "I need a pound of bologny and some cookin' cheese."

"Good idea," Barbara said. "I mean, Okay, Ethan. I'll get it for you." She reached for the telephone and dialed the house. "Aunt Pearl, I'm starting to get busy now. Could you come back over and bring Jaime?"

Chapter XIX

Dog Days

"Here he is, Mom." Jaime held the kitten in his arms.

"So that's the one you picked." Barbara took the gray and white striped kitten from Jaime and held it as it purred. "What are you going to name him?"

"Gray sounds good to me," Pearl said.

"Gray? That's a color, Aunt Pearl – not a name." Jaime took the kitten back. "I don't know what to name him. What do you think, Mom?"

"Give it a day or two and you'll think of something that fits him – her," Barbara said.

"Ouch!" Jaime let go of the kitten and let it fall to the floor. "It put its stickers in my arm."

"Stickers?" Aunt Pearl said as she and Barbara both laughed. "He doesn't have stickers, Jaime. Those are claws and they *will* get you."

Jaime rubbed the scratch and frowned at the kitten which was ignoring him and playing with Barbara's shoestrings.

"Well, it felt like stickers. I need a Band-Aid."

Barbara looked at the scratch and reached for the first aid kit that sat behind the counter. " Here you go, big boy. It'll be all right."

Jaime picked the kitten up again as a light bulb look came across his face. "Hey! That's what I can name her."

"Big boy?" Pearl asked.

"No, Aunt Pearl." Jaime looked at her as if she were silly. "It's a girl and just a little kitten."

"Well, what are you going to name her?" Barbara asked.

"Stickers!" Jaime grinned. "She's got stickers, so I'll name her Stickers."

Pearl laughed. "She doesn't have stickers. Those are claws, I tell ye."

"Well, they feel like stickers." Jaime put the kitten over into his other arm as he walked toward the door. "Here comes Billy. I'm gonna go show him Stickers. Red has one more kitten left for him." With that he ran out the door to meet his cousin and Barbara watched as they both raced up to Red's with Stickers bouncing in Jaime's arms.

A few minutes later the boys were back in the store. Billy had a yellow tabby in his arms. "Look, Aunt Pearl. Look, Aunt Barbara. Mom let me pick out a kitten too. This was the last one. Red said I sure was lucky."

"Yeah, but when we left her house, Aunt Shirley said 'Red was the lucky one. She got rid of all her kittens and it only took three months,'" Jaime said.

"That's right," Billy said. "Mom said she'd be back to get me later. She's taking Mawmaw and Sarah shopping."

"Y'all go up to the churchyard and play with your kittens," Aunt Pearl said.

"And be careful not to let them wander into the road. Don't go near that road," Barbara warned.

As they started out the door, Isaac walked in. "Hey there boys. Whatcha' got?"

"Kittens!" the boys said in unison.

"Well, well. Now I'd say those are some nice looking kittens. Have you named them yet?"

"Mine is Stickers," Jaime said.

"Mom said I could call mine 'Trouble', but I don't think I like that name," Billy said. "I just might give him a different name."

"Well, I'm sure you'll come up with a good one," Isaac said. He wiped the sweat from the back of his neck. "Got a Band-Aid?" he asked Pearl.

"Sure. What's wrong, Isaac?"

"I've just got a little cut on my arm, but these dog days make it hard to heal."

"Yeah, know what you mean," Pearl said. "I'll be glad when they're over. Sure has been hot and humid."

"What are dog days?" Jaime cocked his head toward Aunt Pearl.

"It's when the summer gets hot and sultry. Starts sometime in July and goes through part of August."

"Is my cut gonna take a long time to heal?" Jaime looked at his Band-aid.

"No, I think your scratch will be fine," Pearl said.

"What about Bear?" Jaime asked.

"What about him?" Barbara asked.

"Well, you said it was dog days. Does Bear do something special?"

"No." Aunt Pearl laughed. "Though the animals are kinda cross and funny during this time of year; so y'all be careful and don't be pestering Bear and Stickers. And you be good to Trouble, Billy, or he might just live up to his name."

"I don't like the name Trouble," Billy said.

"I don't pester Bear or Stickers, Aunt Pearl," Jaime said.

"You know, they say snakes are blind during dog days. You have to watch when you're walking in the woods," Aunt Pearl said.

"Actually, I believe that's just an old wives' tale," Barbara said.

"Well, just don't you be so quick to dismiss those old wives tales," Aunt Pearl said. "I've been around a lot longer than you and I can tell you there's a heap of truth in most of them."

"I know, Aunt Pearl. I hear snakes are deaf."

"If you say so. I ain't never known one that had ears."

"I think they're under the skin, but they go mainly by vibrations in the ground."

"How's Gene doing, not to change the subject," asked Isaac.

"He's not doing well at all," Barbara said.

"Betty said she couldn't even cook anymore because he can't stand the smell of food," Pearl said. "He eats very little and keeps even less down. He has already lost about twenty-five pounds."

"Is that so? Reckon it would be okay for me to go visit awhile?" Isaac asked.

"I'm sure. I'll call and tell Ma you're coming. I'm sure that would cheer him up." Barbara reached for the phone.

"I'll take him over," Jaime said.

"That's okay, Jaime. I'm sure Isaac can find his way across the road." Barbara grinned and Aunt Pearl hooted. "Y'all just go on over to the churchyard and play."

"They'll want to see the kittens," Jaime protested.

"Not now," Barbara answered. "Pawpaw is not up to looking at kittens."

"Come on." Jaime motioned to Billy. "Let's take Stickers and Trouble to the churchyard."

"Quit calling him Trouble." Billy followed Jaime out the door.

"Whew! It sure is hot," Bertha said as she walked in the door with a little girl.

"You got that right," Ray said as he walked in behind her. "That garage sure is hot. Those cinderblocks hold the heat in." He handed Barbara $3.00. "For fixing a flat," he said. "Who is your sidekick, Bertha?"

"This here's my baby granddaughter. She's almost five." Bertha grinned as she looked down at the blonde haired, blue eyed girl before her. "She's smart as a whip. I tell ye one thang. Her Ma and Pa are raisin' her right."

"What's her name?" Barbara asked.

"Adie Ann, but we call her Adie for short."

"Adrienne," the girl corrected her.

"Well, yeah, I guess. That's why we call you Adie. Adie Ann's too hard to say."

Adie reached in the box of bananas and picked one up. "Put that back," Bertha said.

"But you said I could get something."

"I know, but you won't eat all of that and I know it."

"Yes, I will."

"No, you'll eat about half of it and then throw the rest away. Too much waste." Bertha took the banana from her and threw it back in the box. Adie stood there with a pout on her little round face. "Here, get ya a candy bar. None of that will go to waste, I'm sure."

Adrienne brightened. "Okay!" She reached in the candy shelves and brought out a Caramello.

"How much?" Bertha asked Barbara.

"Forty-seven cents," Barbara said.

"Here ye go." Bertha counted out the correct change. "Adie, ya ready to go?"

"Uh-huh," Adie said as she bit into the Caramello bar and the caramel oozed from the bar.

"Kerful. You're gittin' it all over ya," Bertha said.

They watched as Bertha and Adie walked out the door.

"I'll tell ye, Barb, that banana would've been a lot better fer that youngun."

"You got that right," Ray interjected.

"It amazes me," Barbara said. "The banana would have cost about eighteen or twenty cents and even if she did throw half of it away, she would still come out cheaper and Adie would have had some nutrition."

"Yeah, but the customer is almost always right," Ray said.

"I guess," Aunt Pearl sighed. "Did ye see the way she threw that banana back in the box? Probably won't be fit to sell by tomorrow."

The telephone rang. Barbara walked over to pick it up. "I hear a siren," Ray said, as he walked toward the door. "Oh no, it's going over to Ma and Pa's. I'm going over."

Barbara hung up the phone. "That was Ma. She said Pa is worse so she called the ambulance to take him to the hospital."

"Why didn't she just ask Ray to take him up?" Pearl asked.

"I don't know." Barbara walked to the door to watch the happenings.

"I'm going over too, Barbara. I'll be back to let you know something."

"Okay." Barbara opened the door as Jaime and Billy came running. "Help us across the road. The am-bu-lance is over to Pawpaw's," Jaime said.

"No, you stay here with me," Barbara answered. "Dad and Aunt Pearl have gone over to see. They don't need too many people in the way."

"Oh, Aunt Barbara, we won't get in the way," Billy said.

"No, we'll stay way back," Jaime said.

"Yeah, way back over here across the road with me," Barbara said.

They watched until Pa had been loaded into the ambulance and driven away with the sirens blaring. "I bet he's sicker," Billy said.

Jaime nodded his head in agreement as Barbara walked back behind the counter to wait on Ethan.

"Anything I can help you with, you just let me know."

"Thanks, Ethan, I will."

Ray and Pearl walked in the door. Barbara raised an eyebrow in question to them. "Pa was throwing up something fierce," Ray said. "I'm going to follow them up to the hospital. I'll be back in time to go to work. Think you'll be okay?"

"Yeah. Pearl and I will be right here."

"Dad, is Pawpaw going to die?" Jaime looked up at his dad as he held the kitten close to his chest.

"Not today, Jaime. You and Billy go on out to the churchyard and play. Be good and don't give your mother any trouble."

"We won't." Jaime and Billy walked out the door and up the driveway to the churchyard.

"I was hoping that doctor was wrong," Aunt Pearl said. "But Gene looks worse and worse everyday."

"I know," Barbara said. She sighed as she picked up the cigarette order form.

"Doesn't seem fair," Aunt Pearl barely whispered.

"I know." Barbara looked at Aunt Pearl. "It's not easy watching your older brother suffer, is it?"

"No." Aunt Pearl walked back to the kitchen.

Barbara sat down on the stool and laid her head in the circle of her arms on the counter.

"Whatcha doin' sleepin' this time of day?" Granny Johnson had walked through the doors.

"Not - just thinking," Barbara said.

"Oh. Well...okay. We'uns in the bottom saw the am-bu-lance. Gene done got worse?"

"Yes, Ma thought it best to take him to the hospital," Barbara said.

"Anythin' we can do?"

"Thanks, Granny, but I don't know of anything right now. Ray has gone up to the hospital. I guess he'll be back soon and give us a report."

"Okie-dokie. You just remember whar' we're at. Whar's Pearl?"

"She's in the kitchen."

"Good, I want me some bologny sliced. I'll go see her."

Ray was back in a couple of hours. "They're keeping him," he said. "Mary Ann will be down to get Ma some clothes and necessities. She's going to stay at the hospital with Pa." He looked around. "Sure is quiet. Where is everybody?"

Just then Jaime and Billy burst through the door. "Dad, how is Pawpaw?"

"He's real sick," Ray said. "The doctor decided to keep him."

"Will the doctor make him better?" Billy asked.

"We can hope so," Ray said.

"And pray. Don't forget to pray," Jaime said. "Hope and pray."

"That's right," Barbara said. "That's one thing we can all do."

Sunday morning Barbara got Jaime dressed and they all went to the hospital to see Pawpaw. It was the only time the four of them could go together.

"I tell ye, when I was up here with Shirley last night he looked much better," Pearl said as they walked down the hallway looking at room numbers.

"He's in 314. This way," Ray said.

When they walked in the room, Ma was sitting in a chair and Pa was sitting up in bed. "Pearl said you looked better and I reckon she was right. How do you feel?" Barbara asked.

"Better, thanks," Pa said. He looked toward Jaime. "And how's Jaime?"

"I'm okay Pawpaw. Guess what? I got me one of Red's kittens. I was gonna bring him over for you to see, but Mom wouldn't let me. Then that am-bu-lance came and got you."

"That's okay." Pa grinned down at Jaime. "I'll see it when I get back home."

"The doctor's are making you all better, ain't they Pawpaw?"

"Sure. I'll be home in no time. Then you can bring that kitten over."

"His name is Stickers."

"Stickers? That's a funny name. How come you to name him that?"

"'Cause he sticks me!"

"Oh, well, now. I guess that is just the perfect name then," Pa said.

"Billy got one too. He named him Wheatie."

"Wheatie?" Barbara, Ray and Pearl all said in unison.

"I thought his name was Trouble," said Pearl.

"Yeah, he didn't like the name Trouble so he changed it to Wheatie."

"Why did he pick Wheatie?" Ma asked.

"'Cause he said his kitten is stronger than my kitten," Jaime said. "But that's not so. Billy just thinks so."

"Oh…" The room got quiet and everybody had a questioning look on their faces. Finally Pearl brightened. "Okay, I get it. The cereal commercial!"

"Oh, yeah." Pa said as everybody chuckled.

"Do you need me to bring you anything?" Ray directed the question to his mother.

"No, I don't think so, Ray. We're doing okay so far."

"They're going to start chemo tomorrow," Pa said.

"That may make you sick," Pearl said.

"I know. I dread it but guess sometimes you have to get sicker to get better," Pa said.

"What's chemo?" Jaime asked.

"Medicine," Ray said.

"They should have already give you medicine, Pawpaw. Boy they sure are slow around here. Mom gave me medicine when I got sick. I hated it, but I did get better. You'll be okay." Jaime patted his grandpa's hand.

"Y'all skipping church this morning?" Pa asked.

"Yeah, it's the only time we could all come to see you together. We'll have to be leaving soon to open the store," Ray said.

"Dad, you said we could stop by Kentucky Fried Chicken after we leave here." Jaime's face lit up. "He said maybe you'd want some."

"No, I don't think so," Pa said.

"How about you, Ma?" Ray asked. "Why don't you take a break and go eat with us. We'll bring you back in a little bit."

"Yes, do. Go ahead with the kids. I'll be okay," Pa said.

"Well, that does sound good. Sure you'll be okay?"

"I'm sure. Now go along and enjoy yourselves."

Jaime headed toward the door. "Bye, Pawpaw," he glanced back over his shoulder.

"Bye, baby," Pa said.

Jaime stopped in his tracks and squared his shoulders. "I'm not a baby...I'm big!" he said and started on out the door.

Pa laughed with everyone else. *Jaime was some good medicine,* Barbara thought.

Chapter XX

Waiting

"I can't believe it's time for school to start already," Barbara said.

"Me neither." Pearl sat a box of candy on the shelf and pulled another from the big box that held the other boxes of candy they had ordered. "Do you want me to put out this Halloween candy?" she asked as she held up a box of orange wax whistles.

"No, we'll store them back in the office. It's too early for Halloween. Ma said I should order them early because they're hard to get as the date gets closer."

"Where exactly should I put them in the office?" Pearl asked.

"I guess on the shelves with the paper bags – up high so the kids won't spot them. Do you want to go school clothes shopping for Jaime with me?" Barbara asked.

"Might as well. That boy sure has grown this summer."

"Yeah, he sure has. I'll see if Shirley will watch the store Saturday evening and we'll take Ray and Jaime and maybe eat at Godfather's Pizza. Then we'll go visit Pa in the hospital."

"That sounds even better." Pearl disappeared into the office as the wind chimes rang out over the door.

"Hi, Ethan. How are you doing?" Barbara smiled as she sat her bookwork on the end of the counter.

"Fair to middlin' I reckon," said Ethan. "And how are you doin'?"

"Fairly well. It has cooled down a little in the mornings. I like that a lot; even though I hate to see summer end."

"I do too." Ethan nodded his head. "Think I could get about ten of those big hot weinees and a hunk of cookin' cheese?"

"Sure. I'll fix her right up." Barbara walked down the aisle toward the kitchen.

"Where's Pearl and everybody else?" Ethan asked.

"Pearl's in the office and Ray and Jaime slept in. They'll be over in a little while. Jaime starts school next week so he'll be getting up early soon enough."

"Uh-huh." Ethan nodded. "How is Gene doing?"

"Not good, I'm afraid. He's lost so much weight. So has Ma. She stays with him every day and hardly eats anything."

"You know I'll do anythin' I can to help y'all."

"I know, Ethan. I appreciate that," Barbara patted his hand as she handed him his cheese. She spotted Pearl coming down the aisle and Barney walking in the front door. "I'll let Pearl get those weinees for you," she said.

"Hey, Ethan. What else you need?" Pearl walked behind the meat case.

"Hey, Barney. How are you today?" Barbara was half way up the aisle as Barney rounded the corner to the beer cooler.

"Fine, Miss Barber. How you?"

"Fine, Barn..." Barbara stopped in mid sentence as she spotted Ethan's little wire-haired terrier cocking his leg up on the ice chest that sat outside the door. He jumped in mid air, yelped and took off running.

"Ouch!" Barbara yelled and started laughing.

"What happened?" Pearl and Ethan ran back up front. Ray walked in the door almost doubled over from laughing.

"Did you see Benji?" he gasped.

"Yeah." Barbara was laughing so hard she could hardly talk.

"What happened?" Ethan was looking out the door and spotted Benji on the other side of the road – trotting toward home. The dog stopped at the bridge and looked back toward the store.

"What y'all waughin' 'bout?" Barney sat his pint of wine on the counter.

Ethan, Pearl and Barney were all chuckling as Ray and Barbara were laughing hard. "There's a short in the ice freezer and Benji cocked his leg up on it. It shocked his little..."

"Ray!" Barbara stopped him. Pearl and Barney burst out laughing and Ethan gave a half-hearted chuckle as he watched his little dog standing at the bridge waiting for his master.

"Silwe dog oughta know better," Barney said.

"Why should he know better?" Ethan turned toward Barney. "He's no sillier than you were when you wet on that policeman out town last year."

"I heard about that," Ray said.

"Well, I didn't." Pearl wiped a tear from her cheek and she tried to quit laughing. " I want to hear about it."

"Now that was different. I was drunk and didn't know what I was doin'," Barney said. He had quit laughing.

"Tell us about it, Ethan," Pearl urged.

"I wanna pay for this wittle quart of wine. I need to git me home," Barney dropped a handful of change on the counter. His eyes pleaded for Barbara to hurry.

"Okay, Barney," Barbara said. She counted the correct change and gave the rest back to him.

"Tell us," Pearl said.

"Maybe I ought not to," Ethan said.

"That's wight. Weave it awone." Barney twisted the top of the paper bag around the neck of the bottle.

"Thank you, Barney," Barbara said.

"Tank you too, Miss Barber," Barney said as he walked out the door glancing back at Ethan.

Pearl waited until the door closed behind Barney. "Did he really wet on a policeman?" she asked.

"Yeah. He was sitting out town on the park bench playing his mouth organ," Ethan said.

"Mouth organ?" Barbara asked.

"That's a harmonica." Ray answered her questioning look.

"Oh."

"Anyways, he plays a mean tune when he's been drinking. And he can talk better too. His favorite song is 'Cotton Fields.' He's always going around singing that song; but when he's sober, he gets the words mixed up. The other day he was singing. 'When I was a wittle bitty baby, I'd rock my mommy in the cradle...'" Ethan grinned and walked back over to the door to check on Benji. His little terrier was still sitting across the road, patiently waiting for his master, but afraid to come back near the ice machine.

"Well, I'll be dipped. I never knew he could sing and play," Ray said.

"That's because you usually only see him when he's wantin' some al-ke-hol or snuff." Ethan grinned.

"Yeah, I guess so," Ray said.

"Well, I better be gettin' back. Gladys will be worried about me."

"Wait a minute, Ethan. You haven't told us about Barney wettin' on the policeman yet," Pearl said.

"Oh, yeah. Well, it wasn't just a police-man. It was the police chief."

"This is gettin' better and better." Pearl grinned as Barbara and Ray kept their eyes on Ethan's humble face. He hung his head and looked at his hands. He twirled his thumbs around each other as if he was trying to think of how this story should be told.

"Well sir, it was broad daylight – a sunny afternoon – and Barney was already lit. He was sittin' out town playin' his mouth organ. Ever once in a while he'd slip behind the doctor's office and come back. Ever-body knew he was goin' back thar to take a nip. Maybe somebody reported him or maybe it was just a co-in-ci-dence but pretty soon here come the po-lice chief. He eyed Barney and had a not-too-happy look on his face. I don't think Barney noticed him, 'cause he got up and walked over to the side of the doctor's buildin'. 'Bout that time 'ole Chief Smith realized what Barney was up to. He walked up behind Barney and swung him around – a little bit too fast. 'What do you think you're doing?' he said to Barney. But it was too late. He found out – the hard way. Barney soaked his uniform."

Pearl hooted while the others chuckled. "Poor ole Barney. He's a mess." Pearl wiped her eyes with her apron. "Sweet, though."

"Well, sir. I better git back home. Gladys is waitin' on these here weenies to fix fer our supper. Oh, yeah. I better git a loaf of bread. She has to have her bread to smother that hot taste. Put this on my bill, Barbara, and I'll see y'all tomorrey."

"Thanks, Ethan, for the business and the story." Barbara wrote the total on his charge book.

"You're welcome, but I wouldn't be teasin' Barney about it. You can tell it's a sore spot with him."

"You're right. We'll steer clear of that subject when he comes in. He usually doesn't say more than a sentence or two anyway. I still can't imagine him singing and playing a harmonica," Barbara said.

"Yeah, well, al-ke-hol does change a body, I reckon...Bye."

"Bye, Ethan," Barbara, Ray and Pearl said in unison.

Saturday evening after clothes shopping, they all went up to the hospital to see Pa. He had lost even more weight and looked so sick.

"Don't y'all be worrying about me. I know God's going to heal me and

I'll be going home soon enough. I'm so tired of staying here and I know your mother is."

"Good. You still haven't seen my Stickers, Pawpaw."

"No, Jaime. I bet the little thing's growing, just like you."

"Yeah. I'm going to be in first grade. Mom says I will learn how to read books in first grade. I already know some words…and I got me some new clothes."

"Good. You study real hard and I'll let you read to me when I get home."

"I don't know big words, Pawpaw."

"Okay, little man. You do your best."

"I will."

"Ma, we're going to Godfather's for pizza. Why don't you go with us?" Ray asked.

"That sure does sound good to me. Think you'll be okay, Gene?"

"Sure. This medicine is making me sleepy. You guys go ahead and have fun."

"Want us to bring ye back something?" Pearl asked.

"No, I can't eat right now." Pa closed his eyes.

Ma rubbed her hand across his forehead and motioned for the others to follow her. In the hall, she said. "He doesn't eat hardly anything. What he does manage to eat he can't keep down."

"He looks so weak," Barbara said.

"He is weak. He can hardly sit up. It's a struggle to get cleaned up or go to the bathroom. Unless God intervenes…" Her voice trailed off.

"Pawpaw needs some of Mawmaw's chicken and dumplins. I bet he'd eat that," Jaime said. Ray reached down and took Jaime's hand and walked ahead.

Barbara took the cue. "We'd better get down to the Godfather's before they run out of pizza or places to sit, huh?"

Ma raised her head and smiled a smile that didn't quite reach her eyes. "Yeah, we'd better do that."

"How was your first day in first grade?" Barbara reached out her hands for a hug, but Jaime laid some papers in them instead.

"You have to sign these papers and I have to take them back to school tomorrow. I have a real nice teacher. Her name is Miss French and she has yellow hair. She said we're going to learn to read this year."

Barbara took the papers. "That's right, you will."

"Then I will read you some books, Mom."

"Sounds good to me. We'll..." Barbara's voice trailed as she turned to pick up the ringing telephone. It was Mary Ann.

"Barbara is Ray there or did he work today?" she asked.

"No, he's off. He has to work the weekend. What's wrong?"

"It's Pa. I need to talk to Ray."

"I'll get him," Barbara said as she laid the phone down and headed out the door. "I'll be back in a minute, Aunt Pearl. I have to find Ray. Mary Ann's on the phone."

"I saw him go into the garage a few minutes ago," Aunt Pearl called to her. Barbara was back with Ray in a few seconds. Pearl was holding the phone and she didn't look any too well. Ray reached for the receiver.

"Yeah, Mary Ann. What's up?...Okay...I'll be up there in just a little bit. How's Ma?...Okay...See you then."

"What is it?" Barbara looked into Ray's eyes. They looked darker than usual.

"Pa has contracted a staph infection. They don't expect him to pull out of it. The doctor said to call the family in."

"Oh, no." Barbara whispered.

"Ma wants us all up at the hospital after everybody gets home from work this evening. We'll take turns watching the counter and getting ready and then close early. All of us will go up together." Ray sighed. "I need to finish Mr. Gillespie's car. That'll take me a few minutes and then I'll go home and clean up first."

"Okay." Barbara rubbed her hand along Ray's shirt sleeve.

"I'll fix a bite for us to eat," Pearl said.

Ray walked out the door and slowly up to the garage. Barbara noticed for the first time that his shoulders were slumped. Ray was 6'3 ½", and she had never seen him not walking tall.

"Can I go, Mom?"

Barbara had forgotten Jaime was standing there taking everything in.

"Go where?"

"To the hospital with y'all," he said.

"Of course you can go Jaime." Barbara smiled and hugged him. This time he didn't object.

"Mom, I thought the doctors were going to make Pawpaw better."

Barbara had taken Jaime home to get him and her ready to go while Ray watched the store.

"Jaime." She sat down on the bed and patted the place beside her. He walked over and sat down next to her and then she slipped down on her knees in front of him, laid her hands on his hands, and looked into his questioning eyes. "Jaime, Pawpaw is very sick. He probably won't come home. God is going to send an angel down from Heaven to get him and the angel will take Pawpaw back to Heaven with him."

"Why?" Jaime's eyes were glistening.

"Sometimes when people get old and sick, God heals them by taking them to Heaven to be with him. Then they won't be sick anymore. Heaven is a beautiful place and I know Pawpaw will be very happy there."

"But I don't want him to go."

"None of us want him to go, Jaime; but God decides when our time on earth is up and when we should go to Heaven. Pawpaw won't hurt anymore in Heaven."

"But won't Pawpaw miss us?"

"He'll be so happy, and he will know that one day we will be there with him. He won't be sad in Heaven. He will get to see his mother and father and two brothers in Heaven. We will be the ones that will be sad because we will miss him." Barbara's eyes were now glistening.

"Mom, does God only take old people?"

"No, sometimes he takes young people, children, babies. It is sad, but we have to remember that Heaven is the best place to be. He mostly takes old people though. Now raise your arms and let me put this clean shirt on you. Dad and Aunt Pearl are waiting on us to get ready so we can go to see Pawpaw."

"Before the angel comes and gets him?"

"Yes, before then."

Pa's complexion was turning yellow. Barbara knew that wasn't a good sign. He opened his eyes as they walked in the door.

"Hey, Ole Man," Ray said. "Looks like you're having a really bad time of it."

"Yeah, I don't feel too good."

"How are they treating you?"

"Fine, but I can't eat this food."

"Want us to go out and bring you back something?"

"No, I don't feel like eating, Ray."

"Okay, then." Ray dropped his head and walked over to the corner of the room. Ma walked over and touched Ray's arm. Pa had closed his eyes and she motioned for Ray to follow her. Barbara, Jaime and Pearl followed them into the hall. "The doctor says he's contracted some kind of staph infection. He's only giving him twenty-four to forty-eight hours."

"I know. Mary Ann called. What can we do?" Ray asked.

"I don't guess there's anything to do, except pray...and tell him goodbye. But don't let him think this is the end. He doesn't know what the doctor said. He's still hoping he'll be healed. I don't want to take his hope from him."

"Okay, Ma."

They all went back into the room. Ray walked over and laid his hand on his father's arm and stood there looking down at him, saying nothing. Pa opened his eyes and tried to smile, then closed his eyes again. Ray caught Barbara's eyes and nodded for her to bring Jaime over.

Barbara bent down to Jaime. "Jaime, go tell Pawpaw bye. We have to leave now."

Jaime grabbed Barbara's hand and shook his head no.

"Jaime, this may be the last time you get to see Pawpaw," she whispered.

He looked down at the floor and shook his head and held her hand tight. Barbara gave him a gentle nudge, but Jaime stood his ground. He looked up at her and said, "No!"

"Jaime?" Barbara gave him a pleading look and then noticed the fear in his eyes.

"Don't make him," Aunt Pearl said.

"No, I won't. Jaime, I'm going over to kiss Pawpaw goodbye."

Jaime gave her a frightened look. Barbara pried his hand from her fingers and walked over to the bed. Pa opened his eyes and Barbara kissed him on his forehead. "Goodbye, Pa," she said with her voice faltering and tears trailing down her cheek.

"See you later, Barbara," he murmured as he stared at her with a questioning look on his face. She knew he was wondering about all the strange behavior.

"I have to go," she smiled and patted his hand and left the room in a hurry. She rounded the corner and hid her face on the first windowsill she found. She was sobbing when she felt arms around her. She looked up into the face of a nurse.

"What's wrong, honey?" the nurse asked.

"My father-in-law is dying."

The nurse patted her hand and told her she was sorry. She stood there with her a few minutes until Pearl and Jaime came down the hall. Barbara had composed herself. Pearl wiped her eyes and asked her to walk down to the cafeteria with them.

Barbara turned and thanked the nurse and took hold of Jaime's other hand.

"Ray, Mary Ann, John, Peggy and Ellen are all with him. Ma asked if they could have some time alone."

"That's a good idea." Barbara nodded her head and gazed ahead.

About an hour later Ray found them and they all quietly got into the car and drove home.

After they had all gone to bed, Barbara asked Ray about their time alone. "Pa doesn't know he's so close to death, does he?"

"I think he's figuring it out. It was so heartbreakingly hard to tell him goodbye. Yet it was a privilege not everybody has. We each took turns sitting by the bed and reminiscing about our growing up days. We laughed and cried. It was a chance to thank him for all he has meant to each one of us."

"He was so sleepy. Was he able to talk to you all?"

"Yeah. His medicine must have been wearing off. He became more alert but he looked like he was hurting toward the end, so Ma asked the nurse to give him something. We left soon afterwards." Ray paused a minute. "He looked so tired – so drained."

"I know. It bothered me that Jaime wouldn't go over and hug him goodbye."

"I know. I thought that was a strange way for him to act, but he's so little and I guess he was scared."

Barbara stared up into the darkness. "I know. You could see in his face that he was afraid. I'll talk to him about it tomorrow."

"Good idea." Ray found her hand and squeezed it. "We'd better get some sleep. The next few days are going to be long ones."

Chapter XXI

The Answer

Barbara jumped as the telephone rang. The paperwork dropped to the floor as she stood up to answer it. Relief spread across her face. "Let me check and see." She rested the receiver against her leg. "Aunt Pearl, do we have crushed pineapple and how much is it?"

Pearl dropped the feather duster to her side and blew a sigh from her mouth. She walked around to the other side of the shelves. "Yes, we do. It's fifty-nine cents."

Barbara relayed the information and hung up the phone. She picked up the scattered papers and daybook from the floor.

Pearl had walked to the counter and stood staring at Barbara. "It's nerve wracking."

"Sure is. I wish we could just call in sick and stay at the hospital with Ma."

"Believe me, it is better to stay busy," Aunt Pearl said. "Waiting with nothing to do is ten times worse."

"I guess. It's still hard."

"Did Ray talk to you last night?"

"No, we were exhausted. We both thought it strange the way Jaime was afraid to hug his grandpa."

"No, that's not really unusual." Pearl reached across the counter and patted Barb's hand. "He's so young and doesn't really understand. I know I'm prejudice, but it seems to me he's more sensitive than most younguns his age."

"Yeah, I think so. Wonder how he is doing in school today. Do you think last night will affect his school work?"

"Probably not. Kids bounce back real easy." Pearl turned toward the kitchen. "I'd better get some lunch packed for Ray. I guess he'll go to work. Don't you?"

"He didn't say, but since he didn't get up when we did, he must be planning on going to work this afternoon." Barbara picked up her pencil and hit the total button on the adding machine. "The ledger shows where we closed early. Do you reckon any customers got mad when they saw the sign?"

"Not if they realized why we closed. We can explain it one by one if they ask." Pearl stopped and stood at the door. "Here comes Ray now."

Ray pulled the glass door open and touched the chimes to stop their ringing. "What's for breakfast?"

"Didn't know you'd be up so soon. Jaime ate cereal and Barb and I ate toast with apple butter. How about I whip you up some eggs and bacon?" Pearl started toward the kitchen again.

"No, don't bother. I'll just grab a honey bun and a pint of milk."

"Why are you up so early?" Barbara asked.

"Couldn't sleep. Have you heard anything from the hospital?" He pulled the top open on the pint of milk.

"No. It's been right quiet this morning."

"Yeah. With all the kids in school and it being a weekday morning, it would be slow. I don't know if I should call in to work or not."

"Ray, think about going to work," Aunt Pearl said. "There's nothing you can do sitting at the hospital. You need to earn money while you can."

Ray shook his head. "Yeah, Ma told me last night that we shouldn't be closing early. She said the customers depend on us and we'll lose business if we close very much. People get used to stopping by the same store, she said, and we don't want them getting used to another store."

"Yeah, I remember her telling me that during those two months she was training me," Barbara said. "It does make sense."

"Not only that," Ray said, "but we need to remember it is our store payments that they are living off of right now. If something happens we can't make the payment, they wouldn't have any income that month."

"Don't worry, Ray. I've already thought of that," Barbara said. "We will let the restocking go before we miss one of our payments."

"You could, but think about it Barbara. If you don't keep what people want, they will go elsewhere. Not to mention that if we don't have it to sell, we lose that profit."

"Yeah, I know. I don't know how we would make it if you weren't bringing in extra income from the railroad."

"Barbara, did you tell Ray what Brenda and Dianne told you?" Pearl asked.

"What's that?" Ray pulled the paper back from the honey bun.

"They said that when and if something does happen to Pa, that they will come in and work for us for a few days, so that we won't have to close the store."

"I guess that would work. They were good workers for Ma and Pa. Only I think we should close for the funeral – just out of respect," Ray said.

"Of course," Barbara said, "and the night of the wake."

"Yeah. If I get a chance, I'll talk to Ma about it. I don't want her feelings hurt, but I don't want her to worry about money problems either." Ray downed the last of the milk and threw the carton in the trash can that sat at the end of the counter. "I'm going to get ready and go up to the hospital. I'll decide after that if I should call into work."

"How about dropping off a bank deposit on the way," Barbara said.

"Sure. Get it ready." Ray walked back out the door and toward the house.

"He's tired," Pearl said.

"And worried," Barbara added.

Barbara watched as Jaime jumped the last step off of the school bus and ran toward the door. She grinned and opened the door for him.

"Hi, Mom. Look what I did today in school." He held up a piece of paper with his complete name written on it.

"That's good, Jaime. Why you'll be writing everything before you know it."

"Let me show Aunt Pearl." He took the paper from Barbara's hand and headed toward the kitchen. Barbara could hear his chatter and Aunt Pearl's praises.

The door of the store pushed open and a stranger walked in. She had grey hair piled on top of her head, and wore a long skirt and long sleeves. Her walk to the counter was more of a march than a stroll. "Think I could lay these on the counter for you to give to your customers?"

Barbara hesitated for a moment and then said, "Sure, I guess so."

"Good. The last store I was at wouldn't let me." The lady slapped some tracts onto the counter with a thud. "I'll not be shopping there anymore. I'll do my business here from now on. Where are the grocery carts?"

"About half way down that front aisle." Barbara smiled as she pointed to the carts.

"Thank you," she said and marched back to the two carts that sat in front of the windows.

Barbara turned her attention away from her as she heard the chimes ring again.

"Hi, Barbara."

"Hi, Charlie Bob. How are you doing today?"

"Fine. It's a bit nippy but the sun's shinin'. I can feel fall comin' on." He gave a little laugh.

"I've noticed it too," Barbara said.

"Yeah, but it might rain tomorrow. You just gotta be enjoyin' today, 'cause you never know. It just might rain tomorrow."

"That's right, Charlie Bob."

He laughed. "I'll be right back." He headed toward the wine cooler.

Barbara looked for the lady. She was picking up cans and looking at the prices and then sitting them back on the shelves. Charlie Bob walked back to the counter and sat a quart of wine down with a handful of change. Barbara started counting it.

"I got me a fifth today. I think I've got enough."

Barbara counted. "I'm afraid you don't, Charlie. You'll have to get a pint today."

"How much do I like?" Charlie dropped his gaze to the fifth that sat on the counter.

"Fifty-three cents," Barbara said.

"Can't I charge it 'til check day?"

"No, Charlie Bob. It's against the law in Virginia to be charging any kind of alcohol. You'll have to put it back and get the little one."

"Okay." He laughed and picked up the fifth and headed back toward the cooler.

Barbara let out a soft sigh. She had told Ray she was surely glad that they weren't allowed by law to charge beer and wine. She knew that it would lead to big charge accounts that the customers couldn't pay. This way they considered the law and not her to be the bad guy. The new lady walked back to the counter pushing the cart in front of her. She had a pint of orange juice and a tub of butter in it. Barbara stared at the cart in amazement and then looked up at the lady. The woman was glaring at Charlie Bob, who had just sat his pint of wine on the counter. He noticed her and looked down at the floor.

"Will that be all?" Barbara said trying to hide the curtness in her voice that would reveal the irritation she felt toward the woman.

"Yes, that will be quite all I need." The woman sniffed as she turned her attention toward Barbara with a look of disdain written on her face.

"That will be $1.64." Barbara didn't try to hide the irritation she felt this time as she held out her hand for the money. The woman gave Barbara two dollars and turned her attention again toward Charlie Bob and his pint of wine. Charlie, head down, shifted his feet, drawing attention to his too-worn, dirty shoes.

"Thirty-six cents is your change." Barbara held her hand out and the woman stuck the coins in her purse as she looked at the wine again. She slung her purse over her shoulder, picked up the small package and turned to walk out the door, but not before she gave them an emphatic "Humph."

Barbara turned her attention to Charlie Bob and gave him back two pennies of the change he had laid on the counter. She smiled at him as she put the wine in a paper bag. "Thank you, Charlie Bob. You come back."

He looked at his feet again and let out a small laugh. "I will," he murmured. He stopped at the door and looked outside as if he was making sure the woman was nowhere in sight.

Jaime and Aunt Pearl had walked back up to the counter about midway through the two transactions. "Was she a mean lady, Mom?"

"Not really. Just a little pious, I think."

"What's pious?"

"That's when you think you're better than somebody else." Aunt Pearl said.

"Aunt Pearl." Barbara shook her head. "That's not what it means. It really means showing holiness. I guess I was using it to mean 'holier than thou.' – which wasn't nice."

Jaime looked up at Barbara as he furrowed his brow. "I still don't understand. She just looked mean to me the way she looked at you and Charlie Bob."

"I know, Jaime, but I don't think she meant to. She just doesn't think Charlie Bob should be drinking that wine."

"You said that too, Mom, but you don't look mean at him."

"I know, Jaime. It's hard to explain. You just don't worry about it." She saw Shirley's car pull up in front of the door. "Look, there's Billy. You two go play for awhile."

Billy pulled the door open. "Mom said she's going to the hospital to see Pawpaw." Sarah and Seth climbed out of the back seat.

"Mom said she would pick us up after awhile," Seth looked from Barbara to Aunt Pearl. "What are we having for supper?'

"Hamburgers," Pearl answered.

"Mom said we could each get one thing on the bill." Sarah reached into the candy case.

"I want ice cream," Billy said.

"Me too?" Jaime looked at Barbara with hope written on his face.

"Go ahead," Barbara said. "Now you can either work or you can go outside and play."

"Outside," said Jaime as he opened the door.

"Outside," the others echoed as they followed.

Aunt Pearl rolled her eyes. Barbara laughed. "Doesn't take long to clear them out does it? Give 'em a piece of candy and a choice and they're gone."

"That's okay now, but you know soon it will be cold and sometimes raining. You won't be able to send them outside. We already know how that can be."

Barbara sighed and now rolled her eyes. "Don't remind me."

"That lady was downright rude, don't ye think?" Aunt Pearl picked up one of the tracts.

"I do. I should have looked at what she had before I told her she could leave them on the counter."

"You didn't look at them first?"

"No. She took me by surprise with that attitude. I just noticed the cross on the front and thought there couldn't be any harm to lay Christian literature on the counter for our customers."

"Well, she didn't seem very Christian to me," Aunt Pearl said.

"I was thinking the same thing. I guess she thought she was, but to tell you the truth, Aunt Pearl, I just couldn't see the light of Jesus shining through her. I doubt she will win anyone over to Christ like that."

"I doubt it too." Pearl laid the pamphlet back down on the counter. "Better get to makin'some hamburgers. Those younguns will be back and hungry before you know it." She turned to walk back to the kitchen.

"Aunt Pearl…" Barbara chewed on her bottom lip.

"What?" Pearl walked back to the counter and gazed at Barbara.

"I've been having a hard time lately wondering if as Christians we should be selling beer and wine. I asked Ray if maybe we should stop selling them."

"What did he say?"

"He said that almost every store sells beer and wine. That's just the way it is, he says. He also said that we don't make them buy it and as long as we obey the law then we're doing what we're supposed to."

"Did that not satisfy you?"

"No. He also said we couldn't afford not to sell it. That bothered me - thinking that we may be making a profit off of someone else's misery. He said if they don't buy it here, they will just go to the next store to get it."

"He's got a point," Aunt Pearl said.

"Yeah, I know he's right there. Anyway, I've been praying about it and asking God to show me what's right or wrong."

"And…have you gotten an answer?"

"Maybe. I was just wondering if that woman was God's way of showing me that it is not up to us to judge or decide for other people. I don't believe a person could win anybody to Jesus with an attitude like that."

"You know what, Barbara. I think she just may have been your answer. I have to agree with Ray. What about the cigarettes? People are killing themselves slowly with that. And what about obese people who come in here and spend food stamps on candy, pop and chips instead of apples, potatoes or bread? Are you going to stop stocking those items or tell them what they can and cannot buy?"

Barbara grinned. "You sound just like Ray."

"Well, he is a pretty smart fella, you know. Takes it after his aunt." Pearl reached across the counter and tapped Barbara's hand. "Everything will work out. You can't be taking on the whole world you know."

Barbara hung her head and then raised it back up. She smiled at Pearl. "Guess not. Right now we have enough worries in our own family."

"Right," Pearl said. She turned and headed to the kitchen. As she swiped a pack of buns from the bread shelf, she called back over her shoulder. "One hamburger or two?"

"Two," Barbara said as she looked across the road at the kids playing in their grandma and grandpa's yard. *Poor Pa.*

Saturday morning dawned cold and rainy, yet there was still no phone call. They all agreed Pa did look better on Friday night. Could the doctors be wrong?

"I called Shirley," Ray said. "She has agreed to keep the store tonight while the rest of us go up to see Pa. They are getting ready to go now to see him. She said she'd be back about five o'clock."

"Good. If you'll come in about four, I'll go over to the house and get Jaime and me ready. It will be a good time to talk to him about the other night when he was so scared."

"You haven't talked to him yet?" Ray asked.

"No, something always gets in the way: business, tiredness, other kids around, falling asleep before his head hits the pillow…"

"Really?" Ray laughed. "I wonder where he gets that from?"

Barbara stuck her tongue out at him, then grinned.

Barbara reached her hand in to test the bath water. "Jaime, we're going up to see Pawpaw and then eat at the Tastee Freeze. Does that sound good to you?"

"Yes, I want a hot dog, Mom."

"Okay, but are you going to be all right when we go in to see Pawpaw? Do you want to wait outside with Aunt Pearl while I go in?"

"No, I want to see Pawpaw."

Barbara chewed the inside of her cheek as she turned the faucet off. "Jaime?'

"What?"

"Why did you not want to go and hug Pawpaw the other night?"

"'Cause."

"'Cause, why?"

"'Cause I was afraid to."

"I know, honey. I could tell you were afraid. I just don't understand why you were afraid."

"I was afraid if I was hugging Pawpaw when the angel came to take him that the angel would take me too."

"What do you mean? Why did you think an angel was going to take you?"

"You said that an angel was going to come and take Pawpaw to Heaven. I was afraid he'd come while I was hugging him. I don't want to go to Heaven now."

Barbara broke into a big smile. "Jaime, honey, you don't have to worry about an angel taking you. Only Pawpaw is sick and needs to go to Heaven."

"Yeah, but if Pawpaw is holding onto me…"

"Jaime. The angel knows to take only Pawpaw."

"Well...I still was afraid."

"That's okay. I understand; but you really don't have to be afraid anymore."

"Okay." Jaime nodded his head as he reached for the soap.

Barbara squirted shampoo on his hair. "Scrub your head and I'll rinse it for you."

Later as they walked down the hall to Pa's hospital room, they met Ma. "Good news," she said. "He has survived the staph infection."

"Praise God." Pearl broke into a big grin, and they all walked a little lighter to Pa's room.

Chapter XXII

Saying Good-Bye

Even though Pa had escaped death by the staph infection, he steadily grew worse. The doctors had decided all they could do was give him pain medicine and keep him as comfortable as possible. He told Ma to sell their motor home to help pay for the hospital bills. "My days of camping are over," he told her.

September slipped into October and the vigil continued day after day. He seemed a little better one day and worse the next. He started hallucinating and living in the past. "Ma, they changed me to night shift at the mines…" "Don't pack me such a big lunch…" "We need to get these coolers moved from Anawalt to Pocy." Ma tried to humor him by talking about the past and nodding in agreement when he saw things that she didn't. The five months the doctors had given him were just about passed. Some nights Ma came home and one of the children stayed to watch over Pa. Uncle Hubert and Aunt Gladys had come back down from Indiana and were helping out also. Mostly, though, Ma stayed night after long, lonely night watching him suffer. As the cancer spread through his liver, his color changed to yellow, his weight dropped more and more – only his faith in God grew stronger. He talked occasionally about being cured, but more and more he talked about going to Heaven.

The customers in the store often asked about Pa, but even they were getting used to him being in the hospital and the questions about his health grew further apart. Ray continued to work every night he was scheduled. He had yet to take a turn sitting with Pa since John and Mary Ann's husband were more readily available for the night. He was scheduled to be off on Sunday and that was to be his first night that he would sit with Pa. Saturday night he went to work.

About 4:00 a.m., the phone rang next to Barbara's bed. It was Mary Ann. Barbara knew before Mary Ann could get the words out, "Dad's gone."

"I'll call Ray right now," Barbara said. "Is Ma okay?"

"She's holding up. We'll be bringing her home in a few minutes." Barbara hung up the phone and called Ray. She waited while his supervisor went out into the railway yard to get him. *This doesn't feel real. Even though we expected it, it always seemed it wouldn't be today.*

"Hello." Ray's voice interrupted her thoughts.

"Ray, your Dad…he's gone."

"I'll leave right away. How is Ma?"

"Mary Ann said okay. They're bringing her home in a few minutes. She'll probably be here before you, since it takes an hour for you to drive home."

Barbara looked up to see Pearl standing in the bedroom doorway as she hung the phone back in its cradle.

"I heard the phone ring."

"It's over," Barbara said.

Pearl nodded her head. "I figured that was what it was about."

"What should we do?" Barbara asked.

"Nothing right now. Lie back down. The next few days will be long and hard. We'll need all of our energy." Pearl let out a deep sigh as she turned to go back to her room.

Barbara shook her head in agreement as she lay back onto the pillow. She stared at the ceiling. The dusk to dawn light outside the window threw shadows on the ceiling. She closed her eyes and blew out her breath. As she opened her eyes, the shadows seemed to dance as the wind blew the leaves on the tree outside their window.

It was still dark outside when Ray got home. "I went over to check on Ma. She is lying down and Aunt Gladys and Uncle Hubert were getting ready to lie down too. We'll go over about 9:00 or 10:00."

"Okay," said Barbara. "Do you want me to fix a bite to eat?"

"No, let's lie back down. I feel so tired. I still haven't gotten used to this third shift."

As they lay there, both of them staring at the ceiling, Ray asked, "Do you know what today is?"

"Sunday?"

"It's John's birthday," Ray said.

"Oh…poor John." Barbara sighed for the hundredth time.

The next two days were filled with arrangements being made. Friends and neighbors brought in plenty of food. Long distance families were notified and plans were made as to where everyone would stay. Ma was holding up remarkably well. As promised, Brenda and Dianne opened the store Sunday afternoon and most of the day Monday. It would be closed early Monday for the wake, closed all day on Tuesday for the funeral, and then reopen on Wednesday morning.

Barbara combed Jaime's hair as they were getting ready to go to the wake. He squirmed and looked up at his mom with a frown.

"Mom, if angels came and took Pawpaw, how can we go see him at the funeral home?"

"We're going to see his old body that wore out. The angels took Pawpaw's soul – the part of him that doesn't die, and now He has given him a new body in Heaven – a better body."

"Does he look the same in Heaven?"

"I think so…only not sickly anymore."

"Can he see us down here?"

"I'm not sure. Maybe – but maybe not. He would be sad if he looked down and saw us crying and hurting for him."

"Yeah, but I bet he misses us. He doesn't know anybody in Heaven."

"Oh, but he does know lots of people in Heaven. His Mom and Dad and some of his brothers and a sister and some friends are already there. God won't let him miss us. He'll be so busy having a good time; it will just seem like a little while until we go up to see him."

"But I don't want to go to Heaven. I want to stay here." Jaime looked at Barbara with imploring water-filled eyes.

Barbara drew him closer and hugged him. "Jaime, it will be a long, long time until you go to Heaven. People usually grow real old and sick before they die. You have a long time before you leave here."

Jaime looked hard at his mom, hesitated and then said, "Mom, you're about ready to get old."

Barbara laughed in spite of herself. "No, Jaime. It might seem like it to you, but I'm going to be here a long, long time. I don't want to go to Heaven anytime soon either. I have my little boy to take care of."

"Me." Jaime let out a big breath and grinned.

"Yeah, you big boy." Barbara tickled his belly and he raced off.

"Tell your dad we're ready. Okay?"

"Okay." Jaime let the door slam shut and raced across the yard to Mawmaw's.

Barbara gasped as she walked into the funeral home. Flowers were lined up and down the walls and were in the other room. "So many flowers!" She gripped Jaime's hand.

"Smell," Jaime said.

"Yeah, smells like a funeral home," Ray's mouth curved a little.

"Why do they have all these flowers?" Jaime asked.

"Friends that loved and cared for Pawpaw and Mawmaw sent all these flowers," Pearl said.

"Wow." Jaime whispered. "Pawpaw sure had a lot of friends!"

"He sure did," Ray answered. "Seemed like he knew everybody and everybody knew him."

He left their side to hold onto Ma as she entered the door. John was on her other side. Silently the rest of the family followed into the chapel room where Pa was lying.

"More flowers!" Jaime said. Flowers surrounded the casket and lined the walls in this room too.

"Shhh!" Barbara and Aunt Pearl cautioned together.

The family watched as Ma touched Pa's face and said something. She seemed only one heartbeat away from breaking down and crying. One by one and two by two they all gathered around the casket. Some were staring with sad faces and some were quietly crying.

"Mom, I want to see Pawpaw," Jaime whispered.

"Okay. I'll get your dad to lift you up in a minute."

Ma turned around and went back to the first pew and sat down. Barbara motioned for Ray to help Jaime. As Ray lifted him up, Jaime didn't say anything. He just stared.

"You okay, son?"

Jaime shook his head yes and Ray sat him back down. He took Barbara's hand and they walked back to a pew and sat down.

For the next three hours friends and families came in to pay their respects. The somber air changed to a more relaxed atmosphere. After awhile Barbara let Jaime go with Billy and Seth to the outer rooms cautioning them to be good and be quiet. Many of the people shared their memories about Pa with them. There was laughter sometimes as Pa's friends told of some of the crazy antics he had pulled through the years.

Finally it was time to go. Almost everybody had left and Ma wanted to go back to the casket again before she left. Barbara watched as tears flowed down Ma's cheeks and she rubbed Pa's still hands. She knew Ma was hurting. She realized her own pain could not be nearly as bad. In reality, Barbara hoped she would never have to walk in Ma's shoes. She drew in a deep breath.

As they drove home and rounded the curve at the cemetery, Barbara's eyes automatically fell on the store. She started crying. Ray parked the car in the driveway and took Barbara's hand to help her out.

Barbara didn't seem to notice Jaime and Aunt Pearl as they walked past her to the front door. She stood in the driveway looking across the road at the store with her head on Ray's shoulder. "Pa can't be gone." Her voice broke. "That's really Pa's store."

"It's our store now, Barbara." Ray rubbed her arm.

"It was Ma and Pa's store for so long," she murmured. "It doesn't feel like our store."

Ray buried his head in her hair and whispered, "Someday it will."

Barbara woke up the next morning realizing it was their wedding anniversary. She rolled over to catch Ray smiling at her.

"Happy Anniversary, Charlie," he quipped.

Barbara laughed. "You haven't called me Charlie in a lot of years."

"Yeah, well, you're still my Charlie. I'm sorry our anniversary is going to be such a sad one."

Barbara half smiled and ran her fingers along Ray's jaw line. "Me too, but it can't be helped. I know John will never have another birthday without thinking of his Dad's death, and I imagine it will be the same for our anniversaries."

"True." Ray laid the covers back and climbed out of bed. "I guess we'd better get everybody up and get ready for the funeral."

The funeral service was held. The graveside was the most emotional with the daughters breaking down, but somehow everyone got through it all. Ma seemed to be in a trance. Afterwards everyone traveled back to the home place. To Ma and everyone else's surprise, a neighbor from half-mile down the road had let herself in and was baking pans and pans of hot rolls. She had laid out all the food everyone had brought in and the hot rolls were the crowning touch to a good meal. The mood grew lighter as everyone filled their plates. Afterward, family members gathered in the yard and took pictures – sisters and brothers with one missing...sons and daughters and mother without the father... grandchildren without their granddad.

Finally after the long day, Barbara and Ray gathered Jaime, Pearl and their houseguests and headed home. As they walked across the yard, their eyes fell upon the empty parking lot with a 'Closed' sign in the window. "You're right," Ray whispered to Barbara, "it is Pa's store…doesn't seem like it should be ours."

Barbara shook her head. "No, but someday it will."

Chapter XXIII

Going On

The day after the funeral Barbara and Pearl opened the store. Sadness hung in the air, but waiting on customers and doing their routine work made things seem to be getting back to normal. They were dusting and fronting the shelves on the aisle nearest the door.

"I offered to stay with Betty, but she said she didn't want anybody. Said that she was going to have to make it on her own and she might as well get used to it right now. 'The sooner the better,' she said." Aunt Pearl was poised with her hand on her hip. Body language and tone told Barbara she felt insulted – hurt. After all, it was the unofficial rule that Pearl take care of any of them that needed care.

Barbara hesitated then said, "Well, Aunt Pearl, I'm glad to have you stay with us."

"Likewise." Aunt Pearl sighed and reached for the broom that sat in the corner. "The funeral went real nice, wouldn't you say?"

"Yes, I would. Ma is a strong person. I'm sure she is hurting much more than any of us know." Barbara suddenly remembered Aunt Pearl was also a widow. "Well, not all of us. You've been through it, right?"

"Right," Pearl said. "It will take her a while to get adjusted, but she'll never get over it. Losing the person you love the most in this world changes a body. You're never the same again. It will always hurt, but she will get used to it. Sort of like a wound that heals, but leaves a big scar. The reminder and some pain are always there."

"I never thought of it that way," Barbara slowly nodded her head. "Ma is too young to be a widow. She's only 57."

"Yeah, you're right. I was even younger than her. I had to raise my kids alone. At least she doesn't have that to worry about. But in a way, that was

156

a blessing to me. I had to keep going because of my kids. They gave me a reason to get up in the morning."

The chimes rang and Barbara looked up the aisle. Aunt Annie was walking into the store. "We're on our way home," she said. "Tim is filling up the car and I want to get me some hominy to take back. How much of it do you have?"

Barbara walked up the aisle from the kitchen and stopped to count the cans. "There are sixteen here. Do you want them all?"

"Of course…can't get any of this up North. I always buy all you have when I come in. Don't you remember last summer after Gene's birthday party?"

"I sure do." Barbara grinned. "I ordered another case right away and this is what we have left."

"Well, order another. We won't be back until Memorial Day…" Aunt Annie hesitated, and with a big sigh continued, "unless something happens. But order now 'cause I will be buying you out again."

"That's all right with me," Barbara said. "I'll always try to have you a bunch of cans ready."

"Well, you just better," Aunt Annie towered over Barbara with her hands on her hips. Barbara swallowed and walked past her with an armful of the canned hominy.

"When are Gladys and Hubert going home?" Pearl asked, and then leaned over toward Aunt Annie and whispered, "You scare that girl half to death."

"Ah, I don't bite," Annie said aloud. "As for Gladys and Hubert they said they could stay over another week. They're going to help Betty get some of the paper work straightened out and clean up from the company."

"Well, now, I offered, but she turned me down." Pearl shook her head.

"Seems to me you've got your hands full taking care of Ray and Barbara," Annie said.

"Well, just the same…" Pearl's voice trailed off.

"Just the same, what?" Annie said.

"I'm here iffen she needs me," Pearl said.

"Well, I reckon you oughta know Betty is an independent woman. She's not going to be asking for help."

"We'll all be here to help," Barbara interrupted as she filled her arms with cans of hominy. "Get those last two cans, please Pearl. I can't hold anymore."

"Good grief. I can get my own hominy," Annie said.

"Then why didn't ya?" Pearl asked.

Annie shot her a glare and walked up to the counter. "I need to find out how much gas Tim got. We need to be getting on the road."

"Is Ray still asleep?" Tim had walked in the door. "I'd like to tell him goodbye and thank him for the hospitality."

"I'll call him. It's about time he was getting up," Barbara said. She dialed the house number. "He's supposed to work tonight."

"Who are you calling?" Ray said as he walked in the door.

"You."

"Well, hang up, 'cause I'm not home."

"You're not?" Barbara said. "Could've fooled me."

Tim reached across the counter and gave Barbara a quick hug. "Thanks for the bed and board."

"You're always welcome, anytime," Barbara said warmly.

Ray and Pearl walked Annie and Tim to the car as Barbara stayed to wait on the next customer. "Bye," she called as they walked out the door. She turned toward the aisle that held the bread. "Hi, Ethan. How are you doing?"

"Doin' good…and how are y'all doin'…how's Betty doin'?"

"She's doing pretty well," Barbara said.

"Well, ye know if ye need anything, just let me know." Ethan laid a loaf of bread and a pack of sandwich cheese on the counter. "Will Ray be going back to work soon?"

"Yeah, he's going back tonight."

Ray and Pearl walked back into the store. "Aunt Annie and Tim are on their way back home," Ray said. "How's thangs?" He looked at Ethan.

"Jest fine. I told Barbara anything y'all need to let me know."

"Thanks, Ethan, we appreciate that." Ray touched Barbara's shoulder. "I'm going over to check on Ma. If you need me, holler."

"Will do," Barbara said as she added the bread and cheese to Ethan's bill.

About thirty minutes later, Ray walked back into the store. "Mornin', Glory." He grinned at Barbara.

"Mornin' yerself." Barbara laughed in spite of herself. "What's got you so all fired into a good mood."

"Well, sir, I was wondering how you would like to take Jaime out of school for a week and go to Florida?"

"Florida? For a week. How could we manage that?"

"I've been over to Ma's. Uncle Hubert – well, really Aunt Gladys – came up with the idea. Said they had been talking and decided we needed a vacation."

"That would be nice, but there are too many obstacles. Jaime has school, the trip would be expensive, you are working on the railroad and who in the world would keep the store? Not to mention the fact that Pa just died."

Ray picked Barbara up and whirled her around. "That's just about the same argument I had, but they crossed off every reason that I said we shouldn't go."

"Yeah, well start listing and crossing off." Barbara laughed as Ray sat her down.

"Number one: Jaime's only a first grader and doing well. The trip would be educational for him, he can take his school work with him and he would love it."

"Okay," Barbara said. "That's an easy one. How about number two... What about your job?"

"I've been working almost a year now. I'll talk to my boss tonight. I bet I could schedule a vacation soon. He was real nice about the funeral...told me to take as long as I needed – that they had my job covered."

"Yeah, well who would cover my job?"

"You're not indispensable, Mrs. Kidd." Ray grinned and caught himself as he noticed the look on Barbara's face. "Well, maybe you're indispensable to me and Jaime, but the store could hold out for a week without us. Aunt Gladys had already called Shirley and asked her if she would keep the store if we decided to go. Shirley said she would."

Barbara grabbed her stomach. "Oh Ray, it would be so nice. Do you think we could afford it?"

"We've worked that out too. Ma said she would give us the key to her trailer and we can stay there. It's only forty-five minutes from Disney World and a whole bunch of other attractions. We're crossing them off, one by one." Ray raised five fingers and lowered them as he watched Barbara's eyes light up a little more.

Not noticing that Aunt Pearl had walked up behind her, Barbara said, "What about Aunt Pearl. We couldn't just leave her here."

"Oh yes you can." Barbara jumped as Aunt Pearl spoke. "I'm staying here and helping Shirley keep the store and keep an eye on Betty. You kids could use some family time together."

"Well, it sure sounds good." Barbara's tone was hopeful, and then she searched Ray's face. "What about Ma? Doesn't it seem disrespectful to take a vacation so soon?"

"Uncle Hubert said now is the time to go and so did Ma. Ma said she would be fine and Aunt Gladys said she and Uncle Hubert will stay until we get back to help with things. That makes it the perfect time to go. I'll take you out every night to eat to make up for not taking you anywhere on our anniversary. Jaime can chaperone."

Barbara laughed. "Then let's do it. Oh, Ray, this is so exciting. Remember when we took Jaime when he was only two years old. He can't even remember it. He's old enough now to remember. Do you think your boss will let you off for a week? What clothes should I pack? I don't know if we have enough..."

"Whoa," Ray interrupted her. "Slow down. I can't even understand half of what you're saying."

"Me either." Aunt Pearl patted Barbara's shoulder. "Everything will come together. You'll see."

"Jaime will be so excited. I can't wait until he gets home," Barbara said.

"Hold on a minute. Don't say anything until I check with my boss tonight. I don't know for sure if he will let me off – pretty sure, but not certain. Better not get his hopes up and then have to disappoint him... or you either."

"Too late. I'm already on a roller coaster ride...looking down on Mickey from the sky."

"Silly girl." Ray laughed as he started around the counter. "Ouch!"

"What?" Barbara watched him lift his foot.

"God Bless America and my poor toe."

It was Barbara's turn to laugh. "Clumsy boy," she said.

"Hey, watcha you mouth."

"Ditto."

Aunt Pearl shook her head. "You two are too much. I'm going over to check on Betty and the others."

"Okay, Aunt Pearl," Ray said as he hugged Barbara. "You feel better now, don't you?"

"Yes." Barbara looked up into Ray's eyes. "I guess I forgot for a minute your dad was gone."

"I know...me too. Maybe that's the way it's supposed to be. After all, we won't be able to run this store wrapped in sadness every day. Pa wouldn't have wanted that. He was so full of life." Ray sighed.

"Fun-loving...we can say that for him. Sometimes he was temperamental, but usually he was happy."

"One thing we can say for him and Ma," Ray said, "was that they never interfered with our business once they sold us this store."

"That's for certain sure. Ray, did I tell you the advice he gave me before we actually took over the store?"

"I don't remember. What was it?"

"He was sitting right there on that stool and I was standing next to him. He said, 'Always remember this: Treat the customer that buys only a can of pop just as nice as you treat the customer that comes to the counter with a buggy full of groceries, because at the end of the day, those small sales will add up to more than the buggy full of groceries.'"

"That was mighty good advice, I'd say. He liked his customers and I think they all liked him...so many of them became his friends."

"I'm already feeling friends with some of them," Barbara said.

"Yeah, well, they like you too. I've gotten a lot of good compliments on you."

"Oh, really...tell me."

"Tell you what?"

"Tell me who said what," Barbara pleaded.

"Nah, Can't do that. Your head might swell up like a dead possum... make you rotten."

"Yuk, Ray, do you have to be so graphic?"

"No, I don't have to be."

Barbara put her hand on her hips and rolled her eyes.

"Now don't be standing there hugging your hips, woman, there's work to be done!"

"I oughta kick you!"

"That's right, but ya never have and ya never better," Ray grinned at her twinkling green eyes.

"You're right." Barbara hugged him this time as she remembered the time during their third year of marriage that she had gotten so mad at Ray that she had started slinging her fists at him. He held her back with his long arms and looked right into her flaming eyes and said, 'Listen, Barbara, I have never hit you and I never will. I expect the same respect from you.' That one statement was all it took to drain her anger and make her realize what a good man she had married. They had now been married fourteen years and he had kept his promise, and she never felt obliged to vent her anger that way again.

"Happy belated anniversary," Ray whispered in her ear. "I'm sorry it couldn't have been a happier one."

"I know. Happy anniversary to you too, darling."

"There are better ones ahead." Ray brightened his voice.

The chimes rang above the door. Barbara looked at Ray. "Yes, but we'll never have another one that won't be tinged with some sadness – always remembering."

Chapter XXIV

The Spongers

"Can you believe today is our first anniversary in the store?" Barbara grinned at Ray as he nodded his head.

"It sure was a year we'll always remember. So much has happened. Jaime started school, we started in business, we lost Pa, I got a job on the railroad, and we sold one home and bought another."

"Yeah and Aunt Pearl came to live with us. A lot of good and a lot of bad," Barbara said.

"Well, which category do ye think I fit in?" Aunt Pearl asked.

Barbara and Ray laughed. "Well...." Ray looked at Aunt Pearl and ducked as she hit him with a folded newspaper.

"You were one of the best, Aunt Pearl. Don't pay any attention to him."

Ray put his arm around Aunt Pearl. "She's right, of course. We love ya and don't know how we would have made it through all of this without you."

Pearl smiled and said, "I'm glad I was here for ye."

"You know this anniversary snuck up on us. We haven't planned anything to celebrate," Barbara said.

"Well, I guess we can celebrate by working hard. I'm working tonight and we can't close the store. School's going on. I'd say we just count our blessings we made it through the first year." Ray gave Aunt Pearl a squeeze. "I've got to fill a hundred pound LP bottle the Jefferies left here and get ready for work."

So it was...the first year had slipped into the second year and life was starting to settle down to a routine. Ray, Barbara and Jaime had taken their week's vacation to Florida and enjoyed it immensely. Jaime was still talking about it and hoping they could go back next year. Ma was back to painting her landscapes that she loved to do. It was good therapy, because they knew she was hurting. Ray would check on her every day, usually finding her in a bedroom she had converted into her studio. "I can tell you what everybody will be getting for Christmas," he reported back one day to Barbara and Pearl.

"I'm glad she is staying busy," Aunt Pearl said as Barbara nodded her head in agreement.

One day about the middle of November, Barbara was making a display of Thanksgiving foods on a table by the door. She stacked cans of pumpkin, sweet potatoes, green beans, stuffing mixes, brown sugar, cranberry sauces, spices, etc. "We should have done this at the first of the month. I don't know why we didn't think of it sooner," she said to Aunt Pearl.

"Yeah, you know we need to start getting the Christmas stuff ready." Pearl said as she arranged some marshmallows next to the sweet potatoes.

"Oh, that reminds me. I've ordered the candies and next week we are going to make our trip to Cana and Fancy Gap for the produce and gifts to sell for Christmas. I'd better call Shirley and see if she can work for us next Friday. Ray will be off work and he said we can go then."

"What about the box of Santa Claus candies you had me store back in the office. Do you want me to go ahead and put them in the candy shelves?" Aunt Pearl asked.

"Yeah, we'd better do that before we forget them completely," Barbara said.

"That's what I'm thinkin'. K-Mart and all the other stores start putting some of their Christmas stuff out before Halloween."

"I know. I never did like that. Seems like to me it takes away from the other holidays."

"I agree," said Pearl. She walked back toward the office as Barbara scooted back behind the counter to wait on a customer.

Pearl walked out of the office and stood beside Barbara as she finished waiting on the customer. As soon as he left, she held the candy box up to show it to Barbara.

Barbara looked at her with a question on her face. "Yeah, that's the right one...the only one we put back in the office."

Pearl opened the box. It was empty.

"What...?" Barbara said. She couldn't believe her eyes. "It's empty!"

"I know," said Aunt Pearl.

"What could have happened?"

"Four little munchkins is what happened. I also found a bunch of the wrappers hidden."

"You mean the kids got back there eating all of that candy?"

"That's exactly what I mean," Pearl said.

"Why those little scoundrels...Jaime couldn't reach that high. I bet Seth got them down for them."

"Probably..." Aunt Pearl looked up as Ray and John walked in the door.

"Look!" Barbara said as she pointed to the empty box.

"What's that?" Ray asked.

"It *was* a box of Christmas candy, until the kids got into it and ate it *all!*" Barbara frowned.

John started laughing and Ray followed suit.

"I don't think it's funny," Barbara said. She looked around as Pearl started laughing with them.

"Well - well...what do you think we should do?" Ray asked.

"They should pay for it!" Barbara said. "It's a wonder they didn't all get sick."

"How should they pay for it? They don't have any money," Ray said.

"Put them to work," John said.

"They oughta be spanked," Aunt Pearl said.

"Yeah," Barbara shook her head in agreement.

Ray and John laughed harder. Barbara stood watching them and not even smiling. *I guess they pulled enough of these stunts on Ma and Pa when they were growing up. The kids got it honest, I'm sure.* "I guess a whipping is out of order?" she asked.

"Yeah," Ray said. "Let's just give them some chores to do and warn them they're never to do that again."

"I guess you know at their age, they're not much help in the store. In fact, it's more work to go behind them and straighten up what they've done." Barbara sighed and picked up the candy order form. "Guess I'd better order more."

"From now on you ought to consider putting the candy out when you get it in instead of hiding it," Ray said.

"But it's not time to put it out."

"So, who cares? You sell it when you sell it. You wait too late you might not get it sold at all. People buy a lot of stuff early, Barbara." Ray touched her shoulder to try to ease her feelings.

She sighed. "You're right. I guess it was a big temptation to them."

"It sure was," John chuckled. "I wonder when they got the chance to do this."

"They're all the time playing in the office on rainy or cold days," Aunt Pearl said. "They've had a million chances."

"I've got to get to work." Ray said.

"Yeah, I'd better get home too. See y'all later," John said as he walked out the door.

Ray pecked Barbara on the cheek and picked up his lunch bucket. "Thank you, Aunt Pearl. See you later, babes."

"Bye," Barbara said. "Be careful."

"Always," he said.

Barbara stood at the door and watched him get in the car and drive off. Then she turned to Aunt Pearl. "I don't think it was funny. And John made me mad. He should have offered to pay for some of this. It was his kids too. And now we have to find something for them to do so they can learn a lesson. Something doesn't seem right here."

Aunt Pearl nodded her head in agreement and then she smiled. "I guess we had to learn a little lesson too."

Barbara sighed as she picked up the check book to pay some bills. It would be a week or two before she would see the humor in it all.

The chimes rang out over the door. "Hidy, ever-body. It's me...ole Idy."

"Hi, Idy," Barbara said.

"You look a little down in the dumps. What'sa matter?" Ida wiped the drool from her mouth.

"Just bill paying time." Barbara forced a smile.

"Whar did all the candy go in this box? You already sold all the Santa Claus's?"

"You might say that." Barbara said.

"Well...order some more. Them's good candy. 'Course I can't have none. You know how that goes."

"Yeah, you shouldn't be eating sweets with your diabetes."

"It's sugar I got" she corrected Barbara. "Too sweet already. This ole body of mine can't tolerate no more sugar."

"Oh, I see," Barbara said.

"Yeah, that's what the doc told me. Whar's Pearl? I need me some weenies and some hamburger. Think I'll cook a little today and tomorrey. It's gettin' a might nippy outside."

"She just walked back to the kitchen. You can catch her there."

"Good. Y'all closin' Thanksgiving?" Ida asked.

"We're going to close from 1:00 until 4:00. That way we can eat with my Mom and Dad and still give people a chance to get what they need," Barbara said.

"Good. I'll be up here. Granny's gonna fix us somethin' good, I think. She might even let me have a little bit of sweets."

"Good. I hope so, Idy."

The chimes rang again as a man came in the door with his two children. They looked impoverished and dirty. The man headed toward the beer and wine cooler. Barbara smiled at the children.

"Now how come you little ones ain't in school today?" Ida asked.

They shrugged their shoulders and looked at their Dad who was sitting a fifth of cheap wine and a big bottle of beer on the counter. "We overslept this mornin'," he offered. "Missed the bus." He gave a little laugh.

"Dad, can I have a Reese cup?" the oldest asked.

"Yeah, I want one too." the smaller boy asked.

"No, y'all ain't needin' anything sweet. I don't think I'll have enough left over after I pay for this. How much we owe ya, Miss."

Barbara totaled the purchases on the register and told him. He gave her two one-dollar bills and counted out the change for the rest. He had only fourteen cents left in his hand. "Here, y'all get ya some bubble gum."

Pearl reached up on the top shelf and held the bubble gum bucket in front of the boys.

"How many can we get?" the oldest one asked.

"Two apiece."

They each got two and laid them on the counter. "Here, y'all can split this Reese cup," Aunt Pearl said as she laid it on the counter with the gum.

"We ain't got enough left for that." The man scowled at Pearl and then the boys.

"That's okay. I'm buying it for them," Pearl said as she put the bucket back on the top shelf.

Barbara rang the gum up and smiled at the boys. "Thank you and y'all have a good day now."

They nodded their heads as they picked up the gum and the Reese cup.

"Come on ya little brats," the man twisted the top of his bag and gave the oldest a shove out the door.

"Pearl, ye oughtn't not have done that," Ida said.

"Why? The little boys wanted some real candy and the stingy man wouldn't buy it for them. Makes me mad to see these grown men buying beer and cigarettes for themselves and then won't buy anything for their own little flesh and blood."

"Yeah, you're right, but ye oughtn't not have done that," Ida said again.

"Why not? The younguns looked like they could use a little spoilin'."

"That may be true, but you embarrassed that man. He'll take it out on his kids. I'd bet you two to one he gives 'em a whipping when he gets them home."

Pearl's face turned white. "Oh, no. I never dreamed."

"Well, maybe he won't. Good chance he'll forgit about it afore they git home. He's got better thangs to thank about...namely the bottle." Ida tried to smooth over Pearl's feelings.

"I never would have done that if I'd known it would cause him to beat those younguns." Pearl looked at Barbara.

"I know, Aunt Pearl. We all live and learn. It's my fault for not warning you. Ma told me before we ever took the store, not to interfere with a parent when they won't buy their kids something. She said 'Your heart goes out to them and you have all that candy sitting there. You just want to put a little happiness in their lives.' But she said that some parents (especially alcoholics that feel guilty about their drinking problem or just don't have a heart for their kids) will take it out on their kids when they get them home. I'm so sorry I didn't warn you, I just never had the chance to think about telling you before now."

"Well, you can be sure I won't give any kids anything else."

"Well, Ray has a good way of doing it. Ever notice how he gives a lot of the little ones a sucker, but it is before they have a chance to ask their parents for something. And to Ray it doesn't matter if they're rich or poor. I tell Ray though that he'd better be asking the parents' permission anyway. Sometimes they have them dressed up to go somewhere special or don't want them to ruin their supper. He's got so now he just gives them a sucker and tells them they have to ask their Mom or Dad when they can eat it. That seems to work okay. You can't give them candy bars, though, Pearl or they'll be looking for a candy bar every time and that can get expensive."

"Yeah." Pearl hesitated - then blew out her breath. "Still makes me mad...that man."

"Yeah, I know what ye mean," Ida said. "Makes me mad too, but I've seen some of these men beat their kids just 'cause they got embarrassed. But don't ye be a frettin' now, Pearl. I doubt any damage was done and ye learned ye a lesson."

"I reckon," Pearl sighed and picked up the broom. "I'm gonna sweep on the driveway a bit," she told Barbara.

"Hey, hold on a minute. I ain't got me my hamburger yet."

"Oh, yeah." Aunt Pearl headed for the kitchen with Ida right behind her.

Two days later Ray walked into the store with good news. "Guess what?" he grinned.

"I have no idea," Barbara answered as she wrote down the figures from the cash register tape into the day book

"One of the guys on the railroad is redoing his kitchen and putting in new cabinets. He asked if I would like to have the old ones. All I have to do is haul them away. He said they're not in the best of shape but I figure they'll be fine for the kitchen in the store."

"Wow! He's just giving them to you?" Barbara laid the book on the counter and stood up. "Wouldn't that just be great."

"Great? It would be wonderful." Pearl said. "That one old cabinet we have doesn't hold much. We could do away with some of the old shelving that we're storing everything on now."

" I'm taking the pickup to work tonight and follow him home. He said they're ready to load up."

"What a great Christmas present that will be for us." Barbara clasped her hands together.

"What a *wonderful blessing* it will be," Pearl added.

"I'll wait until after Thanksgiving before I start the work. I'll have to move the meat cooler up a little and make room for them. I'll have to stop by Lowe's and get some masonry screws for the top ones that will go on the wall to the outside."

"We'll have to empty the shelves and try to work around the mess," Barbara said. " It'll be a lot of work, but worth it."

"I'll paint after you finish everything." Pearl raised her eyebrows and grinned. "Won't we feel grand with a real kitchen?"

"Don't you think it's a real kitchen now?" Ray asked.

"Oh, you know what I mean." She picked up the day book and swatted his behind. "You're not too big to spank, ye know."

Barbara laughed. "Don't worry, Aunt Pearl. I know exactly what you mean."

Ray was true to his word. The Monday after Thanksgiving, Barbara and Pearl spent the morning taking everything off of the shelves that would be removed and out of the one old cabinet they had. The next day was check day.

"Boy, what a mess." Barbara said.

"Yeah, I guess we oughta thank God again for the big meal your Mom fixed on Thanksgiving, because we'll be eatin' sandwiches for a few days until Ray gets the cabinets in."

"I don't mind that a bit." Barbara said. "Tomorrow is check day anyway and we'll be busy with customers. You probably won't have much time to be cooking."

"No, I just dread slicing bologny, ham and cutting the cheeses, but I'll push everything to one side of the table and put the stuff we don't use very often in some boxes."

"In order to get anything done, I guess you'll have to do that."

The next morning Barbara walked over to the store to open early since it was the first day of the month and customers would be in early - wanting to cash their checks. She got it opened before any customers had arrived. After setting up the cash register, turning on the lights and gas pumps, and making coffee for their breakfast (and to share with customers), she unlocked the door to begin the day's business. Within minutes the store started filling up. She was by herself since Aunt Pearl had stayed to get Jaime ready for school. Four customers stood in line waiting to pay their bills and cash their pension or welfare checks. As Barbara waited on Charlie Bob first, a man called Chuck walked into the store. (Barbara and Pearl actually called him 'Sponger' behind his back.) He came in every morning for the free cup of coffee, but rarely patronized them. He even used the far end of their parking lot to park his car on snowy days. Then he would walk to his home in the Bottom. That was easier than driving on the rough, unplowed road that ran behind the store. He had been asked not to park his car there since it was in the way when Ray snowplowed, but he ignored them and parked it there anyway.

He poured himself a cup of coffee. "Barbara, the sugar canister is empty."

"Okay. I'll fill it up in a minute," Barbara said. "Here's your change and thank you, Charlie Bob."

"I'll fill it up fer ye. Whar's it at?" Chuck stood there holding the small canister in his hand.

"I"ll get it for you as soon as I wait on the other customers," Barbara said.

"Here, Henry, let me sign your check and Idy can sign for the other signature," she said when Henry handed her his check with his X marked on it.

"Sure, I can do that," Ida said as she reached for the pen. "I can sure sign my name. Ye oughta learn how to do your name, Henry."

"I have my mark; and me and Barbara's just fine with it as it is. Right, Barbara?"

"Right," Barbara grinned.

"Barbara, I'm in a hurry. I need to get some sugar in my coffee. I can't drink it without sugar." Chuck shifted from one foot to the other.

"You'll have to wait until I finish waiting on these customers, Chuck," Barbara said deliberately.

"Never mind. I'll find the sugar myself." Chuck started toward the kitchen.

"Chuck, we're remodeling and the kitchen's a mess. You'll have to wait on me."

"I'll find it," he said as he kept walking down the aisle toward the kitchen.

Barbara rolled her eyes and sighed. "Excuse me, please," she said as she came out from behind the counter and followed Chuck down the aisle. It took her only a few seconds to find the sugar. First she put some in Chuck's coffee cup and then turned around to fill the canister, her mouth clamped shut as she did so.

"Well, now, thank ye much," Chuck said as he stirred his coffee and turned back to walk down the aisle and out the door.

Barbara walked back up front with the canister and saw Chuck climb into his car that had been parked overnight in their parking lot. He headed toward town. She knew he would get his check from the post office and shop at their competitors...the ones that didn't give free coffee to their customers.

"Sorry y'all had to wait," Barbara said to the ones that had stood patiently waiting for her to come back to wait on them.

"Oh, that's fine," Ida said. "Reckon he was in a big hurry to get to the post office and get back here to cash his check afore ye ran out of money."

"Yeah, he oughta git up here early and he wouldn't have to wait 'til ya built your money back up," Charlie Bob laughed.

"Don't worry about it," Ethan said quietly. "I'm in no hurry."

Barbara didn't tell them that he rarely bought anything at their store. She just said "Thanks" and kept on waiting on them until they had all left.

In the meantime, Aunt Pearl had put Jaime on the bus and had arrived in time to slice ham and bologny and help the customers with their meat purchases. After they had all left, Barbara told Pearl about the incident. She was still fuming.

"You can't be serious. I never did like the way that sponger would come in here for his free cup of coffee and then leave. I've seen him many a time get in his car with empty pop bottles, drive out town, come back and park at the upper end of the driveway and then get out of his car with a full carton of pop and a bag of groceries. That man has sure got his nerve." Pearl lifted one hand from her hips occasionally to shake her finger toward the parking lot. "Ye ought to charge him from now on."

"I should; but how can I charge just him while the other customers are getting theirs free?" Barbara shook her head.

"Wouldn't bother me none." Pearl sighed as she walked back toward the kitchen. "Ray got a lot done on these cabinets yesterday. I say he'll have them done in another day or two."

Ray came in the store about 11:00. "I'm going to work on the cabinets for a few hours today. I've been scheduled for night shift."

"Good," Barbara said. "Ray I've decided to start charging for the coffee," she said.

"Why?"

She told him about the incident with Chuck.

"You've gotta be kidding," he said.

"Nope."

"Yeah, you're right. Start charging him. Are you sure you want to charge everybody. After giving it away for so long, some of them might be offended."

"No. I've thought it all out. I'm going to set an empty coffee can and cut a slit in the lid. Then I'm going to ask people to donate money for the Rescue Squad. Actually, we'll take turns and every couple of months we'll give the money to a different charity. What do you think about that?"

"Sounds good to me."

"And if they don't have the money - you know like some of the poor ones - I'll tell them that's okay, they can drop a few cents in sometime when they have extra."

Ray laughed and walked back to the kitchen.

The next morning, Chuck was up at the store for his usual free cup of coffee. He had poured it as Barbara was waiting on another customer. She finished and looked Chuck right in the face and said "That'll be twenty-five cents, Chuck."

"What do you mean, twenty-five cents?" he asked.

"I mean we've started charging for the coffee. You put your money right in this can and we're going to give it to the Rescue Squad. There is no more free coffee."

"Oh," he said as he fished a quarter out of his pocket and dropped it in the can that Barbara was holding in front of him.

"Thank you," she said.

Chuck nodded his head and walked out the door. He didn't come back the next morning for a cup of coffee – nor all that week.

The next week it snowed and Chuck had parked his car in the parking lot again. Ray plowed the snow up around his car instead of walking down through the snow filled path to the Bottom to ask him to move his car. Later that day, Barbara and Pearl had to laugh as they noticed Chuck with a shovel working to clear his car. He never parked in the upper end of their driveway again.

Chapter XXV

The Parade

Christmas was fast approaching. The houses were lit and the air was filled with excitement. The high school band program and the town always joined together to have a Christmas parade. Barbara and Ray talked it over and decided to put a float in the parade.

"Whatcha doin'?" Bobby Darling asked.

"I'm making a sleigh," Ray answered as he marked the outline on an old piece of plywood.

"Oh...well, good luck to ya." Bobby didn't question...just acted like it was a natural thing for Ray to be doing. He stood watching a few minutes.

John walked into the garage with another piece for the other side of the sleigh "Found another piece of plywood," he said. Bobby helped him lean it against the wall.

"Good." Ray kept tracing the outline. "What we need to do is paint this red and put some silver tinsel around the edges."

"I've got some red velvet material I bet would look great on it." Ray looked up and saw Bertha standing in the garage doorway watching them.

"Yeah, and I have some tinsel ye can have," Granny Johnson added.

"Now that would sure look good." Ray grinned. "Thank you, ladies."

"Soon as we git our stuff and go home, I'll get that velvet and bring it right back up," Bertha said.

"Yeah...and me too," Granny said with enthusiasm in her usually unruffled voice.

"It'll take a lot of material and tinsel," Ray said.

"Got plenty," Bertha said.

"So have I...and if I don't have enough, I'll buy ye some," Granny added.

Ray and John continued marking and cutting. Bobby helped hold the plywood. Before long they had a sleigh cut and ready to cover.

As they stood checking out their project, Bertha and Granny walked in. Excitement was written all over their faces. "See, ain't this tinsel what ye need?" Granny asked.

"Yeah," John said. "It's exactly what we need."

"See...won't this look purty as can be?" Bertha held out the red velvet material. Ray and John exchanged surprised looks. It was rich looking and a beautiful bright red.

"Oh, wow! Are you sure you want us to cut this up? It looks like really nice material." Ray said.

"Reckon I wouldn't of offered it iffin I didn't want ye to use it," Bertha said.

"*Thank you so much.*" Ray took the bolt of cloth as John reached for the tinsel from Granny.

"You gonna sit this on the back of your truck?" Bertha asked.

"No, we're going to attach it to the side of a riding lawnmower and let Seth drive it in the parade. We're going to put him in a Santa Claus suit and then let some of the kids be the reindeer."

"Now won't that be special." Ida had seen the commotion in the garage and joined them. "How ye gonna make them look like reindeers?"

"I don't know. That will be the women's project."

"Oh..." The three women looked at each other and started toward the store.

"Ray and John told us y'all fixin' the kids up to be reindeers," Ida wiped the drool from her mouth.

"Yeah, I imagine ye might need some help there." Bertha grinned. "Ye oughta see the red velvet material I done give to Ray. He really likes it."

"I give him the tinsel," Granny chimed in.

"It's gonna look right purty," Ida added.

"Well...how did ye say you're gonna fix the younguns up?" Ida stepped closer to the counter.

"We've been talking about that," Aunt Pearl said. "We thought we'd use brown garbage bags...slip them over their heads and then make them some antlers."

"Garbage bags?" the three women said in unison.

"Yes, garbage bags," Barbara laughed. "We'll cut holes for the arms and head to go through. There's no way we would have time to sew them little brown outfits."

"Yeah, I reckon not," Granny said. "Well, I gotta go. See y'all later." She headed toward the door.

"Yeah, see ya later," Bertha said as she reached up and smacked the chimes with her hand as she departed.

"Ole Idy's gotta go too. She reached down into the candy case. "Put this candy bar on my bill."

"But…" Barbara looked at Aunt Pearl. "They just came in to find out about the reindeer?"

"I reckon so," Aunt Pearl chuckled as she walked to the door and watched the three women walk up the driveway and back into the garage. "I guess Ray and John's project is more interesting to them."

"The brown garbage bags and some twine will take care of part of their outfits, but what about their antlers?" Barbara wondered.

"Don't look at me. I wouldn't have the foggiest about something like that." Aunt Pearl shook her head.

"Well, I know who would." Barbara walked toward the phone.

"Who are ye callin'?" Aunt Pearl asked.

"Who's the artist and crafter in our family?" Barbara grinned.

"Betty. Yeah, she'll know what to do."

Sure enough, it only took a few minutes for Ma to figure out what to do. "I'll be right over," she said.

As she walked in, Ma was looking around. "I need some cardboard… and see if you have some brown spray paint," she said.

Aunt Pearl started toward the kitchen. "How much cardboard do you need?"

"How many reindeer are you going to have?" Ma asked.

Barbara walked back from the hardware section. "Here's the paint," she said. "Well, let's see…they'll be Sarah, Billy, Kirsten, Matthew, Adrienne, Renae and Jaime…as Rudolph."

"Well, now, looks like you have plenty of reindeer," Ma grinned. "Looks like this cardboard is going to be too stiff, Pearl. Do you have any poster board?"

Pearl reached behind the spice rack and pulled out a big sheet of poster board. "Is this enough?"

"Probably. If not, I'll be back over to get more."

Pearl scratched her head. "What's your plan, may I ask?"

"Ask all you want to. Don't mean I'll tell you." Ma laughed.

Pearl dropped her hand as her mouth flew open.

"I'm teasing, Pearl. I'm going to cut out headbands with the poster board and then spray paint them brown. While they're drying, I'll run to the Craft Shop in Bluefield and find some fat pipe cleaners. I'll probably have to spray them brown also. I'll glue and staple everything together. You'll see. It'll look as much like reindeer horns as those garbage bags will look like their hide." She laughed again as she bent the poster board. "Yeah, this is going to work just fine. I'll have them ready by Thursday evening." She walked out the door without another word.

A few minutes later Mrs. Fox walked in. "I heard y'all gonna have a float in the parade come Saterdey. Bertha and Granny was a braggin' 'bout it. Now, let me tell ye I've got some jingle bells. Reckon ye could use them?"

"Jingle bells sound real good." Barbara nodded her head as she furrowed her brows in deep thought. Suddenly, her eyes lit up. "We could string them on the twine belts we're fixin' for the kids. That would be a real nice touch. Thank you, Mrs. Fox. That is so kind of you."

"Well, now, looks like I need to be doin' my part, ye know. Only one thang got me worried. Ye think little Seth is old enough to be Santa."

"We're gonna put a white beard and hair on him so everybody will think he's old." Pearl grinned.

"Now, Pearl, don't be sassin' me. I mean to be drivin' that contraption. He might run over ever last one of them younguns. Then whar would ye be?"

Barbara laughed. "You're right, Mrs. Fox. I had the same worry, but John assured me that he has been letting Seth mow their lawn all last summer on that lawn mower and he says he can gear it down so Seth can't go too fast. Besides, he and Ray are going to be walking right near them."

"Oh well, iffen you're sure. I'll bring the bells up next trip I make up here. These old bones don't let me skip around like Bertha does. Say, Pearl, how 'bout cuttin' me a pound of bologny and wrap me up about four of those big weenees...not the hot ones."

"Sure...comin' right up," Pearl said.

By Thursday evening, the sleigh was finished and attached to the lawnmower. Henry and Charlie Bob stood at the garage doors admiring the work.

"Wow, that really looks great, don't it Henry." Charlie Bob laughed.

"Sure does," Henry answered as he looked down the parking lot. "Hey, Ethan, come look at the Santa sleigh Ray and John done made."

Ethan walked up the driveway to the garage. "Yeah, it sure does look purty," he said as he admired the work.

They stood talking awhile as Bertha walked up. "Oh...Wow!" she gasped. Suddenly she turned and walked back down toward the Bottom. In a few minutes she came back with Mrs. Fox, Granny, Chuggles, and Idy. "See, didn't I tell ye it was beautiful."

"Yeah, but I never imagined it would look so good," Mrs. Fox almost whispered.

"Well, now, Ole Idy could've told ye. I knew it was going to be beautiful...just not *that* beautiful," she added in her strong voice. "Come mer, Eddie. Look what ole Ray's done went and made."

Fast Eddie was walking toward the store. "What y'all gawkin' at?" he asked. Before they could answer he saw the sleigh. "Woo-Wee! Now I bet y'all could sell that thang to Santa Claus. He probably needs a new one after crash landing into Flannigan's barn last year."

"What's goin' on?" Junebug asked.

"See fer yerself," Eddie answered.

"Wo – boy. Whacha goin' do with a sleigh, now, Ray?" he said.

"Well, Junebug, thought I might hook the snowplow up to it when it snows...just in case the truck don't start." Ray grinned.

"Whaaat?" about three voices said in unison.

John laughed and slapped Ray on the shoulder.

"Smart-alec. He's gonna put it in the Christmas Parade out town come Saturdey," Mrs. Fox said as she looked at Junebug and Fast Eddie.

"I bet ya take first place," Ethan said in his soft voice. "Sure is a elegant thang."

"Yeah, I supplied the red velvet cover," Bertha said proudly.

"Yeah and I give them the shiny tinsel fer the trim," Granny answered.

Red walked up to the small crowd. "I wondered what was going on. I could see y'all from my front room window. You boys did a real good job. Now if the reindeer turn out so nice, you'll probably take first place."

"We hope," Ray and John said together.

"Barbara, Ma, Shirley and Pearl are in the store working on that part right now," Ray said.

The women looked at each other and started toward the store. As they walked in they saw Ma trying the antlers on Sarah, Billy and Jaime.

"What we need is something to tie these little reindeer together," Shirley said, "or they'll be wandering all over the street."

"Tie them together?" Barbara asked.

"Yeah, like a team of horses," Shirley added.

"Hmmm…" The women stood with thoughtful expressions on each face.

"Anybody got enough rope to do that job?" Idy asked.

Each one shook their head no.

"Got plenty of twine," Barbara said. "Guess we'll have to use that. It'll look kind of plain next to all the other stuff we've fixed."

"That won't keep them from running into each other," Shirley said. "We want them to stay spaced about two or three feet apart, don't we?"

"Got it!" Red nearly jumped on top of Idy's foot.

"Watch it," Idy hollered as she jumped back and looked down at Red.

"What do you have?" Granny asked.

"Yardsticks!"

"Yardsticks?" Everybody looked at her.

"Yeah, I have about a dozen yardsticks…you know, those flat wooden ones they give out for advertising. We could attach them to the twine, and then attach the twine to their belts and they'd have to walk three feet apart from each other."

"Well, now, don't ye think yardsticks would look a little ridiculous in a Christmas parade?" Mrs. Fox said.

"No…" Shirley said thoughtfully. "We could disguise the yardsticks. I've got a couple of strands of gold tinsel out at the house. I'll bring them out and we'll fix it up tomorrow evening after the kids get home from school."

"Yeah, that sounds like it would work," Barbara said.

"It would add even more glitter to the whole thing," Red agreed.

"I've been thinking," Ma said. "Do you realize you've left little Susie out?"

"We talked about it, but she's so little we were afraid she wouldn't understand how to walk with the others as a reindeer," Barbara said.

"That's true, but I was wondering why I couldn't make her up like a little angel and let her walk in front of the others."

"Yeah, sure, that would be nice!" Barbara exclaimed with a smile. "I wish I had thought of it myself. I'll tell you what I did think of. We have a torn white sheet that I put back to maybe cut down into a twin size sheet. We could make a sign out of it and let Susie carry one side and, well… Ma maybe you could carry the other side. Y'all could walk ahead of the reindeer."

"What would the sign say?" Aunt Pearl asked.

"How 'bout 'Christmas and Santa'?" Granny Johnson said.

"What? No. How 'bout 'Eight little Reindeer'?" Mrs. Fox said.

"There's only seven, can't ye count," Ida said.

"How 'bout 'Twas the Night afore Christmas'?" Bertha added.

"How about…'Through the Eyes of a Child'?" Barbara said.

Everybody stood silently for a moment and then Ida said, "I like that."

"Yes, I do," said Bertha.

"Suits me," Granny said.

"Oh, well, then if it suits Granny, then that's fer sure what it will be," Ida retorted.

Everybody laughed.

"I'll work on it tonight," Barbara said. "I know Ray has some stencils out in the garage and we have blue spray paint up in the hardware section. We need to make sure all of the kids are here by 10:00 a.m. Saturday morning since the parade is at noon."

Saturday morning dawned sunny and cool. Barbara and Ray walked over to the store, made the coffee and Barbara got her checking up done early.

"It looks like a fine day for the parade," Ray said.

"Yes, aren't we lucky. It could be snowing or raining," Barbara added.

"Or freezing cold. Are you sure everything is ready for the kids?" Ray asked.

"Far as I can tell. Are you sure the sleigh is ready?" Barbara grinned.

"Far as I can tell." Ray playfully punched her arm.

By a quarter 'til ten most of the kids were lined up in the kitchen of the store - excited and jabbering. Barbara walked back after Ray came in to relieve her behind the counter. Granny walked in and walked past the counter and straight back to the kitchen with her little granddaughter in tow. Ma was slipping a white garbage bag over Susie's head.

"Do ye think my little Missy could be in the parade?" she asked.

Barbara, Ma and Aunt Pearl exchanged glances. Ma was the first to speak. "Of course, she can. We'll make her into a little angel like Susie here. She can help carry the sign."

Barbara breathed a sigh of relief.

Granny said, "Well, now, that will be right nice, won't it Missy?"

Missy nodded her head excitedly and walked over to Susie.

"I'll go home and fix another set of wings and halo and be right back. Granny, do you have a long sleeve white sweater she could wear under the garbage bag? Her coat will be too bulky and it's too cold for her to go sleeveless."

"I think we can scarf one up. We'll be back in a few minutes." Granny took Missy by the hand and led her back out of the store.

Barbara shook her head and smiled at Aunt Pearl as she leaned over and said, "Poor Ma's gotta scramble to get that done, but I'm glad she's got a good heart for the kids. She'd never let one be left out, but I was about to panic trying to think of a place to put her all of a sudden."

"Yeah, me too," Pearl said.

"Here, Jaime, let me put this on your nose and cheeks," Barbara said as she reached for her son and started marking his face with red lipstick."

The other kids all started laughing.

"Hey, surely you kids know that Rudolph has to have a red nose," Aunt Pearl said.

"Yeah," Jaime said as he held his face up toward his mother's.

"All right, everybody, climb in the truck," Ray hollered over the noisy children. They all scrambled and Barbara climbed in the car with a few of them. Ray led the way as John followed with the lawnmower. Barbara followed John with her flashers on to make sure no one ran over him for the almost mile they had to drive to the parade line-up site. It took several minutes to hook them all up with the tinsel and yardsticks.

Finally the judges finished walking up and down the line-up. They placed a second place sign on the back of the sleigh. First place went to their church which had a flat bed trailer fixed up with children singing around a Christmas tree in a made up living room.

The judges motioned for the parade to start. As the float went up the street with Susie and Missy carrying the banner and Jaime's red nose following not far behind, the crowd cheered as they passed. Seth sat on top of the lawnmower and yelled "Ho..Ho..Ho" over and over again. Barbara and Shirley walked close by the little angels to keep them moving and Ray and John walked close to the sleigh to make sure Seth did a good job.

Charlie Bob and Henry were the first to spot them. "Hey, y'all look good." Henry yelled.

"Hey, Santa, bring me a Mustang for Christmas," Charlie Bob yelled.

"Ho! Ho! Ho! to you, Santa," Barney yelled.

"Hey I helped build the sleigh, ya know." Bobby Darling puffed out his chest.

"Well, I supplied the red velvet," Bertha said. "That's the purtiest thang about the whole git-up."

"Yeah, well don't forgit I helped too," Granny said.

"Me too," Mrs. Fox added. "Y'all should be first place," she yelled.

"Look how purty the angels look. Hold the sign a little higher, Missy," Granny said.

"Look at Rudolph! Hey, 'member last year you was a-lookin fer Rudolph, Jaime," Fast Eddie yelled. "Didn't know ye was a-gonna take his place this year, did ye?"

Ida wiped what appeared to be a tear from her cheek as she punched Red. "Don't they just look like the sweetest thangs?"

Red shook her head. "Yeah, but ya don't have to knock me over, Idy."

"I didn't," Idy shot back.

"Now pay attention to the little ones," Ethan said.

"Yeah." Ida shot Red another look.

As the parade came back to the starting line, which was also the finish line, Ray walked up to Barbara and put his arm around her waist.

"They did a good job. Don't you think? Seth did a good job with the mower." Ray beamed.

"He sure did…and the reindeer did really well. They were the best in the parade," Barbara said.

Bobby Darling went by in his El Camino and blew his horn at them. Chuck followed in a pick-up truck blowing his horn. Charlie Bob, Henry, Barney and Ethan were in the back and the women packed in the front, except for Ida. She was in the back with the men. They all waved and yelled greetings to them.

Isaac walked up to them. "Ray, Barbara," he said as he also nodded to Ma, Pearl, Shirley and John.

"Hi, Isaac," they said in unison.

"Just fine," he answered. "It was a good parade. You did a good job on your float. Kidd's Country Grocery did themselves proud. I just wish Gene could have been here."

Ray let out a big sigh. "Wouldn't Pa have loved this. I do wish so much he could have been here to see it."

"Me too," John said as Shirley nodded her head. Ma and Pearl wiped away tears.

Ray looked at Barbara and squeezed her hand.

"He sees," Barbara whispered as she looked up into the cloudless sky. *Everything is going to be all right.*

About the Author

Patricia Woodard Synan, along with her husband, David Woodard, owned and operated a small country store on the border of West Virginia and Virginia. Here she met and became friends with many colorful mountain people of which she writes. This is her first book. After David's untimely death in 2004, she sold the store to her son. She has since remarried and lives on Peeled Chestnut Mountain outside of Pocahontas, Virginia with her husband, Russell.